THE HITMAN

THE FAMILY

KATRINA JACKSON

Mentions of domestic abuse
Mentions of child abuse
Murder
Shooting deaths

BEST LAID plans lead you straight to hell.

That's the saying, right? If not, it should be, and we should start saying it to all the Type A little girls with extensive notebook collections, color-coded digital calendars, and a favorite stationery brand. Me. I'm saying someone should have said this to me. Someone should have told little me that all my vision boarding and extensive wedding planning was bullshit. And after today, every time I see a little girl who even vaguely reminds me of myself, I'll tell her to pack it in and do whatever she wants, if no one else will.

I've lived my life following all the rules. I've done it all the right way, and what do I have to show for it right now, at this exact moment?

An $80,000 bespoke couture wedding dress that's covered in so many crystals, I've only been wearing it for two hours and my back aches.

An engagement ring so simple and elegant and expensive that the jeweler who made it has been begging me for a week to model some less expensive knock-offs for the summer engagement season because every woman of a certain class will want a ring like mine. Because so many women dream about being engaged to A-list action star Ryan Fuller.

I have so many pins in my head that my scalp has gone numb.

And I have a full-body flush while watching breaking news on every entertainment website show footage of the man I was supposed to be walking down the aisle to marry twenty minutes ago, stumbling into his hotel room last night with Candee Caine, the most famous exotic dancer in the tri-state area and reality television star.

I also have the profound pleasure of feeling that flush turn to fire threat level when I see hotel surveillance footage — almost certainly obtained illegally — of my best friend and MIA maid of honor, Trisha Mays, sneaking down the hall to my fiancé's room the night before she was supposed to stand next to me while I married him.

And maybe worst of all is that I can hear my sister Zoe's voice in my head. I can practically hear her sucking her teeth and telling me, "I told you so." I can hear her in my head because she's not in my bridal suite, because I asked Trisha to be my maid of honor and not Zoe. So, no, I stand corrected. The worst part of all this is that I'm watching the two people Zoe told me I shouldn't trust betray me, knowing that I betrayed her for them.

I'm watching them make a literal fool of me, and on my wedding day, no less.

So yeah, you can bet that from here on out, I'm going to tell every little girl I see that plans don't mean anything. Mine sure as shit didn't.

But first, I'm going to kick my ex-fiancé's ass.

"Zahra." Anna, the producer who's been tasked to follow me around for the past two months, says my name quietly as if she's afraid she'll disturb me. Joke's on her; nothing will ever disturb me more than the footage I'm watching on a loop on the real news station now.

I shake my head but don't answer her. I turn the volume on the television up so that I can hear Chip Collinson — respected entertainment journalist and supreme asshole — talk about my life falling apart. He hates me. The feeling is mutual. I bet he's loving this. I turn the volume on the television up because I want — no, need — to hear Chip tell the world with barely contained glee that my fiancé cheated on me the night before our wedding. It's shit icing on a shit cake.

"Our exclusive source says the actor spent nearly ten thousand dollars at the strip club," Chip gloats. "We can only estimate what portion of that he spent on the dancers before he went into a private room with Candee Caine.

If that name sounds familiar, here's footage of Candee from her reality show Candee Shoppe, which chronicled the dancer's jet-setting lifestyle. Confidential sources indicate that a private session with Candee costs at least twenty thousand dollars. And if this is the kind of service she offers, I'd argue that she's worth every penny.

How many times have we reported on a celebrity cheating on their long-suffering girlfriend? It's basically a genre of its own, but *this* is an exciting twist, the likes of which we hardly see anymore because, honestly, what celeb is this sloppy in the age of cell phone cameras?"

I laugh sardonically because that's a damn good question, Chip, you jackass. He might suck as a person, but at least he's a journalist who does his job well, and that's the only reason I even entertain our professional relationship. Getting one of my clients a one-on-one interview with Chip is worth the hassle. Also, if Chip is reporting on this story —

God, my life is a story! — it's true. There's no convincing myself that I'm not seeing what I'm seeing.

"If you don't recognize the *second* woman on the security footage, that's celebrated entertainment journalist Trisha Mays. I hate to speak ill of a colleague, but it seems Ms. Mays is willing to go above and beyond for the scoop, even if it means betraying her best friend and Ryan's fiancée, public relations wunderkind Zahra Port.

We have no idea what happened in that hotel room, but we do have live footage of Candee leaving the hotel thirty minutes ago. And if you're keeping track, that's nearly an hour after guests started arriving at the uber-posh Grand Garden Plaza Hotel for Ryan and Zahra's wedding. I'm going to go out on a limb and say the wedding of the season might be a bit delayed. But the real breaking, still unfolding, scandal is that Ryan and Trisha have yet to emerge from their sordid love nest. To stay up to date on this story as it unfolds, make sure to keep an eye out on our website—"

I finally shut the television off. Chip's giddy laughter is ringing in my ears even though the suite is so quiet it's deafening. My heart's pounding and my dress feels heavier and more oppressive than it did two minutes ago. I feel like I'm suffocating under the designer creation and the ashes of my life.

"Zahra," Anna says again.

I turn to her this time, not because I want to hear whatever she has to say, but because now that I can't see the video footage of my life going up in flames, the righteous indignation is already seeping from my pores, and I feel helpless. I hate feeling helpless. Not feeling helpless is the literal point of all the notebooks and calendar alerts.

I turn to Anna, but I come face-to-face with the camera,

because, oh right, Ryan and I have been filming a reality tv wedding special. I'd forgotten that.

Apparently, so had he.

"What are you feeling, Zahra?" Anna asks in a voice I know they'll edit out in post because there's no chance they won't release this footage.

I should call my lawyer and get her started on fighting the television network, looking for a loophole — any loophole — that can bury this footage deeper than my garbage relationship. But I'm still frozen.

What am I feeling? I consider that question, but I can't land on a single answer, because I feel nothing and everything all at the same time. I'm angry as fuck. I'm embarrassed. I want to murder Ryan for putting me in this position. I want to pull out Trisha's bonded extensions one by one. I'm ashamed of myself for choosing them over my sister who hates me now. I feel hollow.

"What are you thinking?" Anna prods, trying a different tactic.

That's an easier answer to pin down. I can't name all the things I feel, but I'm thinking of gathering my big ass train in my hands, running through the lobby of the hotel I spent a fortune reserving two years in advance, and jumping into the limo we rented to take us to the airport after the reception. I want to drive across town to Ryan's hotel like I'm in some late 90's Julia Roberts movie and punch Ryan in the perfectly-formed jaw his agent paid a fortune to craft early in his career.

Okay, now that I think that all the way through, it feels right. It taps into that part of me that loves a bullet-pointed to-do list. And even though I've just decided that all that's a scam, I think I have one more well-executed to-do list left in me.

Normally, I like to think and rethink all of life's important decisions — and if you'd asked me two days ago, I'd have told you that all decisions are important — but I don't have the benefit of time to give this scheme more than hasty consideration. Besides, why should I put more effort and thought into this than Ryan put into preparing for our wedding day? Why should I be more caring or careful than my best friend? And why the fuck should I be the only one feeling like this right now?

I shouldn't, I realize, so I rip my veil from my head, barely feeling the sting of the strands of hair I pull out with it. I bunch the overlarge skirt in my arms — as much of it as I can gather, at least — and head straight for the door.

"Zahra, what are you doing?" my cousin Shae calls after me, but I don't stop because I don't want to fuck up my momentum. I've started, and I need to keep going, or I might break into tears and collapse in a heap of lace, chiffon, and Swarovski crystals instead of getting justice. Also, hearing Shae's voice reminds me that Zoe isn't in this suite, and Zoe, of all people, would have led the way to Ryan's hotel for vengeance. That makes me feel comforted and miserable. Yay, two more emotions to add to the mix.

Why didn't I choose Zoe as my maid of honor? Because she never trusted Trisha, and she flat-out hated Ryan from the moment I brought him home for Thanksgiving six months into our relationship. She took one look at him, Google-investigated him, and then told our entire family over the sweet potato pie, "This white boy is trifling. Zahra can do better," and she'd never changed her mind.

I'd made excuses for him; stupid ones, now that I think about it. I told myself that she was jealous of me, that she hated me, that she was crass. When I announced that Ryan and I were engaged in our family group chat, her response

— the one that arrived before anyone else's congratulations — was a simple and devastating, "Why?" I'd been steaming mad and complained to Ryan and Trisha, but I also buried the question in my subconscious, too afraid to tell her, let alone myself, that I actually didn't have a great answer to that oh-so-simple question.

And now everyone knows that Zoe was right — Shae, our parents, my Aunt Caroline. Everyone.

A small part of me is thankful that I don't have to face Zoe right now, though. I don't have to see the "I told your fool ass so," in her eyes or the pity on my parents' faces. Even though I know I need my family right now more than anything, I'm pretty sure that minimizing the sadness I feel is crucial to keeping the embers of my rage burning. Besides, I have family. I have Shae, and she's hot on my heels as I stomp out of my bridal suite.

When I get to the elevator, I press the call button a dozen times. It doesn't make the elevator arrive faster, but I need to do *something* so my mind stays focused on the task at hand and doesn't have the bandwidth to consider the very real question: *What am I going to do now?*

Shae rushes to stand next to me, and I look at her out of the corner of my eye. She looks pissed, which is so unlike her. Of all the cousins, Shae's the nicest. Too nice if you ask me, but her sunny disposition is part of her charm. Seeing her angry makes me feel less emotionally frazzled for half a second, at least.

Shae's fingers brush the back of my hand and wrap around my wrist. She squeezes me briefly, and I feel tears building at the back of my eyes. I hate it. I don't want to cry. Not now. Not yet.

But when I turn my head, I see the small camera crew that's been following me around for months, and the tears dry up. If I'd had my way, the only cameras here would be our personal videographers, but as soon as we got engaged, Ryan's management pitched a reality television special to him, and he'd said yes. I heard about it only when the contracts arrived. I should have called off the wedding then, or at least put my foot down, but I didn't. I listened to Ryan's sob story about how great the series could be for him during awards season, and I caved. I knew it was bullshit — Academy voters hate reality tv — but he'd wanted it badly, and I loved him. And look at what that got me.

I've compromised a lot of myself in all the years I've been with Ryan but crying on camera isn't an option. I refuse to let Ryan or his PR machine have that last tiny shred of my dignity.

I wrench my hand from Shae's grasp and cover my face as best I can. I go back to pressing the call button again, this time like my life depends on it. I'm thinking about taking the stairs when the elevator doors finally slide open. I practically throw myself inside, which isn't easy with my big ass dress. I have to whip around to pull the train fully inside, and Shae helps, bending low to gather it delicately. But I don't want to be delicate with this dress Ryan paid a fortune for, so I snatch it from her hands and pull it inside.

I press the button for the lobby. One of the cameramen tries to rush inside, and I take a deep, terrified breath at the thought of riding down to the lobby with a camera trained on my face. I don't know if I'll start cursing Ryan out or break down in tears, but I'm certain that either of those responses will elicit yet another wave of online abuse from his batshit fans. I've had years of that. I don't want more.

The fear makes me freeze, and Shae unexpectedly takes charge. She covers the lens with her entire hand and pushes the cameraman back with a dainty yelp. And then she glares at Anna and the crew, silently daring them to step a single foot on the elevator car until the doors slide closed.

I finally exhale.

"Shae?" I breathe, unable to say more. Not even sure what I would say if I could keep speaking.

My cousin turns to me with fierce eyes and a small grin, as if she can't believe what she just did either. "So, we going to fuck him up?"

I'm still worried that I might fall to the ground in tears, but I smile and then burst into surprised laughter. Shae doesn't join me, but she does put her hand on my shoulder. She squeezes and mercifully doesn't say anything more.

I'M TRYING to channel Zoe. The car ride to Ryan's hotel is short. Honestly, it might have been faster to walk, even with the twenty pounds of crystals I'm lugging around. In transit, I ask myself one question over and over again: What would Zoe do in a situation like this?

When we were kids, I used to ask myself this question when it seemed beneficial to be as unlike myself as possible. When the cool kids at school bullied me for my Coke-bottle glasses with the headband. When my teachers took off half a point on a math quiz because I didn't follow the formula they were trying to teach, but I got the right answer anyway. "What would Zoe do?" was my shorthand for, "How would someone with more bravado and a louder mouth right this wrong?"

Unfortunately, I had the same problem as a kid as I do right now, namely that I'm nothing like Zoe. I don't have bravado, I have strategies. I'm not brave, I'm organized. I'm not brazen, I'm competent. I'm nothing like Zoe.

Also, no matter how hard I try, I can't imagine my older sister ever letting anyone — especially a man — treat her the way I've let Ryan treat me. I've made a lot of compromises to make him happy. Zoe doesn't believe in compromises. She also doesn't believe in monogamous relationships, but I digress. My point, though, isn't that no man would ever dare cheat on Zoe — people cheat, that's not up for debate — but that Zoe wouldn't let a man get close enough to actually hurt her. So I can't fathom what Zoe would do in this situation, because Zoe has never been in a relationship long enough to get too attached.

I'm attached, and I'm angry as hell about it.

I loved Ryan against my better judgment — my better judgment being Zoe's judgment — and I sacrificed so much of my relationship with her to be with him. That's another problem, Zoe would never choose any of her romantic partners over me. *It's just the three of us,* Zoe always said, *you, Shae, and me. Forever.*

I feel sick.

I think about calling Zoe. I think about it so hard that I'm forced to realize I have no idea where my cell phone is. I think I left it back in the not-quite bridal suite. My eyes drift to Shae. She's holding her own cell phone in a death grip against her stomach. I'm just on the verge of asking her to let me borrow it when the limo pulls along the curb in front of Ryan's hotel.

"Fucking paparazzi," she breathes.

My eyes widen in shock. Shae almost never curses. But then my eyes drift to the small cluster of photographers milling about in front of the hotel entrance, just far enough away not to bring hotel security out of their offices, but close enough to get a good shot of me looking devastated or of Trisha's walk of shame. Whichever. My stomach clenches.

"You want to go around the back?" the driver asks.

I take a deep breath. I should say yes. I've become

uncomfortably comfortable with sneaking around to meet up with Ryan. When we first started dating, we hadn't wanted to tip off the celebrity media since his whole PR schtick at the time was the young Hollywood heartthrob, but also because I was terrified of getting on his fans' radar. I'd seen how they'd run his last girlfriend off. Going "around back" is second nature by now, and I almost tell the driver to do just that, but I stop myself.

In the cold light of my ruined wedding day, I begin to ask myself questions I should have considered years ago. If Ryan was trying to be the single heartthrob, why did it seem like he was always going on publicity dates with his co-stars? Why didn't his fans attack those actresses, but they did attack me? And why did he allow it? Why had I allowed it?

"No," I say in a brittle voice. "You can let us out right here."

I don't know why I did so much to protect Ryan's reputation in the past, but what's the point now? He's blown years of good PR work to smithereens in a single drunken night. What I do from here on out doesn't matter at all, so I'm going in through the front door.

Shae's hand covers my tightly balled fists. She squeezes gently. "Can you wait for us here?" she asks the driver. Great question.

"Sure thing," he replies casually as if this kind of thing happens to him every day. Maybe it does.

The driver gets out of the car, and I watch as the paparazzi turn to him with interest. Their hands move to the cameras around their necks as they get ready, just in case the person in the back of the limousine is interesting. It doesn't even need to be me; I know that from prior experience. They eye the driver as he walks briskly around the car to the back door.

He pulls the door open and offers Shae his hand. She steps quickly from the car, and they both have to help me maneuver myself and my big, heavy ass dress onto the sidewalk. By the time I'm standing on the curb, my pristine white dress is wrinkled and dragging along the dirty New York streets — and heavier than when I climbed into the car, I swear — and the sound of the camera shutters is deafening.

They start calling my name, excited at the sight of me in what is hands down one of my worst moments. I tuck my chin against my chest and ignore them. Shae laces her fingers with mine and pulls me toward the hotel entrance. The doorman and our driver hold the doors open for us and try to block the paparazzi's view of me with their bodies, not that it matters now.

In the lobby, the sound of the paparazzi screaming my name thankfully fades away in the cavernous room. I normally love hotel architecture and décor — I'm not sure why — but I don't even get to appreciate all the marble and carved wood. This room could be a dank cave, and I would still feel grateful that I can't hear the commotion outside. I also appreciate that no one who accidentally makes eye contact with me pretends not to know what's going on or why I'm here. And the next thing I'm grateful for is that Shae and I don't even make it to the check-in desk before a concierge intercepts us and leads us to the elevator bank.

We step into yet another elevator car. I feel as if none of this is real, that is, until I make quick eye contact with the concierge as the elevator door slides closed.

She smiles sympathetically at me and winks. "Fuck him

up, sis," she whispers. I have no idea why, but those few words from that complete stranger buoy me.

Shae's nervous laughter fills the elevator as we head up to the penthouse. "VIP treatment to get into my first fight. This is the weirdest fucking year."

I don't look at her or reply just in case it makes me cry, but I do smile to myself at her adorable enthusiasm. I can't speak, but I feel very grateful that she's here.

I wrap my arms around my waist, trying to hold myself together just long enough to make it to the penthouse and face whatever awaits me there.

Wʜᴇɴ ᴡᴇ ʀᴇᴀᴄʜ the top floor, I straighten my back, square my shoulders, and lie to myself that I'm a brand-new person right now. I'm not whoever I was when I woke up this morning. I'm not the kind of person who's going to take this. I'm some new person — some person more like Zoe — and this new version of me is mad as fuck.

When the elevator doors open, I rush across the short hallway to the penthouse door. I bang my fist against the wood so hard it hurts, but I can't stop, and I can't knock less forcefully. Or I should say I don't want to soften my blows. The pain is cathartic.

"What?" someone yells on the other side in a dry, scratchy voice.

I can't immediately tell if it's Ryan or Trisha or hell, maybe even someone else I don't know about, but when the door opens, I come face-to-face with the woman who I thought was my best friend and the person who should have been in my bridal suite twenty minutes ago, holding me while my life fell apart, not helping the destruction along.

When she sees me, her eyes widen in shock. She starts

shaking her head side-to-side as if that can erase what's happening.

"It's not what you think," she mutters, because that's what they all say, isn't it? I stayed up on weekends to watch *Cheaters* in high school like everyone else; I know the script.

My mind cobbles together as many of those episodes to concoct all the ways this moment could unfold. I could talk to her, listen calmly as she tells me what this is, since it's apparently *not* what I and the gossip news sites think. I could push past her and find Ryan. Or I could punch her.

I'm a rational human being.

I punch her.

"Oh shit," Shae yells in a shocked, excited gasp behind me.

I'm not proud of myself, but when my fist collides with Trisha's face, I feel...well, not quite free, but light. She stumbles back and crumples to the ground, her hand covering her right eye. I look down at her and exhale a breath. Yes, light is the right word for how I feel. And then I lift my dress and step demurely over her, the sound of Shae's cackling laughter following me into the room.

I head straight to the bedroom because where else would my garbage almost-husband be? On the way, I see empty liquor bottles and takeout boxes, and I take some small comfort in knowing that his agent is going to be pissed at him for blowing his diet. I hope it costs him the movie role he shortened our honeymoon plans to take.

The bedroom door is open. I see the bed and Ryan's body under the wreck of sheets before I'm even halfway across the living area. A quick scan of the bedroom floor tells me everything I need to know and squelches that tiny bit of hope I hadn't realized I was harboring that what the news had reported might not have been true. The tornado of clothes scattered around the floor are a mix of Ryan's and Trisha's, the sheets, covers, and pillows are a rumpled mess, and Trisha's whining crying from the hotel room door mixes with Ryan's loud ass snoring. At least I'll never have to hear that freight train in his nose again after today.

I take a deep breath and rush to the foot of the bed. I grab the comforters and yank them from his body. "Wake up, you piece of shit," I yell as loud as I can.

"Yeah, girl," Shae calls from the living room.

"Five more minutes, babe," Ryan mumbles groggily.

"Fuck five more minutes, you shit stain. Get up. Or do you want me to let the camera crew in?"

At that, Ryan sits up quickly, red-faced, rumpled blonde hair and dazed blue eyes. God, how had I wasted so much time with this man?

"Zahra?" he says, rubbing at his eyes and looking around the room in confusion. "What's going on? You shouldn't be here. I'm not supposed to see you in your dress."

I rear back in shock.

"Is this bitch serious?" Shae asks, coming to stand in the threshold of the bedroom.

I glance quickly at her before turning back to Ryan just in time to see the reality of our situation begin to dawn on him.

"Fuck. It's not what you think, babe," he says, scrambling out of the bed completely naked.

My eyes go to his shriveled dick, and somehow, that sight makes me even angrier. When I raise my eyes to his face, I'm shaking. "That's what my best friend said when she opened your hotel room door, in a robe. Are you sure it's not what I think?"

He's speechless. Good.

"And before you answer that, you should know that you're all over the gossip sites. You, my *former* best friend, and Candee Caine, you absolute piece of fucking garbage. On our fucking wedding day."

"Let me explain," he says, having the nerve to walk toward me.

I let him grovel as he approaches, but I don't hear anything he's saying, because I don't care. When he's within arm's reach, I rear back. His eyes widen, and I silently thank him for making my target bigger. And then I punch him square in the face.

I feel the ruin of my $300 wedding manicure as my hand collides with his chiseled jaw.

"Ow, Zahra, what the fuck?" he screams, his hands going to his face.

"What the fuck? The fuck is that you cheated on me."

"I was drunk."

"Then go to rehab, you piece of shit. Or don't, I don't give a shit anymore. We're done." I grab the skirt of my dress and turn dramatically from the room.

"Zahra, please, let's talk about this," he calls after me.

When I'm back in the sitting area, I see Trisha cowering on the couch looking...not sorry, but terrified. The part of my brain that was certain that these were two people who loved me wants to think she looks shocked because she can't believe what she's done to me, but I'm not that foolish.

"How long?" I spit at her.

Her eyes lift to mine, and she shakes her head.

"How long?!" I scream.

She swallows. "It's not... I didn't... We didn't..."

I stalk toward her with my fists clenched. "Six months!" she screams, crawling away from me. "It...was an accident."

"The first time. What about all the other times for six fucking months?"

She shakes her head, and her eyes get watery. "I never meant to hurt you."

"It's not what you think," Ryan says, standing near me, but not close enough for me to hit him again.

"She meant nothing, Zahra, I promise. It was just sex. I love you." Why do men always say that? I wonder. Why the hell do they think that sounds comforting?

I scowl at him and turn to Trisha. I watch as her face caves in on itself, and her eyes become glassy with tears that fall down her red, embarrassed cheeks.

"I love you, Z. I've only ever loved you. This won't happen again. I promise," Ryan says.

I don't even look at him, because I don't care. I'm not proud of it, but watching my former best friend realize that she ruined our friendship for a man who doesn't even care to spare her feelings in this moment, makes me feel triumphant. And that more than anything saps all the energy I have left.

I'm not a new person, I'm still just me, and I've never been happy at someone else's devastation, nor do I want to be.

But I do like having all the information, and since I'm here, I need to make sure that I say all that needs to be said. I don't want any regrets, and Zoe wouldn't either.

"I hope his dick was worth it," I spit at Trisha. "When the next shitbag you date cheats on you, gives you an STI, or empties out your savings account again, and you realize that you can't call me, that's there's no one left to call because you're such a shitty person that you've run everyone away, I hope fucking my fiancé for six months and having a three-some with him — even though we both know you said you'd never do that again — the night before my wedding was worth it. When you walk out of this hotel room and realize that his crazy fans hate you now, and your entire career is ruined, and you can't show up at my apartment to cry on my shoulder, I hope you think fucking Mr. Two Strokes was worth it. Come on, Shae," I say and turn quickly toward the door.

"Zahra, wait," Ryan calls.

I turn to him with hard eyes.

"What...what about us?" he has the fucking audacity to ask me.

My eyebrows furrow. "What about us? Do you really think I'm going to stay with you after this? I might have respected you more if you'd loved her, but you don't love anyone but yourself. There is no us." I turn back to the door again, but I stop and turn my head to Trisha with a laugh because I've just remembered something that makes this new bitter note in my chest that I hate but can't get rid of — not right now — swell with sad glee.

"You should call your editor," I tell Trisha. "Didn't you tell me she said she'd fire you if you fucked another celebrity?"

Trisha's tears fall faster now. Apparently, she hadn't thought of that when she was betraying our ten years of friendship.

I roll my eyes, shake my head, and walk out of the penthouse suite on surer steps than when I entered. Shae follows me and slams the door behind us. The elevator door opens as soon as I press the button, and I stuff my big ass dress inside it.

"How do you feel?" Shae asks quietly as we ride back down to the lobby.

"Numb," I tell her, feeling the pressure of tears again.

"That's okay," she says reassuringly. She opens her purse and pulls something out and offers it to me.

It takes me a few seconds to realize what I'm seeing is Ryan's wallet in her hands. I look at her in confusion as she pulls Ryan's credit cards from the worn leather wallet and hands them to me.

"Shae?"

"For when you feel less numb, and you want to buy yourself a small island to ease the pain," she says matter-of-factly.

I squint at her. "What the fuck has gotten into you?"

She shrugs, and I don't know what to make of that small gesture. "You deserve the best," she says without any elaboration as if that answers my question. Her eyes dart to the elevator panel. "Here, take these and hide them," she urges.

And I do, because I'm so tired and sad and confused that it's just easier to do as Shae says than to try and figure out what the fuck is going on with my cousin. I shove Ryan's credit cards in the bodice of my wedding dress. When the doors open, I can feel the small plastic things pressed against my titty by the hard structure of the delicate lace bodice. We step back into the lobby. Out of the corner of my eye, I see Shae shove his wallet into a plant pot. I look quickly away — plausible deniability and all that — and the two of us walk through the hotel lobby hand-in-hand.

This is the weirdest fucking day.

Outside, the paparazzi start yelling at me again, but hotel security are holding them back. They still take pictures of me, but at least they're not so close. My limousine driver rushes to open the door, and Shae helps me shove my dress back inside before crawling in beside me.

"Where to?" the driver asks once he's pulled away from the curb, but I can't answer him. Now that it's all over, I can feel the exhaustion spreading slowly through my body, and I know I won't be able to stop the tears from falling now. I've expended every bit of energy I have in the past hour or so, and I don't have anything left.

But Shae pipes up and comes to my rescue. "The airport, please," she says confidently.

I turn to her in confusion.

"Just because you didn't get married doesn't mean you can't go on your honeymoon."

GIULIO

Salvatore told me to skip town as soon as I completed this job. I follow all of his orders without hesitation, but I want this holiday so badly that I've been using it as motivation. Between hunting my targets, I've booked my hotel, bought my plane ticket, and stocked up on condoms. I'm ready, and by morning, I'll be gone.

First, I just have to check this final thing off the list Salvo gave me, but it's taking forever, and I hate waiting. There are worse ways to spend an evening, but there are definitely better ways as well.

Sure, I'm not shuffling to the communal shower in a dank gray prison with a homemade weapon hidden under my folded clothes, the disgusting slapping sound of sandals over wet concrete heralding the time of day, but I'm also not in a luxury hotel suite, on my back with one woman riding my dick and another sitting on my face either. Hell, I'm not even sitting at my nona's dining room table, letting her feed me too much roast chicken and freshly baked bread. So yeah...my night could be worse, but it also could be so much better than sitting in a cold car outside a rundown house on the wrong side of town, waiting.

I like to think of myself as a man of action. Not in the impulsive knobhead kind of way, but in a "point me and my gun at the problem and let me kill it" kind of way. I'm not interested in waiting for backup. I like to get in, get it done, and get out, but here I am, with my gun, ready to get the job done, and my target is MIA.

I hate it.

I huff out another sigh and check my watch. Five hours. I've been sitting in front of this house in a cold car, waiting, with a Berretta in my lap for five hours. I have a flight I need to catch in six hours. If I miss it, I'm going to take my frustrations out on this asshole I've been waiting all night for. He's the last name on the list. His time has run out, and if he makes me miss my flight, he'll spend his last few hours as a living man regretting it.

And then I'll book another flight, make it to this hotel that's costing me a fortune per night, and finally let some woman I hope to never see again use my face like a chair for as long as she likes.

What I'm saying is that I have plans, and nothing is getting in the way of that.

I can't speak Italian.

I bought a phrase book. It's probably somewhere in the bags I packed nearly a week ago, but I don't look for it before I land in Milan, because I don't care. I'm dehydrated from all the crying and champagne I drank on the flight over, and the last thing I want to do is speak to anyone in any language, so who cares?

Ryan doesn't speak Italian either, but we'd talked about how romantic it would be to spend an entire week on our honeymoon, struggling to communicate in a new language together. I'd imagined our honeymoon as a kind of team-building exercise, a time to focus on each other and our relationship, while eating all the pasta and gelato we could stand. I'd imagined the joy of not worrying about work or paparazzi or Ryan's social media content. It was supposed to be perfect; we'd paid damn good money for perfect. The reality is far from perfect. I'm not married. Ryan's not here.

I'm going to drink all the Italian wine instead of eating all the pasta. This is me, learning how to pivot in my new life without lists.

"Reason for visiting Italia?" the bored border agent drones at me without looking up from my passport.

I take a deep breath and bite the inside of my cheek, trying to stop the tears from forming in my eyes. I fail.

"Madam? Reason for visiting Italia?" he asks again, his voice much less bored the second time around. He sits up in his chair and finally looks at me. I'm guessing that he sees a tired, slightly hungover American with wet eyes and a trembling lower lip, and that gets all his attention. Unfortunately.

I can feel the weight of his heightened scrutiny. I know I'm playing this all wrong. I already look...well, unhinged might be optimistic. I've had a headache for a full day. My curly hair is still pinned in an elaborate twisted crown around my head, and there's a bobby pin literally digging into the back of my head. But nearly thirty-six hours since my hairdresser shellacked this style into place with half a bottle of hairspray, after ripping my veil from my head and sleeping fitfully on the plane *without* my silk scarf, I know without even checking that the elegant style looks less like the regal crown I was going for and more like a bird's nest.

And I can't even imagine what my face looks like. Every time I stumbled to the first-class bathroom on the plane, I conveniently avoided looking at my reflection. I couldn't bear it. So I don't know if there's even any makeup on my face. My throat is dry, my skin is drier, my eyes are so puffy they hurt, and I smell. Like, I can smell myself, and I hate it. So yeah, I can only imagine what the border agent is thinking as he looks at me. And even worse, I can imagine what I'll look like on the front page of every gossip magazine with the bold headline: "Ryan Fuller's jilted fiancée has been detained in Italy trying to go on their honeymoon alone." I can literally visualize it in my head. I can't let that happen.

Especially because hair and puffy face aside, I'm also dressed in an all-white Adidas tracksuit with the word "Mrs." written across my ass — without the accompanying man in the matching "Mr." outfit. I'm not particularly confident in my own abilities to save myself, but I need to try. I need to pull myself together at least long enough to get into this damn country.

I unclench my teeth but clench my fists. I dig my jagged nails into my palm and take a deep breath. I blink away the tears in my eyes, just enough to see the border control agent clearly; well...mostly clearly.

I've never been a great liar, and I don't have enough energy to try, so I decide to tell this random man the truth.

"I'm here," I start hesitantly, "because this is supposed to be my honeymoon. But yesterday — my wedding day — I turned on the news to find out that my fiancé had spent the night before fu—" I cringe, lick my lips, swallow and course correct. "The night before our wedding, my *ex*-fiancé had sex with my former best friend and a really famous stripper. So instead of being here on my honeymoon and doing a bunch of romantic and touristy stuff, I'm here to get drunk and eat a lot of carbs and probably cry myself into a coma. I don't know how you note that on the forms, but that's my reason for visiting Italia."

Some people say that when you unburden yourself, you feel free. Not me. Now that I've told someone about the soap opera I'm trying to escape, I feel more fully like the disheveled, stinking mess that I am. I hate Ryan and Trisha anew. I press my lips together and wait for some kind of response, and I get it. I watch as the light of interest fades from the passport agent's eyes slowly as he processes what I've said.

He sighs at me as if I've just told him that I'm here to count churches and statues. "That's it? I was hoping for something illegal. This job is so dull," he mutters the last sentence to himself. He rolls his eyes, stamps my passport, and slides it across the counter back to me. "Benvenuta a Italia, I guess," he says, eyes already shifting away. "Next," he yells before I can even scramble away.

I follow the signs to baggage claim. I'm so weak that when I finally see my suitcases, I struggle to get one off the conveyor belt and have to wait for the second one to do a full rotation on the carousel before I can grab it. I struggle to pull that one onto solid ground as well. No one helps me. I feel very alone.

I roll my baggage cart into the main terminal and come face-to-face with a small crowd of people milling around the entrance to the main airport terminal. In my mind, I know these are people waiting for their loved ones to arrive, but they remind me so much of the paparazzi that I freeze as spikes of fear shoot up my spine. Ryan's not here for me to hide behind or to give me cover to duck out of the way. Zoe's not here to throw a drink at anyone who gets too close. I don't even have Shae to grab my hand and endure this with me. There's only me, and being alone sucks. I haven't been alone since I started dating Ryan six years ago, and before that, I'd always had Zoe and Shae.

Thinking about Zoe is a mistake; it only deepens my paralysis. Even though she and I are polar opposites and fight constantly, she's never hesitated to put herself between me and the world, and I'd stupidly let Ryan come between us. And now she's half a world away. She didn't even come to the airport to see me off, not that I was particularly coherent when Shae and I met up with my mom and Aunt Caroline. I kept waiting for her to show up for me while I cried and changed out of my wedding dress in a bathroom stall that smelled so strongly of industrial-strength disinfectant that my eyes hurt.

Now I want to cry again. How do I turn my tear ducts off?

Thankfully, I might be frozen in despair and wallowing, but no one else has time to be inconvenienced by me.

A man in a business suit pushes past me, barely even registering that he's collided with a human being as he shouts at someone in Italian on his cell phone. It's rude as fuck, but it jostles me out of my paralysis. I step out of the way and open my shoulder bag. I snatch the big glasses case from the bottom of the bag. The relief I feel when I shove my new Chanel sunglasses onto my face is palpable and pathetic.

The glasses were Shae's idea. When I dug Ryan's credit cards out of my bodice, she'd snatched one at random and dashed off into the airport terminal. She returned with a Chanel bag and no credit card and told me not to ask her any questions while she shoved my new glasses onto my face.

If I'd been less distraught, I'd have wondered what the hell had gotten into my cousin, but I had been distraught, and apparently, very conspicuous, so who was I to complain? And even though I have a small crumb of wonder about whatever is going on with Shae, I do have to give it to her; these big ass, expensive glasses make me feel like less like a train wreck and more like a classy train wreck. They're cute, expensive, and cover half of my face.

And I'm not worried about Ryan. He's rich enough not to miss the money, and knowing that he's paid for them soothes a piece of my broken self. It's all about the details.

I still smell, and my hair is still a mess, but at least the sunglasses let me hide my bloodshot eyes and obscure my identity. That's all I need to give myself the courage to keep moving forward, literally.

So two claps for Shae.

Unfortunately, my luggage trolley is heavy as hell, and I can't rush past the crowd the way I want to, but I do get past them. I wheel my bags into the terminal and spot a line of suited men holding signs. I find the sign reading "Mr. and Mrs. Fuller" and head straight for it even though I feel sick at the words.

The driver holding my sign smiles at me. "Mrs. Fuller," he says in thickly accented English.

I burst into tears.

One step forward. Two buckets of tears dumped right on my head.

That's the saying, right?

We chose Villa San Marco in the mountains outside of Milan because even though all of Ryan's famous friends said the paparazzi were less ravenous in Europe, we still wanted some privacy.

The hotel sits on top of a hill just above a small village with a population so negligible that most of the guidebooks combined its figures with the three other villages nearby. The close proximity to Milan, plus the isolation and luxury amenities were part of the pitch Ryan's business manager made while selling this place to me. It wasn't my first choice, but as the limo winds through the village and up the mountain toward the hotel, I'm glad they pressured me into this choice. At least I can wallow in my heartbreak and humiliation in peace and style. Ryan owes me at least that.

I press my face against the passenger side back window and look down at the neat rows of the vineyard below. The driver says something to me in Italian; I assume he's telling me that we're almost at the hotel or that I'm smelling up the car. Both are viable possibilities, and neither really matters in this moment, so I turn to him, smile, nod, and then turn back to the view. There's a grease smudge on the window where my face touched it.

Jesus, is this rock bottom? Because it sure feels like it.

When the car pulls into the hotel's gravel driveway, there's a smartly dressed man standing at the wrought iron entrance.

I press my oily face against the glass to get a look at all the small terracotta-colored buildings. They look exactly like the brochures. The villas are three stories each, reaching into the sky. Apparently, the penthouse suites can get a clear view of Duomo, and all the villas surround a main pool that looks right out of some design magazine.

There's lush greenery everywhere, beautiful shrubs and flowers that make me think of summer and renewal even while I want to shrivel up and die. It looks like paradise, just like the brochures promised. I hope this place can accommodate me, my luggage, and the hole in my chest where my heart is a festering, dying thing.

I swipe self-consciously at my eyes. They're mercifully still dry even though I can feel a sob lodged in my throat.

Actually, I think I might be dehydrated.

The car rolls to a gentle stop in front of the hotel. The driver pushes his door open and stands. I grab my purse and hold it close to my chest as I wait for him to open my door, but I still jump when the rear passenger door wrenches open. I think I might be more tired than I realized. All that champagne and crying during a transatlantic flight has me really fucked up, and suddenly, all I want is a bed. And a shower. And maybe some more wine.

"Siamo arrivati," the driver says with a bright smile, offering his hand to me.

I push my sunglasses up the bridge of my sweaty nose and try to smile at him as he helps me from the car.

"Non parlo Italiano. Grazie," I say, officially exhausting all the Italian I learned in preparation for this trip, excluding the list of food to eat that I memorized.

"Si," the driver says. "Welcome to Villa San Marco," he says in charmingly stilted English.

I reach into my purse and pull a hundred Euro bill from my wallet. "Thank you," I say again.

"Grazie. Thank you," he says with a playful tilt of his eyebrows.

"Grazie," I say back, wondering how to get the hell out of this thank you loop.

He smiles indulgently at me and shakes his head. "Prego," he corrects. "That is how you say, 'you are welcome.'"

"Oh." When I realize what he's doing, I'm genuinely excited and then shocked that I'm feeling something besides...well, nothing. "Prego," I stutter hesitantly.

"And now you know a new word in Italiano," he beams at me.

I laugh, and it sounds weak and dry to my ears, which is accurate since that's exactly how I feel. But some feeling is better than nothing. That's a good sign, right? A sign that I'll be okay? I hope so, and I cling to that hope desperately.

I turn toward the hotel as the driver and a porter unload

my suitcases. I vaguely wonder if this is one of the stages of grief or if I've reached the phase of deliriousness that comes with exhaustion and dehydration. Maybe those feelings are the same.

Either way, when I step inside the lobby and look around, I feel as if I'm in a dream. Everything looks exactly as it had on the website, just maybe a bit smaller than I'd imagined, but not in a bad way. Quaint. That's the word that comes to mind.

I think Ryan might actually have hated the adjustment to scale, and that makes me happy in a vague sort of way just before an uncomfortable realization hits me. As much as he used to complain about the ostentatiousness of fame and celebrity, Ryan sure did love the attention. And now that I think about it, that explains the reality tv show he said he didn't want to do, and why he cheated on me with another reality tv star and an entertainment reporter. Attention. Ryan is an attention whore, and 'quaint' isn't really his bag. He'd apparently do anything for just a bit more attention, even torpedo his life and career.

"He's shameless, attention-seeking trash." That's what Zoe had said the day after she met him during an argument when I'd said things I still regret all these years later. What a terrible way to realize that she'd clocked him right from the start. God, what might my life be like right now if I'd listened to her?

I can feel myself spiraling as I think about it. My vision blurs with exhaustion and a few tears at the corners of my eyes. My head is pounding harder again, and the feelings of regret and self-recrimination are breaching the barriers of my mind.

Okay, I am definitely dehydrated.

"Checking in, madam?" a woman calls to me from the front desk with a bright smile on her face.

She's perfectly professional and put-together in the way most people who work in hospitality usually are. Looking at her makes me feel grubby and pathetic. Well, grubbi*er* and *more* pathetic, which is a feat because I also feel like whatever shit steps in when it's having the worst day ever.

"Y-yes," I whisper, walking toward her. "Yes, I am."

"Name, please."

I swallow.

When Shae took me to the airport to go on my honeymoon sans husband and with purloined credit cards, she clearly didn't think this through, and neither did I. I was devastated, what was her excuse? Never mind, that doesn't matter now. What were we thinking? We really should have taken a beat and considered if it was the best idea to go on a trip where all the arrangements had been made in my ex's name because he was footing the bill and made far more money than me. What if he canceled all the reservations while I was in transit? What if he canceled his credit cards after the expensive sunglasses purchase? Why is this the first time I'm thinking about these possibilities!?

I swallow a wave of bile in my throat before I can answer in a shaky, halting voice. "Ryan... Ryan Fuller. Mr. and Mrs. Ryan Fuller." I feel so fucking sick even saying those words that I have to wrap my arms around my torso just to stave off the feeling that I'm going to fall apart again.

The concierge's eyes widen, and she seems to take me in completely all over again. Her mouth falls open in an excited smile that just as quickly crumbles into chagrin, taking away any hope I had that news about my disaster of an almost-wedding hadn't made it to Europe.

I cringe back.

"Ah...yes, signora. Of course," she says, clearing her throat and slipping back into her mask of professionalism. "May I have your passport, please?"

I fumble, trying to find the small pouch with all of my important travel documents inside my purse. I push the garter I'd ripped off in that just barely clean bathroom in LaGuardia — that smelled so strongly of disinfectant that I wasn't sure if my eyes were watering from pain or the chemicals — until I find my passport and slide it across the desk.

"How...um... How would you like to pay for incidentals?" she asks with a red face and eyes that refuse to meet mine.

I don't know what it is about the fact that she can't look at me — even though I haven't done anything wrong — but it lights a tiny fire under my ass, and I'm pissed all of a sudden. I strain my neck to catch her eyes. I feel myself frown so deeply that I imagine my mother raising her head in alarm at my future wrinkles even though she's thousands of miles away. In that moment, all my sadness and exhaustion burns away.

Is this how the stages of grief work? Not the linear progression they tell you, but a kind of frenetic hopping from one emotion to the next and back again like an emotionally overwrought bunny? If so, I am killing it, and I also would like to be let off this rollercoaster. But right now, I ride the wave of my anger. I use it to do something I'm sure I'll regret at some indeterminate point in the future that hardly matters because it's not right now. I reach into my purse and open my wallet. The sunlight filtering through the windows glints off Ryan's embossed name on his black American Express card as I hand it over. Pettily, my mood lifts.

The woman looks at the name on the card and then at

me. I don't smile — I don't have that much energy — but I don't shirk her gaze either. I remind myself that I'm not actually doing anything wrong because technically, I'm still an authorized user on all of Ryan's credit cards. I don't allow the sliver of reality that this could have changed in the last twelve hours to surface. Lots of things could have changed since I punched him and his little girlfriend in their hotel room, but I can't consider that. Besides, Ryan's not organized enough to have already contacted his accountant. I hope.

I square my shoulders and prepare to tell the concierge that this is all on the up-and-up and to just run the card when she does, without any prodding from me.

We spend a silent, tense moment waiting for the computer between us to respond. I chew the inside of my cheek and try not to look too much like a scammer, and then I hear the sound of a printer turning on. The concierge smiles at me as she slides Ryan's card back to me with a receipt.

"Please sign here," she says in her friendliest, vaguely British accented English.

It's a small, ridiculous thing, and yet, knowing that Ryan will be paying for the next week of my depression-drinking and eating and massages does actually ease some of the ache in my heart. Even if it's only temporary, I sigh in relief and then instantly feel so tired I worry I'll fall asleep in the middle of the long-overdue shower that's first on my list when I make it to my un-honeymoon suite.

But I can't risk being awake any longer than is necessary, so just in case I don't fall asleep quickly, I need to be prepared. "Can you please send up a bottle of white wine?"

"There's a bottle of champagne in the room already, madam."

"Great, that'll be a good start while I wait for the wine."

I don't see judgment in her eyes. I'm tired as hell, but I'm pretty sure that what I see there is mild amusement, and you know what, I'll take it.

"Might I suggest a bottle from our local vineyard?"

Maybe she sees the way my face scrunches at that because she smiles wider, leans over the desk, and lowers her voice.

"We have a few very expensive varieties," she whispers.

I huff out a dry laugh. Lord, I need to drink some water. I imagine that the mild amusement I saw earlier might have been tinged with a bit of grudging respect. Maybe she's had someone cheat on her, or she just likes crime. Either way, I decide that I like her.

"Send two of the most expensive bottles you have," I say.

Her smile is wide enough that I assume she must be getting some kind of commission. "Of course, madam."

I turn to the elevator, and a porter follows behind me. I ride up to the honeymoon suite — which is really just one of the larger penthouses on the top floor of each villa. I'm still dehydrated, exhausted, maybe hungry, and I definitely still stink, but there's a bit of pep in my step. Whatever stage of grief this is, it's the best by far, even if I know it's fleeting.

GIULIO

This isn't a holiday. Not really. I know that, and so does Salvo, but I've never actually taken a holiday in my life so, I decide to treat this trip like one instead of like the hideout that it is. I don't have the kind of job that allows for much leisure time, and I'm not looking to change careers, so I decide to take this unprecedented break with both hands. This might be the only holiday I ever get, and I want to feel it in my bones for a few weeks after I'm back in the muck that is my life.

Villa San Marco is just far enough away from Naples and remote enough that the likelihood of running into anyone who knows me is slim, but it's still close enough to get back to Salvo just in case I'm needed. This is comforting enough that I hope it means I can relax. If Salvo doesn't need me, the next week is mine to do with as I please, and the only things I want are rest, sun, wine, and figa.

Pussy. I want all the pussy I can handle and more. I want to drown in the wettest pussy I've ever had the pleasure to taste and touch. I deserve it. I'm also near to bursting with adrenaline in the post-job, pre-holiday excitement haze. My veins feel as if they're coursing with pure lust.

Until the bubble bursts.

"What do you mean, it's booked?" I hiss across the front desk to the concierge — cute, maybe smiles too much, great rack; a definite possibility.

"I am sorry, sir," she says in English. "The room has been booked for months. There was a mistake on the website. The system shouldn't have allowed that booking."

"But it did. Who's in my room?" I ask slowly, each word a single frustrated syllable.

The concierge smiles nervously at me, and I decide that she absolutely smiles far too much. I'd still fuck her. "I'm sorry, sir. We don't share the information of other guests. But we do have another penthouse suite available if you would like."

"Another penthouse?"

"A junior penthouse suite," she corrects. Still smiling. Trying to rush past that word. Junior.

I'm 190 centimeters tall. There hasn't been anything *junior* about me since my balls dropped.

But I don't tell her that because I'm supposed to be laying low, and I feel like an angry guest cursing and grabbing their cock in the middle of the hotel lobby might garner a bit of unwanted attention. I take a deep breath in through my nose and push it out slowly through my mouth. I saw that shit in a movie once. It works.

I need to solve this like a civilized, wealthy traveler who can afford a holiday in the exclusive Villa San Marco, instead of who I really am, even though that might be more efficient and effective.

"This is the only option? The *best* room you have?" I ask in that slow, irate voice.

"Yes, sir. It's next to the superior penthouse suite. I am sorry," she says in a halting voice.

Under normal circumstances, I could have just taken my business elsewhere. Although, actually, if I were in Naples, this wouldn't even be a possibility. If I were in Naples, whoever took the penthouse suite I wanted would have already been dragged to the junior suite — maybe even another floor — so I could have the room I wanted. But I'm not in Naples, nothing about this is normal, and I remind myself, as I take another deep breath, that this is a good thing. Being out of my element is good. Being unknown instead of as Salvo's bullet is a blessing, even if it's temporary.

"Fine," I say, throwing the counterfeit credit card Alfonso procured for me onto the counter. "Give me the *junior* penthouse." I sound like a petty, bitter man when I'm anything but. But this is my holiday, and I can be anyone I want.

"Yes, sir. Wonderful, sir," she says, tapping at the computer. "Please allow us to send a bottle of our best wine to your room. It's made in the valley just below the hotel."

"Make it two," I say like the scheming fuck I am.

"Of course, sir," she says. Still smiling.

I shrug and turn toward the elevator, thinking that I won't be able to see her smile if I bend her over the bathroom sink.

BY NO MEANS is this the first time I've slept alone in six years. Ryan traveled a lot for work, and I never minded because I've always loved having a big ass bed all to myself, especially when the sheets are silk so I can sleep without my scarf. Under different, better circumstances, I would be giddy standing next to a big, plush hotel bed that looks like a firm cloud that's all mine.

But I'm not giddy. I'm standing next to this bed with a towel wrapped around my body because I was too lazy to moisturize, let alone put on pajamas after my shower. I'm clutching a half-full bottle of wine in my left hand, staring at this bed and feeling nothing but dread. I take a deep swig of wine as I pull the covers back and wince. Note to self; wine tastes terrible mixed with the remnants of toothpaste.

I feel hollowed out and skinned raw. It's not the possibility of sleeping alone that's getting to me; it's sleeping alone on the first night of what should have been my honeymoon that makes me feel like the fool that I am.

I crawl into bed with tears already pooling in my eyes. I burrow down into the bed, finding a warm home in the soft silk sheets but still sitting just upright enough that I can empty this bottle. And I do. I take swig after swig as the watery pools of my tears spill down my cheeks. I manage to cry quietly at first, but eventually, a loud, guttural sob bursts past my lips, and I can't stop it or the one after.

I should order food, but I don't. I should drink a bottle or six of water, but I don't. I shouldn't fall asleep, with an empty bottle of wine clutched in my arms like a teddy bear, with a pillow wet with my own tears, but I do.

GIULIO

I don't want to sound like an asshole, but I hate whoever the fuck is in the penthouse suite that should have been mine, and not just because they stole from me, but because they won't shut the fuck up.

Is there any sound worse than a woman crying?

Yes. A drunk woman sobbing like her entire world is ending before she passes out and then the sound of her loud snores.

I'm lying in the best bed I've ever slept in, covering my head with a pillow to hopefully drown her out and failing. This isn't the holiday I planned. This isn't the hotel stay I paid a fortune for.

My fingers flex against the pillow, missing the heavy steel of my gun. I'm not saying I want to kill her or anything, I'm not a monster, but I definitely wish I could shoot something to take the edge off of all the other times I fell asleep with the sound of a woman crying in another room.

I hate it. Fuck, I hate this.

I'm in a right fucking mood as soon as my eyes open the next morning.

I usually get the best sleep of my life the night after I finish a job. I sleep like the dead, to be honest. Is that crass? Maybe, but it's true. I have a conscience — of course, I do — but I take comfort in a job well done. Just because that job well done happens to involve taking out a few low-level hoodlums coming after my boss and burying them and not, say, picking up the garbage, doesn't really matter. Not to me, at least.

But as soon as my bare feet hit the floor, I somehow feel even more tired than I did when I crawled into bed last night.

I need an espresso.

I shower and put on my best holiday casual attire. I might be in a shit mood, but I still need to play the part. I pull on a pair of linen shorts and a button-down shirt that I only button to cover my abs. I haven't been able to make it to the gym for the past few weeks, and they don't look as defined as I like. Not that I plan to ruin my holiday by working on them.

I look at myself in the mirror across from the bed. I slick my hair back from my face and turn my head left to right, checking out the five o'clock shadow that's on the verge of turning into a beard, just the look I prefer. Not that I'm vain or anything. Not really. Okay, I might be a little vain. I like to look good, and I like to snatch a bit of attention when I can — when it's not a hazard — and I don't think I should apologize for that. I'm not the kind of man who apologizes often anyway. Besides, it feels good to be appreciated for looking good. That's not just for women; I don't care what anyone says.

Unfortunately, looking at myself doesn't improve my mood today. I'm too tired and annoyed. I roll my eyes and sigh at my reflection before storming out of my *junior* penthouse suite in search of the hotel restaurant.

As I wait for the lift, my eyes move to the door at the other end of the hall; to the real penthouse. I wait, and I watch that door, willing it to open with a barrage of angry, intense thoughts, so I can have the chance to tell whoever the fuck is staying in *my room* to keep their crying to themselves tonight.

But it doesn't open.

And that makes me even fucking angrier.

ZAHRA

I wake up drunk. Or hungover. Or jetlagged.

Probably all three.

This isn't that far off from the way I planned to wake up

on the first day of my honeymoon, but it sure hits different when I'm single, alone, heartbroken, and still dehydrated as hell. I feel like a wreck, a husk of my former self but now with swollen eyes. Instead of hopping directly in the shower, I have to press two damp towels against my eyes for a few minutes. This definitely wasn't in the cards for my honeymoon.

Once I can see again, and I've showered, I decide that I need to get dressed and leave my room. As much as I want to wallow in peace and quiet, I'm worried that if I don't leave today, I won't leave for the rest of the week, and that's not why Shae sent me here. Also, Zoe wouldn't approve in the slightest.

I finally open my suitcases and stare down into them, trying to imagine if I have an outfit that adequately reflects my mood. I don't. Ryan's stylist helped me pack for this trip. The vibe we were going for was #cottagecore *Under the Tuscan Sun*. I feel very *Eat, Pray, Love* right now, but specifically that scene in the movie where Julia Roberts just cries. Yeah. I feel like that but Black and tipsy.

My best wardrobe bet is to fashion an outfit that's as different from the storm of my emotions as possible. I want to hide away, so I need to stand out. Very Zoe Wardrobe Tips 101. The sheer red wraparound dress shows off the white bikini underneath in glimpses as the light hits it, and the thigh-high slits at the sides show off all the leg I can. To be very candid, I look fucking amazing. I'm still drunk or hungover or whatever, but I *look* fantastic.

Except my eyes. They're still swollen and red — almost the same color as my dress, but that's beside the point — and no outfit can distract from that. Sunglasses can, though, especially big expensive ones that are technically stolen property, just like this is technically a honeymoon. I push my new Chanel glasses onto my face with a relieved sigh. I don't feel any better, but I look like a brand-new person, and that's the most I can ask of myself right now.

I consider going to the hotel restaurant, but I'm not hungry. I have a headache, and I need to drink at least a sip of water to feel normal again, but as I ride the elevator down to the lobby, I realize that I don't want to feel normal. Normal will mean having to process all the betrayal I've experienced. Normal will mean that I'll have to accept that the life I'd been building is nothing more than dust. For the first time in my life, normal is the exact opposite of what I want.

I want oblivion. I want to forget. I want to *not* think or feel.

Once the elevator opens up to the lobby, I turn down a hallway and end up at the gym. I frown and double back to the front desk.

"How may I help you, madam?" a new front desk attendant asks me.

I clear my throat and try to smile like a not-frazzled mess. "Can you tell me how to get to the pool?" I ask in a hoarse voice that makes me feel even worse for some reason. It's been hours since I've spoken or made any sounds besides sobbing. It actually hurts to talk.

"The pool is just down the southern passage," he says, indicating the other hallway I didn't go down.

"Thank you," I croak. "Do you have poolside service?" I remember to ask.

"Of course, madam. What would you like for breakfast?"

"Wine," I say. "White. Expensive. Whatever you sent to the South Penthouse," I tell him.

"Yes, madam," he says, judging me with his eyes, but

not with his voice. I appreciate that. "Would you like anything to eat?" Okay, he's a little judgey out loud.

Not really, I think, but it's only my first day here. I don't want to get a reputation as the sad lush in the penthouse, not on my first day, at least, and especially not while I'm stealing the money for these incidentals.

"Yes," I say. "Some fruit? Maybe croissants?"

"Of course, madam."

"And water," I add since I'm pretending to be a normal, well-adjusted person.

Once my order has been received, I head for the pool with a bit more enthusiasm. This feels like progress.

Here's hoping I don't start crying poolside. Actually, scratch that, I'll cry in my bikini if I want. I've earned it.

GIULIO

I'm a simple man, and after two very strong espressos and breakfast, I feel less angry. Still angry, just less so. Also, I'm easy, and the flirty waitress flashing her cleavage at me as she serves me breakfast lifts my spirits considerably.

I feel like a new man as I walk outside to spend a little time by the pool. The sun is high in the sky, but it's not so hot yet that it feels oppressive. I strip down to my swim briefs and recline on a wooden pool chair with nothing but a stone wall behind me so no one can sneak up on me. Just because I'm on holiday doesn't mean I need to let my guard fall completely.

I forgot my sunglasses and close my eyes as I let myself relax. I sigh contentedly and pretend that my cover is real, and I'm just a businessman taking a break for some sun and relaxation. It's true enough.

I fall asleep in the sun within minutes.

"Vorresti dell'acqua, signore?"

I wake with a start to find a strange woman standing over me. Instinctively, my hand moves to my back, searching for the gun I normally have there. I panic for a second when my fingers grasp at nothing but air. Eventually, my brain catches up with my eyes. It takes a few seconds, but soon enough, I recognize the woman above me as the waitress from the restaurant. Well, I recognize her tits. She has a bottle of water and a glass on a silver tray in her hands, a smile on her face, and a hungry look in her eyes. I realize why as her gaze travels down my body.

I'm hard. Well, half-hard. Just a little belated morning steel. Nothing major. I'm not trying to show off or anything, but like I said, I like to be admired, and the look in her eyes isn't a terrible way to wake up from my little siesta.

"Si. Grazie," I croak as I sit up in my chair.

She tears her eyes away from my cock just long enough to place the water and glass on the table next to me before dragging her gaze back to my lap. This one is good for my ego.

"If there's anything you need, sir..." She doesn't finish that sentence with words, but I get the gist when she licks her lips and waits patiently for me.

"I'm in the junior penthouse," I tell her. I make sure that the word 'junior' doesn't stick in my throat, but it's a struggle.

Her smile lifts. She flutters her inky eyelashes. She's

pretty, but to be honest, even if she wasn't, her breasts are amazing, and I'm on holiday to fuck and relax. I've wasted enough time not doing those things.

"Si, signore," she whispers before turning and sauntering away.

"Perfetto," I whisper to myself.

I open the bottle of water and drink deeply. When I stand from the lounger, I feel light — and not just because I'm not packing a few kilograms of pistol in my belt for the first time in years — but because no one here knows who I am.

Some men in my line of work love to swagger around town like their dick is bigger than the fucking Eiffel Tower, and their balls are dragging on the floor. They enjoy throwing their weight around figuratively and violently. They drink up the deference that comes with the don's cover because they need it to survive. I don't, and thankfully, neither does Salvo. I don't need people to cower when I walk into a room; I need them to be so afraid of me that they cower when I'm not there, a small but important distinction.

I live half in shadow in Naples. Everyone knows who and what I really am, even if they'd never say it with their full voice. But here I can walk in the sun, naked without my guns, and feel more anonymous than ever, and that is intoxicating.

I dive into the pool and feel refreshed as soon as the water fully engulfs me. I swim a few laps from one end of the pool to the other. My muscles stretch as I glide through the water, and the rest of the world disappears. For a few moments, I don't worry that there's a scope trained at my head or a bomb behind a potted plant. I feel free, and I can't even remember the last time I felt that way.

When I surface on the far side of the pool, I'm panting for air, muscles that I don't normally use are burning, and the sun is beating down on me.

I cross my arms over the ledge of the pool. Most of the pool chairs are empty, but I come face to...feet with adorable, dainty white-painted toes, muscled calves, and thick, light brown thighs. The woman lying on the chaise in front of me is wearing a bright white bikini under this deep red gauzy...thing that makes the half-hard rod between my legs stiffen. It's a good thing I'm in the water because my cock is threatening to escape from the waistband of my briefs. In fact, I should stay in the water to hide myself, but I don't. I love legs. Long and trim, short and thick, and everything in between, as long as they look like they'll feel good wrapped around my waist or head, and these legs look exactly like that.

I plant my palms on the side of the pool and lift myself out of the water with my eyes fastened on those legs for the duration. I slick my wet hair back from my face as I walk toward those legs and the curvy body they're attached to; the curvy body of a woman reclining on a lounge chair with a glass of wine in one hand and a large pair of sunglasses covering most of her small round face. I stand over her, wet and dripping, almost wishing that I hadn't just given the waitress an open invitation to my room. Almost. Maybe the waitress will get a look at these legs and be willing to share; this is the holiday of dreams.

"Can you move? You're blocking my sun," she says with a scowl. I watch as her eyebrows come into view over the upper edge of her sunglasses. In contrast, she's much less enamored of me than the waitress. That shouldn't turn me on, but it does. People are complicated. Her scowl deepens the longer I stand over her until finally, she pulls her glasses down the bridge of her nose with a single, elegant finger. She's definitely not as taken with me as the waitress.

A shame. My dick is very interested in her.

"My apologies, tesora, I was just so captivated—" I say, exaggerating the depths of my accent.

She cuts me off before I can fully demonstrate the way my tongue caresses English vowels. She rolls her eyes before pushing her glasses back onto her face. She waves her hand dismissively. "So not interested. You can't even imagine how *not* interested I am."

I laugh despite myself and turn and walk away. Beautiful legs or not, I'm not on holiday to waste time with a woman who's not interested in me. But I'll be here for a week. Maybe next time, I think, as I feel her eyes on my ass.

ZAHRA

I spend the day drinking by the pool.

Maybe not the best decision I make, but I said yes when Ryan asked me to marry him, so it isn't the worst either. Besides, the disrespectful eye candy breaks up the monotony. I can't even remember the last time a man has flirted with me so shamelessly. Actually, it's entirely possible that a man has *never* hit on me so boldly. After I started dating Ryan, I started to feel as if I was living in a glass case and slowly suffocating. Actually, that's generous. I felt invisible while dating Ryan. The only people who ever seemed to see me were his rabid fans. Even he didn't notice me as intensely as they did.

But the hairy Italian man in the tiny swim trunks notices me. I don't want anything to do with him, but God, I love the attention. I love the attention so much that I forget that my life is a mess and that this isn't a regular vacation. When I'm done day drinking, I head into the hotel restaurant to eat a real meal like an adult, and I almost feel like a whole, functioning — slightly tipsy — human being for a few hours.

That is until I head up to my room. I shower, change into one of the many sets of sexy lingerie I packed and open another bottle of wine. Whatever. Don't judge me; this is my Not Honeymoon. I crawl into bed, and that's where I make the mistake.

I start crying again. I don't mean to, but I do, and I can't stop it.

That's a grief thing, right? The sudden, uncontrollable tears? I'm not even sure what triggers them this time. I haven't cried all day, mostly because I was too caught up watching that shameless man's ass and dick in those tiny ass trunks as he strutted around the pool like a peacock, heavy on the cock. Whatever, the point is that I didn't cry all day, so I have no idea why I cry myself to sleep tonight, but I do.

And I hate it.

***

GIULIO

The bitch is crying again.

Great.

I roll my eyes at the sound of her pitiful hiccupping.

"Sta' zitto," I mutter to myself. "Shut up," I yell louder, and in English, just in case she heard me and doesn't understand Italian.

Get out of town.

Lay low.

Get some rest.

Those were my orders. Simple. Easy. Except not.

How am I supposed to get some rest when there's a fucking wailing banshee next door?

When she starts crying again, I mutter to myself for a few minutes before getting out of bed and finding my earbuds, trying to drown her out with a little heavy metal. It doesn't work. I need silence to sleep.

I feel myself getting tired and rip my headphones out of my ears, praying that she's done with her sobbing. She is, but now she's snoring.

"Fucking paper-thin walls," I mutter to myself before falling into a fitful sleep.

I WAKE up in a bad mood. Again.

Not only did I sleep for shit, but I was so angry that I forgot to wait for the waitress to show up at my door. So not only is the banshee fucking with my sleep, she's fucking with my pussy. Unacceptable.

This isn't the holiday I deserve. It's only been two nights, and I'm already nearing the end of my admittedly short rope. I throw the sheets from my body with a roar and jump into the shower on a mission. I pull on another pair of swim trunks and linen shorts and a t-shirt from the closet and rush from my room. I don't even take the time to do my hair or spray on any cologne. The only thing on my mind is getting to the front desk and handling this in the civilized way since I've committed myself to pretending that I'm civilized.

"Ciao, Mr. Rossi. Buongiorno," the concierge says as I rush up to the hotel's front desk. My steps falter for a fraction of a second. Who the fuck is Mr. Rossi? It takes me a few seconds to remember that I am. I blame the lack of good sleep on almost blowing my cover before leaning into my cover identity. That's why I left my pistol in the hotel suite.

I nod at the concierge and force myself to smile. I'm not the kind of person who smiles easily, but I can pretend if it means getting what I want. And what I want is for someone to get the bitch next door to shut up so I can get a good night's sleep.

"Ciao," I grumble as I step up to the front desk. I sound surly, so I stop smiling. Why bother?

"How may I help you?" the concierge asks.

"I'm in the junior penthouse," I spit at him, "and the person next to me..."

"Yes, sir?" the man asks, leaning closer as if I'm about to say the most interesting thing in the world.

I don't like that reaction, and it makes me pause. I'm not a turncoat. I don't snitch. And more importantly, now that I have a second to think about it, I don't know if ratting out the woman in the penthouse is the way to go. Not because I'm not pissed, but because I don't make moves without assessing the potential consequences; that can be deadly in my line of work.

I sigh, exhausted, and defeated for the moment. "Never mind."

"Are you certain?" he asks, and the eagerness in his voice only strengthens my resolve that this isn't the right course of action. At least not right now. I look around the front desk and realize that everyone's paying attention to me — to what I might say next — and there are warning klaxons blaring in my head. I need a new strategy.

"Is the restaurant open?" I ask, instead of telling him to shut her up before I do.

The man deflates, and his smile broadens falsely. "Of course, sir. Just that way," he says, gesturing behind me.

I grunt my thanks and turn toward the familiar hallway to the restaurant, trying to figure out what the fuck that strange encounter at the front desk was all about.

I skulk through the restaurant and fall into a chair by a bank of windows with a perfect view of the pool. There's a family with a small child playing in the shallow end. I don't realize that I'm looking for light brown skin and oversized sunglasses until my mood dips when I don't see the woman from yesterday. I feel worse now.

"Buongiorno. What would you like for breakfast, sir?"

"Espresso," I say, before turning and coming face-to-face with the same waitress from yesterday. Well, face to breasts. My mood lifts immediately. She's not big glasses and brown thighs and dainty white toenails, but her hungry smile is an open invitation.

"Espresso, per favore," I tell her.

She nods and turns away. I watch her hips and ass move as she leaves.

I scan the dining room looking for the woman from the pool again. Sue me. There's no one in the small restaurant except the servers and an old man chain-smoking on the patio.

When the waitress returns, she leans forward, much more than is necessary, to put the cup and saucer in front of me.

She smile down at me.

I smile up at her nipples. It's as if last night never happened.

"I have a break after lunch, if there's *anything* else you need, sir?" she whispers in English.

I reluctantly raise my eyes to her face and nod. "I'll meet you at my room," I tell her as I raise the cup to my lips.

"Yes, sir," she says and turns to walk away again.

I watch her ass again. The view is nice.

She passes the door to the hotel, and I see a flutter of silky black fabric and dark sunglasses. My dick lurches just as the sweet, bitter coffee hits my tongue. I can hear the sound of her sandals slapping against the tile floor over the restaurant's music and the sound of dishes clanking against one another. The background noise fades away, becoming faint as if I'm not in this room, as if I'm out there following the angry woman with the great legs down the hallway.

And next thing I know, I am.

ZAHRA

He's preening.

It's pathetic.

I can't look away.

His body is fucking perfect.

Not like action star perfect. Ryan has a movie star body. It's a contractual obligation. He spends so many hours in the gym that I used to joke that the rowing machine was his other girlfriend.

I have to wonder now, though, if he really did spend as much time at the gym as he said he did. Maybe he was meeting up with Trisha or someone else; anything is possible now, I realize. Every part of the life I'd had with him — the life I'd felt sure enough about to wreck my relationship with my sister — is now up in the air. How do I know what was real or not? How can I tell which parts of our life he'd been honest with me about and which he hadn't? That's assuming, I realize, if *any* of it was real. Just as that thought crosses my mind, I feel queasy.

I down the rest of the wine in my glass and pour another. I want to drink this feeling away. I want to drink all the feelings away.

I take another sip as a splash from the pool grabs my attention.

The peacock is doing laps again.

The wine glass stops halfway to my mouth. I angle my head to the side to catch the pert globes of his ass bouncing above the waterline as he swims a perfect lap toward the other end of the pool. I'm sweating. Could be the sun. Could be the alcohol. Could be all that fucking dark body hair. Could be all of the above.

Either way, Ryan never made me sweat.

I'm sure that sounds bitter and fake, but it's not. Ryan made me blush and giggle, and he made me feel small in his huge contractually-muscled arms. But so fucking turned on, I start sweating just looking at him? Never.

I don't know what the fuck is up with this man and his tiny swim trunks, but he's doing it for me. Big time. He's even sexier than yesterday, and I can't look away.

Okay, never mind, that's a lie. I know exactly what's working for me. I love the way his thick, wet, jet black hair looks slicked back on his head. The way the downy soft five o'clock shadow makes his jaw looker sharper. It makes him look dangerous, like really dangerous, not movie star dangerous. And I love the contrast of all that dark hair across his lightly tanned skin.

The rim of the wine glass hits my lips just as he climbs out of the pool slowly, walking up the stairs as if he knows each water droplet dripping from the thick, dark hair covering his chest and abdomen and legs and arms makes my pussy ache. I wonder how all that hair would feel against my naked skin.

Ryan's waxed smooth, and I never told him, but I actually hated it. I love a hairy man, and this shameless whore in front of me is picture-perfect. Also, those tiny ass swim trunks he's wearing don't cover any of it. Hell, it's barely covering his rigid length.

No complaints. I'm drenched, and I don't just mean my skin.

He grabs a towel from a stand near the pool and doesn't even pretend to dry off. Instead, he throws it over his shoulders and struts around the perimeter of the pool. I take my time sipping the glass of wine in my hand, watching him from behind the big, dark lenses of my glasses, thankful that the pool area is mostly empty, and no one can see just exactly what I'm staring at or how hard.

Okay, I'm a little preoccupied and realize my miscalculation too late. I think no one can see me. I'm wrong. I'm so lost watching the gentle sway of his hips that I don't realize he's headed my way until his dripping body is standing at the foot of my deck chair. Actually, I don't realize that soon enough; I'm too busy licking the rim of my wine glass as I try to visualize every ridge and vein on his penis.

"Do you like what you see, tesora?" he asks in the sexiest Italian accented English I've ever heard, with the cockiest grin any man has ever had the audacity to muster.

Busted. I should be embarrassed, but I'm half a fresh bottle of expensive wine in, so I'm not.

I lift my head — making sure that I take in the hairy, tanned expanse of his chest as I do, because why the fuck wouldn't I? — and then make eye contact with him through my dark lenses.

There's a small tendril of wet hair falling across his forehead, a single droplet of water hanging from the end. It's sexier than every artificially sexy scene in every one of Ryan's movies I've been forced to endure and secretly hate.

"Do you like what you see?" he asks again.

He can't see, but I roll my eyes. Zoe always told me that men are much more attractive right before they speak, and this is one more thing about which she was always right.

I pull my glasses down the bridge of my nose like yesterday and roll my eyes at him again. I don't want him to miss the annoyance on my face. "You're blocking my light again."

My mouth is dry. I'm almost certainly dehydrated again, but also, he's Sexy. As. Fuck. And that's not helping my dry mouth either.

"That wasn't the question," he says with a smile.

Jesus. No man should be able to make a complete stranger wet with just a smile, but this stranger does. He can.

I am. Wet, that is, just in case it's unclear. My eyes move down his body again. I can't help myself. I blame the alcohol and also the fact that Ryan and I haven't had regular sex in three months. I hadn't felt strong enough to tell Shae that on the day of my Not Wedding, but it's true. How could I admit to anyone — even my cousin — that the man who'd convinced me that all the training he was doing for his next movie was fucking up his libido had actually been perfectly fine to fuck my best friend and a stripper? I couldn't, so I hadn't. I'd ignored my unmet needs then, but my body refuses to ignore them now as, I swear to God, his dick flexes inside his trunks as I watch.

My eyes fly up to his face. The answer he wants is hell fucking yes, I like what I see. He's not going to get it, though. I push my glasses back up the bridge of my nose and tip my head back to rest against the chair. He can't see my eyes, so I don't close them, but I do look away. I have to. All that fucking chest hair? I want to rub myself against him, and if I keep looking at him, I just might.

And he knows it. I don't have to wonder anymore. I know that he knows that I like what I see by the soft burr of laughter that rumbles in his chest.

I scowl but refuse to look directly at him. I don't trust myself.

He's watching me as intently as I'm watching him, the only difference is that he's not trying to hide it or pretend it's anything besides naked lust.

And unfortunately, my traitorous nipples return the greeting his dick gave me just a bit ago, hardening to painful points against the fabric of my thin swimsuit.

He smiles at my chest and licks his lips. "I like what I see," he tells me.

"I didn't ask you that," I hiss. I can hear the strain in my voice.

He laughs again, watching me and not leaving.

I need him to leave. I need to leave before I embarrass myself.

Too late.

I rub my thighs together the tiniest bit. I just need the friction to take the pressure off my throbbing clit. I need something to calm my hormones and my pulse.

Unfortunately, he notices and laughs again, but this one sounds different. Can a laugh sound contemplative? If so, this one does. And I don't have to wonder what — or who — he's contemplating. Me. My hard nipples. My aching pussy. His lurching dick.

And so am I.

I haven't had sex with anyone but Ryan in six years, and besides the occasional daydream, I haven't even thought about it. But right now, I'm thinking about it — *really* thinking about it — and the Hairy Italian knows it. I can see it in his eyes. What he can't see is the conflict I'm feeling about Ryan. Not because I still feel some kind of loyalty to my ex and his community dick, but because in six years, Ryan never made me wet just with a look. And I was going to marry him! Why?

If Zoe were here, she'd have told me to put my existential crisis on hold and take this man back to my hotel room. My older sister has a very firm belief in sex before feelings. Actually, scratch that, she's more of a sex, no feelings type of person. She doesn't believe in coincidences or regrets, and she's always said that if more women followed their body's advice on who to fuck — but especially on who not to — their lives would be easier. I usually ignore her and her life advice, but only because I've always known she was right, and I didn't have the guts to follow her lead. My body said Ryan was a good provider, but my pussy's rating of him was... "Meh."

My pussy has a very different assessment of the man in front of me with his short briefs, downy chest, and cocky grin.

A drop of water falls from the tip of his chin onto my foot, and I swear I have to swallow a moan. He catches that too. Okay, there's a definite downside to too much attention.

His eyes watch my throat bob, and he opens his mouth, but whatever he's about to say is lost in the loud intrusion of screeching children.

We both turn to see four kids sprint right into the pool, intruding on the quiet, intense moment we'd been sharing. The quiet, intense moment that was maybe about to end with me fucking a complete stranger on a deck chair for anyone having a leisurely lunch in the hotel restaurant to see.

The intrusion should have doused my mood, but it doesn't. And even though I never take Zoe's advice — to my peril — I decide to do so now. If there are no coincidences, then those loud ass kids aren't an accident. No strange public sex for me, and to cement that fact, I stand from the deck chair in a rush. I set my wine glass down, grab my purse, and clutch it against my chest — to hide my nipples — push my glasses up the bridge of my sweaty nose, and rush back into the building.

"Wait, tesora," the man calls after me.

I pretend not to hear him.

I WANT TO FOLLOW HER, but I can't. My dick is so hard that I practically expose myself when I turn to call after her. I wrap the towel around my waist and grab my clothes from the lounge chair I'd claimed and then rush back into the hotel. She's gone.

I consider asking someone at the front desk if they saw a beautiful woman with big sunglasses and the most perfect nipples ever created and if they can tell me what room she's in, but after the strange encounter this morning, I don't think that's the best idea. I consider waiting around the lobby just in case she reappears, but Salvo told me to lay low, and stalking some beautiful, angry American around seems like the opposite of that. Besides, my dick is so hard that it's actually hard to walk. I slink up to my room instead.

My room door isn't even closed before I drop my clothes and rip the towel open. I let it fall to the tile at my feet and dig my hand into my briefs. My head falls back, and I groan so fucking loudly in relief that I hope the person next door hears me. A small payback for the last two nights.

I push my trunks down my legs just far enough to get

my balls free and lean back against the door. I give myself an exploratory stroke, squeezing the tip hard enough to hurt, and pull back to the root, twisting my hand as I go.

"Ai, cazzo," I hiss. My hand feels great. It's not a warm, wet pussy, but I can get the job done. And I'm about to. I love a good masturbation session, but this is going to be a great one. I'm already pulling up the memory of those sunglasses perched on the tip of a soft button nose and a pink tongue swiping across the rim of a wine glass from my mind. I'm ready to pore over every second I spent with the Angry American to give myself the messiest solo orgasm I've had in a while when there's a tentative knock on my door.

"Merda," I grunt, squeezing my leaking tip.

"Va via," I yell through the wooden door.

"Sono io. La cameriera del ristorante," she whispers through the door.

I pull the door open in a heartbeat. I don't cover myself. Why would I? The waitress's eyes and mouth widen in shock, and because I'm a vain fucker, I love it.

I pull her into my room. She mumbles something about not having a lot of time, and embarrassingly, I know I won't need it. I don't tell her that, of course, I simply pull her into my arms and crush her mouth to mine. My dick is caught between us, and while I don't love the friction caused by her rough nylon trousers, I don't hate it either. I walk her back into my bedroom awkwardly, with my trunks still down around my thighs, and then I throw her onto the bed.

She giggles. I don't like that sound. It's girlish and innocent, and that might get some men off, but not me.

"Nuda," I bark at her to cut off the noise. Thankfully, she stops giggling as she does what I say. I push my trunks down my legs and then move, naked, to the closet. I open my suitcase, an errant ray of light hitting the metal of the case where I keep my travel guns, with a combination only I know, and no one would guess. To a novice, it looks like nothing more than a small suitcase, but I cover it. I grab the brand-new box of condoms I bought for the occasion and rip it open. I pluck a foil packet from inside and do the same. I groan as I roll the latex down my shaft. I definitely will not last long, but I'll make it good for...whatever the waitress's name is. I need to protect my reputation just in case there are other waitresses willing to deliver their pussies to me on a silver platter.

"Si, cazzo," she hisses when she sees me, and I feel the same. She's not fully naked, but she's shimmied out of her trousers and underwear, and her shirt is hanging off one arm.

That will have to do.

I pounce on top of her, burying my face between those deliciously full breasts. I lick at her pink nipples and suck them into my mouth in turn greedily. She squirms underneath me, the soft skin of her thighs caressing my balls. Much better.

She runs her fingers through my hair. I want to tell her that she can tug on it a little, just enough for me to feel a sting at my scalp and the base of my dick, but my mouth is currently busy. I wonder if I would have to give that kind of direction to the Angry American. She'd probably be pulling my hair and scratching at my scalp out of general annoyance. Maybe she'd even bite my shoulders.

My hips jut forward at the thought of her teeth sinking, just the tiniest bit, into my skin. Not enough to draw blood, but hard enough to leave a mark.

And that does it.

I flip the waitress onto her stomach. I pull her onto her

knees by the strands of her long, mousy brown hair at the same time as I shove my hand between her legs. I circle her clit and wrap her hair around my fist, arching her back beautifully.

Her entire body is flushed, and she's groaning softly. She shivers every time I move a finger to her opening, pressing against her firmly, waiting for her to open for me. Waiting for her to beg me.

"Per favore," she whines after a few soft taps of my thumb, and I push forward as if I'm going to give her what she wants before pulling back. She whimpers. "Per favore."

But that's not enough, I realize. I don't just want her to beg me softly; I want her to do it loudly.

My eyes drift to the wall at the head of the bed, and I realize what I want now — besides the Angry American's thighs cutting off my sun and air. I want the bitch next door to be as angry with me as I am with her.

"Píu forte," I hiss at the waitress.

"Per favore," she says, shivering as I push my thumb inside her.

"Píu forte," I bark, moving behind her.

"Dai. Dai. Per favore," she says louder, but not loud enough.

Her entire body shivers as I take my finger from her wet pussy and place the blunt tip of my dick at her opening. I push her knees farther apart with my legs and then scream loud enough that if anyone is next door, I know they will hear me.

"Louder," I say in English as I push my entire shaft inside her in a single thrust.

She screams loudly this time, and she doesn't stop while I fuck her, hard and fast, our skin slapping together each time I bottom out inside her.

I don't even know if the woman next door is in her room, let alone if she can hear me, but I imagine that she is and she can.

I also imagine that the hair wrapped around my fist and the pussy I'm punishing is the Angry American's. There are a lot of people in this room.

I don't hate that either.

ZAHRA

My heart is still racing. I've showered, changed, and drank the largest bottle of water in the minibar. The last couple of days aside, I'm not actually much of a drinker. A glass of wine with dinner or the rare boozy brunch with my friends is much more my speed. I've been overdoing it in my haste to drown my feelings, and I realize that now. Or I realized that when I'd been giving serious consideration to letting a strange man fuck me by the hotel pool.

Like...seriously considering it and about to do it.

I don't know if this is rock bottom, but it sure feels like it.

I sober up and put on a cute little lace teddy I'd hoped to seduce Ryan in because I don't have any real pajamas. I plop onto the bed, feeling more like myself than I have in days. I'm not going to pretend that I feel normal. Who knows what normal feels like for me anymore? But I feel... not like the dregs of a very expensive bottle of wine, and that's a marked improvement.

And then I hear a loud moan from the hotel room next door.

"Per favore," a woman yells. No, scratch that. She

moans, and that makes me realize my grave mistake in my rush to sober up.

I haven't masturbated in days, and I didn't pack a vibrator for this trip. Big mistake.

The woman whines. If she says actual words, I can't hear them, but I don't need to. I know exactly what a moan like that means. I imagine whoever she's with has pushed his dick into her so hard and fast that it took her breath away. I'm jealous. I know what that sound means, but it's been years since I've felt it. It's been years since Ryan and I have been so overcome with lust that we've fucked each other in the middle of the day. Well, it's been years since I've experienced that. Who knows what Ryan and Trisha have been getting up to for the past six months?

The honeymoon was supposed to help us reset, but I'm here alone.

Alone and horny.

I don't even think. I crawl to the head of the bed and settle against the pile of pillows. I press myself against the wall I apparently share with some unknown couple fucking each other like rabbits in the middle of the day. When I'm this close to the wall, I can hear their whines and panting breaths.

I bend my legs at the knees and spread them wide. I shiver as the room's cool air hits my sex. I'm not even wet, but the kiss of the air conditioning is like a firm slap. I love it. I gently caress my breasts, massaging them, tweaking the nipples, thrilled at my own touch. Thrilled at any touch after the past two days.

The woman moans again, and my hips begin to circle unconsciously. My pussy clenches, unhappily empty. Can a pussy be unhappy? Whatever, mine is. And while I can't go back in time and make Ryan not be a garbage human being, or even better, go further back to never having dated him at all, I can fill my empty, aching pussy.

I move my hand over my bare sex and caress my clit with the pads of my fingers. My head falls back against the headboard, and my mouth falls open. I sigh contentedly.

Is it narcissistic to enjoy my own body as much as I do?

Ah, who cares?

I circle my clit and caress my lips until I'm wet. Until I'm dripping excitedly. Until I can push two fingers inside myself with ease.

My sighs turn to moans.

My hips circle again, and my fingers sink deeper inside myself.

The woman's not whining or moaning anymore; now she's yelling and cursing — I'm assuming — in Italian. I can hear their bodies slapping together, and best of all, I can hear the man's wild grunts. I like them.

I pinch my left nipple and move the hand between my legs faster. And faster. And faster.

I'm obscenely wet now.

Has Ryan ever made me this wet? Has he ever fucked me hard enough for our neighbors to hear? Why haven't we ever fucked each other while listening to our neighbors or at least while watching our favorite porn together?

Why did I waste my twenties on a man who boxed me in to protect his own public image instead of letting me be free and growing with me? Thank God I didn't marry him, I think, just as I come in a wet rush all over my fingers.

SHE'S CRYING AGAIN.

As soon as the waitress leaves, I shower quickly and crawl into bed. I'm asleep practically as soon as my head hits the pillow, and it's the best rest I've gotten in weeks until the weeping bitch wakes me up. So not only is she keeping me up at night, she's waking me up too.

"Sta' zitto," I scream, and she mercifully stops.

I sit up and stare at the wall, wondering if it could be so easy.

It's not.

"Fuck you," she yells and then starts crying again.

"Bitch," I hiss under my breath and scramble from the bed.

I walk naked into the living room to find the pile of my clothing still by the front door. I throw the t-shirt over my head and shove my legs into my shorts. I grab my room key and pull the door open so hard it slams into the wall.

I'm really not sure where I'm planning to go, but I head toward the elevator. Maybe I should go down to the front desk. Who cares what they think if it means I don't have to toss and turn in bed listening to her cry? But I pass the elevator and walk directly toward the door of the other — bigger — penthouse suite.

I don't have a plan. Normally I would set about charming a woman to get what I need. And if charm won't fix my problem, guns usually will. But neither of those tactics seem particularly useful when the problem is a woman who won't fucking stop crying. I know I should take a second to think, but instead, as soon as I reach the penthouse door, I pound my fist against it so hard my knuckles hurt.

I can still hear her crying, but it's faint. "Sta' zitto," I yell through the door.

The crying fades away. I pound on the door again two more times, so she knows I mean business. I'm about to turn and walk away when I hear footsteps on the other side.

"Go away," she says in a quiet whisper.

And I unleash. I spit sarcastically that now she wants to be quiet. I tell her that I haven't slept well in two days because of her fucking crying. I tell her that this is my first holiday ever, and she's ruining it. And I even tell her that her room should have been mine because I'm still furious about that. But I say all this in Italian, so she cuts me off mid-rampage.

"Non parlo Italiano," she says in a tentative voice.

I exhale in frustration.

"Stop fucking crying," I say in slow, irate English.

The silence on both sides of the door stretches long enough that I start to wonder if she's still there or maybe she's calling hotel security.

Just as I'm certain that she's gone and resolve that I should leave too, the door wrenches open.

"Fuck you," the woman says once we're face-to-face.

And even without her big sunglasses, I know it's her. I would recognize those lips anywhere.

ZAHRA

"You?" the man from the pool says. I watch as his face transforms from frustrated rage to shock and then...arousal.

"You?" I echo, my body already responding to him like I did earlier at the pool. What are the fucking odds that the same man who's been preening for me at the pool for two days is staying in the other penthouse suite? And what are the odds that he'd show up at my door when I'm at my weakest and most pathetic? "What are you—?" I can't even finish that sentence for so many reasons.

On the one hand, I'm feeling...warm in so many places, mostly from arousal, but I'm also annoyed because this man — this sexy, hairy man — was just pounding on my door like the fucking police, *and* he's interrupting my nighttime routine of drinking wine and crying.

Whatever the odds, I'm horny and pissed. It's confusing, to say the least.

"What are you—?" he starts, and then his sentence cuts off just as abruptly as mine did.

I don't know what he's thinking, but I do know that he's staring at me — looking me up and down like he wants to strangle me. Or fuck me into next week.

Or both.

My pussy and thighs clench at the thought, and that's as disorienting as the lust. The newness of these emotions... Yeah, Ryan and I never traversed these boundaries.

But bitterness aside, I know that I need to pull myself back together. I have to. It was dangerous to be this close to him — and want him — by the pool; it's even more dangerous to feel whatever the fuck these feelings are with no other rooms on this floor besides ours and a lot of privacy to behave in ways I know I shouldn't.

I frown at him so hard my cheeks hurt. I may not speak Italian, but I'm very certain that he'd just been calling me everything but a child of God, and I focus on that, not — if anyone is wondering — the bulge tenting his shorts. "What the fuck do you want?" I'm finally able to spit at him, channeling some of the venom I feel for Ryan and aiming it toward him.

And do you know what this cocky motherfucker does? He has the nerve to grin at me — much like he had earlier today — as if he knows the flint in my voice is false. The arrogant asshole.

"I want you to stop fucking crying," he says in a calm voice that almost erases the rage I'd heard when he'd been yelling at me just seconds ago.

"Fine. Noted. Got it," I say, and try to close the door on him.

He stops me. And then his eyes dip to my chest. I watch as that grin — that sexy fucking grin — widens, and he licks his lips like a Cheshire cat.

What are the odds that this horny bastard would show up at my door the same night I decided to dip into my honeymoon lingerie? High, apparently, because I watch as this man runs his wet tongue over his lips, taking in all the flesh that this very expensive teddy shows off. My shoulders, my legs, even patches of skin under lace inlets, and if I move too quickly, my bare ass. There's almost as much skin on display right now as by the pool, but maybe it's worse that the lingerie leaves some of my skin to the lacy imagination; more for him to see and guess about.

There's more I want him to see and touch with the tip of that wet pink tongue, I think.

This is a mistake. I know that, even though it doesn't feel like one exactly. Well, not like other mistakes I've made. I'm not sure what it *does* feels like, though, but definitely more right than wrong.

When he finally speaks, it's in a whispered, seductive tone. "What does a beautiful woman like you have to cry about?"

"I didn't realize tears had an aesthetic," I say, rolling my eyes.

I try to close the door again and then jump as the palm of his left hand slaps against the wood.

And then I shiver.

I blame Ryan for this thing I'm feeling, somehow. But Mr. Tiny Swim Trunks doesn't even let me wallow in that.

His eyes meet mine, and he licks his lips at me again as if he can taste me on his mouth. Or he wants to.

He wants to. "Invite me inside," he whispers.

His accent is so thick each word feels heavy as it falls from his lips and travels the short distance between us. His voice is so deep that I can feel it tickling the sensitive skin along my inner thighs and circling my nipples.

"No," I whisper, but there's no conviction in that soft breath. I know it, and so does he.

"Why not?" he asks, tilting his head to the left and smiling down at me from a brand-new and unfortunately very attractive angle.

"Because I don't know you."

He leans against the doorjamb and shoves his hands into the pockets of his shorts. "Yes. That's why you should invite me inside. So that we can become acquainted."

The uncomfortable truth about this moment is that I hear him say these words, and my rational voice thinks he's whatever the Italian for 'fuckboy' is, but my pussy...sigh... She doesn't give a damn. My pussy hears this man say this cheesy ass pickup line, and she's absolutely here for it. Like...probably-ruining-this-very-expensive-lingerie here for it. I'm wet beyond belief in couture lingerie in a Not Honeymoon Suite for a man who is not Ryan.

Disconcertingly, I can hear a voice in my head that sounds uncomfortably like Zoe, telling me to "bust it open" for this absolutely random, unknown, deliciously hairy man, and even in my brain, my older sister is very hard to argue with.

"I want you to stop crying," he says.

I feel... To be honest, I feel all the warm fuzzies when he says these words even though I know I shouldn't, and so, true to form, I do the thing all my exes have accused me of doing: I deflect. "Fine. Got it. I'll keep the volume of my quarter-life crisis down. Sorry."

I try to close the door again. His hand stops me again.

"Who has made you cry?" he asks. I wish he hadn't.

There's no chance that I'll tell him about the farce that is my life, but for a split second, I want to. I want to explain to him how and why Ryan's betrayal hit all the most tender parts of my soul, but I have no idea why I want to do that. I don't know this man. "That's none of your business," I spit out.

"Not yet," he says definitively. He leans forward, but he doesn't move to step inside my hotel room. I notice that, because I know that it matters, even if I want to ignore it and be annoyed at him instead.

I move my hands to my hips. "Why do you care?" I ask again.

"I told you," he says. "You are too beautiful to cry."

"Oh," I breathe in the softest whisper because I can't think of anything more complex than that single word at the moment.

"You've been keeping me awake at night," he adds. There's a playful smile on his face, and I don't need to think too hard or too long to know what he's insinuating.

And goddammit, keeping him up all night is all I can think about now as well. Dangerous.

"I heard you earlier," I whisper.

Most men would deflate when a woman they're shamelessly flirting with tells them they've heard them fucking, but this man doesn't. His eyebrows lift, and that grin widens into a cocky smile. "Did you?" He steps forward, the toes of his bare feet just crossing the threshold into my room. "Did you like what you heard?"

I did.

I swallow before stepping back and to the side, the invitation clear. He doesn't hesitate to take it.

I feel more naked than I actually am for some reason.

It could be his presence. He's not the biggest or tallest man I've ever met — Ryan has at least a few inches and a few pounds of muscle on him — but he takes up space in the not small foyer of my room in a way that's baffling and intoxicating. I swear, as soon as the door closes, I feel smothered by him, and I don't hate it.

He doesn't touch me, but I feel as if he's everywhere when he turns to look at me with dark eyes, lifted eyebrows, and a devilish smirk on his face. I can feel his gaze on me, all over the exposed skin, but also slinking under the lace, teasing me.

"What's your name, beautiful?" he whispers as his gaze moves down my body.

"You don't need to know that."

He chuckles warmly as he raises his eyes to meet mine.

I shiver — violently — at the intensity I see there. I'd let the playful grin fool me into thinking whatever *this* is was light, nothing of consequence, but it's not. When we make eye contact, his eyes bore into mine and pin me in place. There's nothing light about the way he's looking at me, and his heavy presence feels very consequential.

"You don't have to pretend to be cold with me."

"I'm not pretending," I say, wishing the words weren't true. I'm not a full-on ice queen yet, but I'm getting there. I've been feeling myself crystallize ever since I saw the footage of Ryan drunkenly stumbling back to his hotel with a casual arm over Candee's shoulders, and it hasn't stopped. No matter how much wine I drink or how many tears I cry, I can feel it happening. In a few days, when it's time to go home to some shitty version of my post-Not Honeymoon life, I know I'll be someone different. I'll be some bitter, jaded, wary, mistrustful version of myself. I know that, and I've been trying to drown that realization out with all the wine I can get my hands and Ryan's credit cards on, hoping to stave it off for as long as I can.

But I'll fail. I know that as surely as I know that letting this stranger into my hotel room was the wrong call.

"This was a mistake," I breathe.

He shakes his head as he steps forward, crowding me

with his body instead of just his presence, and once again, I don't hate it. He's still not touching me, but now I can feel the warmth of his body on my skin. The clean scent of his soap fills my nostrils.

I take another half step away from him, and my back hits the wall.

I should freak out in this moment, now that I'm trapped between a complete stranger and an actual hard place, but I don't. I'm not.

He's still not touching me. There's a sliver of distance between us, enough that I can feel the slightly cooler air of my room brush between us, tickling the tips of my nipples and making me gasp.

I'm eye-level with his throat, and I watch as his Adam's apple bobs as he swallows thickly.

"It doesn't have to be a mistake," he whispers, his breath kissing the baby hair on my temple. "And you don't have to cry yourself to sleep tonight."

I lift my eyes to his and shiver again. That playful grin is gone, and there's something about seeing him from this close and this vantage point that accentuates his sharp cheekbones and rounded jawline and the contrast of his dark beard and tanned skin.

"He's not worth it," he says, startling me. My eyes widen, and I press myself harder against the cool wall, letting it ground me in this moment. I ball my fists until my still-jagged nails bite against my palm. "Whoever you're crying about isn't worth it. Trust me. You can cry yourself to sleep tonight or let me take your mind off of him." His head dips lower as he speaks. Our lips are a hair's breadth away.

"How did you... I don't even know you," I say, tripping over my words and his very accurate assessment of my pathetic predicament. "Why should I trust you?"

He grins again, and it's even more devastating somehow. Maybe all of his facial expressions look this good up close and from below. And even though this moment is *a lot,* I wonder if he would look even more attractive if I were to lower myself to my knees in front of him.

I shiver, and the tips of my nipples brush his chest.

His Adam's apple bobs again.

"You're right," he says. "You shouldn't trust any man. Especially not me. But even more so, anyone who would make you cry. No man is worth your tears."

"Is this why you wanted to come in? To tell me that all men are scum?"

He grins and lifts his hand to my face.

I swallow, lick my lips, and then nod once, giving him permission to touch me. Finally.

And then he does.

His skin is rough. Not calloused, like a man who does manual labor for a living, but rougher than an actor who has monthly spa appointments. He's not like Ryan, I think again, and this time, I don't let it stop me. I lean into his touch.

He grips my chin with his thumb and forefinger for a second, before his thumb moves from my chin to the curve of my bottom lip. He traces the line of my lip with his nail. "You need to forget him," he whispers.

"I'm trying," I say, shaking my head.

He tips my head back until I have no choice but to look at him. "No," he says. "You are crying over him. Wallowing. You need to forget him. I can help you."

"I don't fuck strangers," I blurt in a shocked whisper.

He smiles and presses the tip of his thumb firmly against my lip. "Then let us become acquainted," he says again.

I don't give myself a moment to think. I spread my lips and lick at the tip of his thumb with the tip of my tongue.

His smile is lowkey devastating.

"Okay," I whisper to him. "Let's get to know each other."

I LIKE to think that I'm an average man — even with my line of work — and by that, I mean that I don't like to work too hard for pussy. I don't have the time or energy to put much of an effort into getting a woman to fuck me. And even if I did, I know that This Woman would be too much. Getting her attention would require the kind of focus I'm only willing to expend on finding, killing, and disposing of the men Salvo tells me to. And keeping her... No. She's so far out of my league I'm practically exhausted thinking about it.

Unfortunately, I know she'd be worth it. I can tell that every bit of time and all the money she'd require — based on the quality of her lingerie — to remain in the luxury to which she's clearly accustomed would be more than worth it. Too bad I can't afford her.

But something about knowing that she's out of my league makes my dick twitch in my shorts. She's the kind of woman I'd pass on the street, do a double-take — maybe even a triple-take — because she's so beautiful, and then I'd think about her for the next few days, weeks, maybe even years, but nothing more.

We're not on the street right now, though.

We're so close that I can smell the clean scent of her soap and a floral scent that I assume is her perfume as I follow her into the penthouse suite that should have been mine. I won't need to do a double- or triple-take with her because I don't plan to look away, especially not when she looks at me over her left shoulder. The glance is shy, tentative as if she's afraid I'll disappear while she's looking away.

She's made a mistake. I know it, not that I'll ever tell her that. She shouldn't have invited me inside her room. She has no idea what I am. If she did, she wouldn't be looking at me with red-rimmed brown eyes and dark lashes clumped together from her tears and beautiful, plump lips stained red from the wine, begging me silently to stay with her.

I will. I couldn't leave here even if I wanted to; my mind and my body are decided on the matter.

There's a half-full glass of wine and a bottle on the coffee table. She snatches the bottle by the neck as she passes and then sits, elegantly, in a straight-backed chair.

She nods at me to sit on the couch. She's watching me with those eyes I want to fall into, even though I shouldn't. I don't know what I'm most attracted to, the sadness or the lust. Maybe both.

Maybe *I've* made the mistake.

"Why are you crying?" I ask again. I shouldn't. This isn't the kind of acquaintance either of us wants, and considering the circumstances of my life, this isn't one I should court. And yet I am.

"None of your business," she bites back. She's much better at staying on task than I am right now. Her voice shakes, but she's not afraid of me. She should be, but she's not. My stomach tightens with desire.

"I thought we were getting to know each other, tesora," I tease.

She eyes me slowly, those sad, dark pools traveling from my face down my chest. She lifts the wine bottle to her plump lips and takes a long sip as her eyes drink me in.

I lean forward and grab the glass of wine from the coffee table. I imagine that my lips touch the same place hers did as I take a sip from her discarded glass.

"I don't want to talk," she whispers, still watching me. "That's not why I let you in."

"What do you want to do?"

She licks her stained lips. I swallow a groan. "I want to..." Her words trail off as her eyes dip. I swear I can feel her attention on the tip of my dick, which is hard and uncomfortable trapped inside my shorts.

"I should apologize for my temper earlier," I tell her.

"Were you really angry with me?"

"Yes."

"Then, don't apologize. Don't lie."

I wonder if she knows how much she's told me in that simple request. "Fine. I won't apologize for yelling at you through the wall or pounding on your door or all the things I've thought about you over the past two days."

"Good. Now stand up."

The wine glass is halfway to my mouth, but my hand freezes, and my eyebrow lifts. "Excuse me?"

"I know what I want to do," she says in a deep, sultry voice.

"And what is that?"

"I want something real," she says. I know she's swallowed something, hiding some explanation from me. "I want to see you come," she whispers as if she's scared of the words.

I'm energized by them.

That admission should be dirty, but from this woman's burgundy-tinted lips, they sound like a filthy command, and I like that. I like it a lot.

I watch her as I bring the glass in my hand to my lips. I drain the rest of the wine in a single gulp and set it on the table. And then I do as she commands. She's watching me. I'm watching her. There's something about this moment that I like more than I can understand. It's the way she's looking at me — assessing, scrutinizing, and lustful — combined with how small and vulnerable she actually is. This slow collection of moments feels powerful and heavy as it settles on my shoulders and in my chest. I've never felt anything so enormous and fragile at the same time.

I should leave.

I'm not the kind of man who can afford to have enormous moments. I shouldn't spend any time with a woman who makes a tingle zip up my spine just from her words. I'm made for women like the waitress; women who want to use me — and let me use them — for a few minutes or hours but no more. And even though she's looking at me as if that's all she wants, I know, just as certainly as I know that the lingerie she's wearing costs more than my favorite sidearm, that this is not a woman who should ever settle for less. I've caught her at a low moment, and I shouldn't take advantage of it.

But then she takes another slow sip of wine from the bottle. A rivulet slips from her lips and drips down her chin. I watch the dark liquid cut a path over her jaw, down her neck, and then straight for her cleavage. I can't get any harder, but I can feel my dick pulse in my shorts trying.

"Do you know what I did when I heard you earlier?" she asks.

"No."

Her fingers disturb the red path before moving down her neck to her chest, over her stomach, and then stopping right at the top of her mound. I couldn't have looked away if I'd tried.

I don't try.

"I touched myself," she whispers.

My eyes fly to hers. "Don't say it like that."

"Like what?"

"Like it's something to hide behind flowery language. Don't lie." I echo her words on purpose, challenging, settling into this moment when I should be leaving.

Her arm moves. I want to see her hand between her legs almost as much as I want to see what her sad eyes look like when she comes.

"I was fucking myself with my hand. Every time you made her scream, I pushed another finger into my pussy."

I unbutton and unzip my shorts and then push them over my hips. I haven't even touched myself, and I'm breathless. My hands are shaking. I don't care if she sees. And she does see because she's watching as my dick springs into view.

Her small gasp is like an electric shock that I can feel circling the base of my dick.

"Are we going to do this together?" I ask her as I sit. I scoot down in my seat and spread my legs so she can see me clearly. I have all of her attention, and I plan to keep it.

"Yes," she whispers, bringing the bottle to her lips.

I lick my palm and grab ahold of the head of my dick with my right hand. I circle my left hand around the base and squeeze tight. My gaze darts to her hand. She's rubbing the pads of three fingers over her mound in circles and then up and down. Light caresses. I use her hand as a cue and begin to slowly jack my cock up and down, squeezing rhythmically at the base just the way I like. I move at the same rhythm she touches herself.

I want to come. I want to sink balls deep inside her, and yet, I also don't want to rush this.

"Do you know what I was thinking about when I was fucking her?" I ask.

"What?"

"Who?" I correct. "Do you know who I was thinking about while I was fucking her?" I lift my eyes to hers.

"Me," she whispers. I like that she's not pretending to be naïve to seduce me. That wouldn't work, and just watching her breathe is enticement enough.

"Was I wearing something like this? When you were thinking about me?" she asks, moving the bottle of wine over her breast.

I smile, realizing she's using it to stimulate her nipple. This Woman will kill me.

"You were naked. I'm not the kind of man to worry about lingerie."

"Good to know," she says and shifts. She raises her right leg and throws it over the arm of her chair.

I can't help but laugh. When I look back between her legs, I see that she's moved the lacy gusset of her lingerie aside. Her lips are a slightly darker shade of brown with soft downy hair over her mound. And wet. Mio Dio.

She's soft and meek and demanding and shy and playful and bold and nervous and brave. I've never met anyone like her. I'm certain I never will again. What kind of fucking dimwit breaks the heart of a woman like this? I know the answer. I don't even need to think deeply about it. He's probably a piece of shit just like I am. He didn't deserve her, and neither do I.

But he's not here right now, I am. And so, I smooth my palm over the leaking slit at the head of my dick. It's not enough moisture to ease my strokes, so I lick the palm of my hand. I taste myself — salty and earthy — and then grip myself again.

She mirrors me, lifting her left hand, and slips two fingers into her mouth. I stroke myself with renewed vigor as her dainty fingers circle her left nipple and then move back down her stomach. I watch her movements intently. How can I not?

She moves that scrap of fabric aside again to stroke the hard bud of her clit. I can see it now, peeking between her lips, and I want to taste it. I want to taste her.

"No," I bite out in a sharp command.

Her fingers still. My balls tighten against my body at how easy that was; how easy all of this has been.

"You watch me. And then I watch you," I say through clenched teeth.

"You don't want to play together?" she asks as her index finger moves over her lips. She presses at her opening but doesn't push inside.

I have to tear my eyes away, force myself to meet her gaze. "If we play together, you're going to end up over the back of this couch," I tell her.

"I don't fuck strangers," she says. I believe her. She's playing with fire because her defenses are down, and I'm a terrible man, but even I have a faint whisper of morality, so I need to keep ahold of this moment for the both of us.

She looks frustrated, as if she wants to change her mind, but can't, and that hesitation is all I need to know that I've made the right decision.

"I come, and then you come," I repeat.

There's a moment of hesitation before she sighs in resignation. "Fine," she says, "then come."

And I do. As soon as she says those three words, I groan loudly as my cock jerks and spurts messily over my lap and stomach. But I don't stop, because she's watching me, and I want her to remember this moment as surely as I will. I stroke myself furiously with a tight grip trying to wring every drop of come from my aching cock for her. I want her to watch me come and know that all of this is for her. Like a tribute.

I don't know if she understands — I hope she doesn't — but she does watch me, cupping her sex and sipping wine straight from the bottle the entire time.

I hope she's enjoying the view.

ZAHRA

For a man who liked to show off, Ryan never once masturbated for me, and I'm suddenly resentful, even though I never even considered that this was a thing we could do. Still, I'm borderline pissed the fuck off that he didn't consider it either, and this anger is something completely separate from the betrayal.

That's foolish, right, that I even care about this, since... you know, everything else? But I do care. I can't explain why I'm so pissed off except that watching this stranger — Jesus, I don't even know this man's name! — come all over himself uncovers a small door inside me that I didn't even know existed. It's like a lightbulb goes off in my head at the sight, and I suddenly know something new; something I hadn't even realized was a possibility one second is a sure thing the next.

That new self-realization? That I feel powerful in a way I never have before knowing that I can make someone come so hard, they turn into a sweaty, shaking mess. Because of me. Because I wanted it. Because I told him to do it. None of the very expensive wine I've been drinking like water has made me feel so light or intoxicated. And shockingly, nothing has made me feel so completely over Ryan than knowing that he deprived me of this feeling.

Just as I think that, this strange man stands from the couch, stuffing his wet dick inside his shorts. His t-shirt sticks to the mess he made on his stomach.

Dirty. This entire situation is dirty. I'm shocked by how much I like it.

He steps around the coffee table and then sits on it, right in between my legs. He grabs the bottle of wine from me, careful not to touch my skin. He tips his head back, and I watch his throat bob as he takes a deep drink from the bottle Ryan is paying for.

"Your turn," he says, eyeing me casually as if this moment is nothing spectacular or special or new. And he's so effortlessly sexy and filthy that I think that's a very real possibility.

"Can you see?" I ask playfully.

"Con chiarezza," he says very seriously.

I don't know what that means exactly, but I'm pathetically obsessed with the way the Italian rolls off his tongue.

I watch his face as I pull my lingerie aside again. He groans.

I watch as he uses his free hand to reposition his dick. I wonder if he's hard again. I slide two fingers down my slit, feeling the wet warmth of my sex. He licks his lips and takes another sip of wine.

"Are you wet, tesora?"

I use my fingers to open my slit for him.

He licks his lips. "Si," he whispers, answering his own question.

"What would you like me to do?" I ask him because it feels right. I'm not sure why, but it does.

He lifts his eyes from my pussy and stares at me with a quiet intensity that makes me shiver. "I want to watch you pleasure yourself. I want to see what you like."

"Is that what you showed me?" I ask, even though I know it was.

He nods and tips the wine bottle to his lips again.

I push two fingers inside myself as slowly as I can manage.

He moves that fiery stare back between my legs. Where it belongs. He watches as I begin to fuck myself in deep, agonizingly slow strokes, soaking my digits.

"Touch your clit," he demands. And it is a command.

"You said you wanted to see what I like," I tease even as I do as he says, shivering as I toy with the bundle of nerves with just the right pressure.

"Did he ever make you feel like this?" he asks me out of the blue.

"I don't want to talk about him," I huff and then groan as I accidently apply too much pressure to my clit in irritation. My toes curl.

He smiles wickedly.

"I will take that to mean he did not," he replies smugly. "Did I tell you to stop?"

His voice is a deep, demanding whisper, and it makes me shiver again.

We make eye contact, and his bright brown eyes are warm, clear, and sympathetic. "You should not overthink this, tesora." His voice isn't cocky or teasing now. He sounds almost kind. As if he knows what I'm thinking, and he wants to distract me.

I so desperately want to be distracted.

That's what I've been trying to do with the wine — we both know that — only I know that it hasn't worked, not really. No matter how much I drink, how much money I charge to Ryan's black card, or how many tears I shed, when I close my eyes, I still see the news footage of Ryan and Candee and the security footage of Trisha slinking down that hotel hallway. I can't escape it, except I did, for a few minutes, while I watched him masturbate for me. That distracted me, and so I lean into the escape he's offering, even if it's only for a few moments.

I start to rock my hips against my fingers, trying to get deeper. I circle my clit with a bit more pressure.

He smiles and obscenely palms his dick through his shorts. There's a wet spot where the head would be.

Watching him watch me turns me on so much that I'm moaning now, and he so obviously likes the sound that I spread my lips and moan louder.

I also catalogue the way his breath hitches when I briefly move my hand to my breasts to pinch my nipples through the lace. I watch with rapt fascination as his dick stiffens in his shorts, and he rubs his palm over it. I watch as that wet spot grows. I enjoy the way our breaths quicken at the same rate, and our moans mix.

I'm so close.

"Come here," I tell him, shocking us both.

His hand stills. "Have you changed your mind?" His voice is full of hope. It's a thrill to be wanted so thoroughly.

"Don't you wish," I pant, still fucking myself. "On your knees."

"I do," he says, lowering himself in front of me.

When he's eye-level with my pussy, he moves his hands to the chair. He doesn't touch me, but the chair moves. He pulls me closer; he pulls my pussy closer to him and his mouth.

"God," I groan. My back arches, my eyes close, and I full-body shiver.

When I look back at him, he's watching my face again.

I think this moment will last for just a second, but it doesn't. I'm fucking myself so hard we can both hear the sound of my fingers invading my wet core, but he doesn't look away from my face.

"I want to see you come," he says.

This isn't a command. His voice is softer, slightly pleading. I like this tone almost as much.

My body starts to shake as I get closer and closer to the edge.

And then I feel his touch, just a soft brush of his fingers against my hips, and then the sound of the chair scraping against the floor as he pulls me closer still.

My hips jerk, my back arches, and I cry out as the orgasm washes over me.

His hands are on my knees, keeping them apart as I shudder and spasm through one of the most intense orgasms of my life. His touch only intensifies the moment, and the orgasm begins at my core and radiates out again and again and again.

I try to fold in on myself, but his hands keep my legs wide. He wasn't playing. He wants to see me come, and he does. Every gushing spasm, every loud cry, every wracking sob when it's just too much, and I have to finally stop touching myself. He sees it all, and I imagine that he catalogues every second just as I did when I watched him.

I don't know how long or how hard I come, but he doesn't move from the floor where I've placed him.

Eventually, I begin to settle. I slump into the chair with his hands still pressing my legs apart. My muscles are starting to ache. I feel as if I've fucked a mile. Is that a saying? It should be. I'm spent. I can feel the small electric aftershocks of that orgasm in every muscle and tendon and hair follicle. I look down my body, and he's still there, on his knees in front of me, his mouth dangerously close to my pussy.

I shiver again.

He notices with a smile.

And then I remember why I wanted him on his knees in front of me — besides just wondering if he would do as I said.

I straighten in my chair and lean toward him. I feel his fingers flex around my knees.

I move my wet fingers to his lips. At some point, while we were performing for each other, the sun set. He looks amazing and slightly menacing in this new light.

I smear my essence over his smile and push my fingers between his lips. I skim the pads of my fingers over his soft tongue.

He doesn't look away as he sucks every drop of me from my digits.

I sigh in a kind of contentment as I pull my fingers from his mouth. "What's your name?" I ask without thinking.

"Giulio," he says, and I don't know if it's the postorgasmic haze or his accent — or both — but that's the sexiest name I've ever heard in my life.

"And yours?" he asks with a playful lift of his eyebrow.

"Zahra."

He tightens his hold on my knees as he stands. The weight of him makes me groan because I'm absolutely imagining him on top of me in that moment.

He brushes his mouth across my left cheek up to my ear. "The next time you think about crying over that stronzo, remember that I'm just next door," he whispers to me.

"What's a stronzo?" I ask, stumbling over the word.

He turns and walks away, smiling at me over his shoulder. "I will tell you next time, tesora," he says.

"There won't be a next time," I call back.

His laughter rings out as he pulls open the door and walks through, cool as you please, as if my pussy isn't still thrumming at the thought of "next time."

GIULIO

I shouldn't have told her my real name. I don't even realize what I've done until I've showered again and collapsed into bed. And by then, it doesn't matter, because as soon as I close my eyes, I can see her pussy and her heaving chest and the look of pure bliss on her face as she came.

For me.

THE SUN IS BRIGHTER when I open my eyes this morning.

That's just the orgasms, I know, but when I stand in front of the bedroom window, looking out at the canopy of trees down the side of the mountain, I'm naked and in the best mood of my life. The sun feels brighter, the air is cleaner, and my dick is definitely harder. That's a great morning if you ask me.

And it's ruined as soon as I see my mobile phone blinking with a new message. There are only two people with this number. I grab the phone from the bedside table and see Alfonso's number. Salvo's would have meant the world was falling apart. Alfonso's means there's probably still time to stop it. I exhale slowly and then laugh. The text message is ridiculous.

Took mama to the sea. It's dry, but I heard there might be a storm soon. Hope you packed your umbrella.

I roll my eyes and laugh. Alfonso's always been shit at these hidden messages, but he's still better than me. I prefer obvious and clear to poetic and gets me killed. I'm still laughing as I walk to the bathroom to get ready for the day while trying to decipher his warning. It could be something; it could just be chatter. Who knows? A real warning in my line of work is rare. All that matters is that I don't let my guard down, and I never do that anyway.

Well, rarely. Last night, I absolutely let my guard down with Zahra. Had it been worth it? Absolutely? Should I do it again? No. Will I do it again?

"Non si può avere la botte piena e la moglie ubriaca," I whisper to myself.

Last night was last night. Today is a new day, with a too-bright sun and the possibility of danger in the air. The best kind of day, in my opinion. I get dressed and add my favorite accessory to my outfit for the first time since I arrived. I strap my holster onto my body under my shirt and shove my Sig Sauer into it at my back.

I look at myself in the mirror. What I see is a rich man, not a dangerous one. Well... Not any more dangerous than most rich men.

I'm ready for an espresso or two and maybe even a few laps in the pool later. There's a lightness in my steps as I walk toward the door. A soft knock against the wood slows my steps. Danger only announces itself with a bang in the movies. I've known a lot of dangerous men in my life — too many, to be honest — and the deadliest have always been eerily quiet. *I'm* eerily quiet when I need to be. This knock could be house-keeping or the storm Alfonso said might be coming.

This knock is faint, tentative even. My left hand goes to my back, and the smooth steel in my palm calms me.

I inch forward, brushing the soles of my shoes across the thick carpet to muffle my steps.

There's another knock.

I should have grabbed another clip.

"Chi'e?" I call out from a distance. There's no answer. I pull the gun from my holster. "Chi'e?"

There's a sound of muffled movement from the hallway, and my thumb goes to the gun safety.

"Um. Non parlo Italiano," a small voice says in halting, terrible Italian that makes my dick hard in an instant.

"Who is it?" I translate for her, even though I know exactly who's on the other side of my door now. I huff out a breath and reholster my gun. I'm not running, but I reach the door in half a breath. I pull the door open so fast she jumps away.

The sun is brighter. The air smells cleaner. My dick is harder. And Zahra is fucking beautiful.

ZAHRA

I sleep soundly for the first time in days. I wake up feeling refreshed. No sore, puffy eyes, or wracking sobs, making my throat feel like a desert. Even the heavy weight of grief has lessened. It's still there, but it feels lighter. I feel almost like myself again.

My good mood is abruptly interrupted by the hotel phone ringing. A feeling of dread washes over me.

I pick up the receiver. "H-hello."

"Yes, hello, Mrs. Fuller—"

That hurts. That's not my name, legal or otherwise. I clench my left fist and dig my broken nails into my palm. "Yes?" I whisper.

"Hello, this is the front desk."

"Yes?"

"We're calling about your reservation to tour the vineyard today."

"Um...yes?"

"Would you like to keep your reservation?" the woman on the phone asks.

I can't be certain, but I think it's the woman who checked me in. Not because I recognize her voice, but because of the hesitation I can hear there — now that my heart isn't beating so hard against my chest that my ears are ringing. And in truth, I'd forgotten about this reservation.

"Um...yes?"

"Splendida," she exclaims. I can hear the relief in her voice, and I feel exactly the same because, to be honest, I've been waiting for Ryan's financial analyst to shut his cards off and reject the hold from the hotel, and then, I guess, for hotel security to throw me out on my ass. I don't know why that hasn't happened yet, but I'm grateful, nonetheless. I should probably come up with a contingency plan for when that inevitably does happen; that's the kind of thing I would normally do, but these are not normal times, so I jump out of bed with a smile.

"Great. Thanks. Grazie," I say as if all is right with the world.

"Will you..." She hesitates, and my stomach twists. "Would you like to modify the reservation?"

I'm silent and confused.

"Would you like a single reservation instead?" she whispers, confirming that she's absolutely the woman who checked me in.

My stomach plummets to the floor. "No," I say automatically, but I can't for the life of me say why.

This woman knows I'm alone. I know she knows, and

yet... I lick my lips and clench my fist again. "No," I say again, "there'll be two."

I can hear the confusion in her voice, and once again, I feel the exact same way.

"Splendida," she says again. She sounds much less relieved this time. "We will have a car to take you...your party to the vineyards at eleven. Please meet the driver in the lobby."

"Okay. Will do." I cringe at the false cheer in my voice, and then I hang up.

The lightness I felt when I woke up is gone, completely evaporated. Now I feel heavy with grief again. I think about crawling back into bed and sleeping the day away. I turn around and look for another bottle of wine, but I'm out. I didn't order any more from room service last night because... A mental image appears, of Giulio's lips wrapped around the wine bottle, drinking casually as he palms his dick through his shorts and watches me get myself off.

I shiver, and then my eyes land on the wall we share.

I have an idea.

I take more time getting dressed than I have since I arrived. I shower and wash my hair. I don't have the energy to blow-dry and straighten it, but I've always loved it curly. Besides, the sun is already high in the sky, and it probably wouldn't stay straight for long anyway. I dig my favorite white sundress from my suitcase. It's linen and very wrinkled, but it's clean, and I know that it makes my tits look amazing. I even swipe my favorite glossy lip paint on my mouth. I stand back to look at myself in the full-length mirror in the suite's closet.

I look like myself. Well, myself on vacation. Well, I don't look like my life went to shit three days ago, and that's an improvement.

But do I look good enough for the strange man next door to agree to spend a couple of hours touring a vineyard with me because I don't have the guts to go on my own?

Let's see!

I throw my sunglasses, room key, and my phone — even though it's been turned off since I arrived — into a purse. I walk on unsure steps down the hallway to the other penthouse suite. I feel like I'm going to throw up, and I really want to run back to my room and hide in the closet with a couple of bottles of wine, but I refuse to let myself lose my nerve.

I stop in front of his door and suck in a deep breath. I hold it. I'm too terrified to let it go, but eventually, I have to. I take another, slower breath. It does nothing to calm my racing pulse or mind. I knock on Giulio's door.

No answer.

My pulse somehow finds the ability to race just a little faster, and my stomach is doing for real somersaults in my gut. I feel queasy. "I need to stop drinking," I mutter to myself, shrugging at the irony of my words and my current plans. I knock again.

He yells through the door in Italian, and I stutter what is clearly going to become my mantra for this trip. "Um. Non parlo Italiano."

I think I hear him chuckle as he translates. "Who's there?" he says, and then he pulls his hotel room door open.

Lowkey, I forget my name because holy shit, this man is fine. I don't think I had fully appreciated that before this morning. Or maybe the orgasms make him look better? That's also a distinct possibility.

"You look..." I say and then stop. I try to swallow the drool in my mouth without him noticing, but I'm not really sure if I succeed.

"I look?" he asks, leaning against the doorframe. He crosses his arms over his chest and smiles at me. "How do I look, tesora?"

Like I should've sat on your face last night. Thank God I only think that.

I have to look away to regroup for a second before I can make eye contact with him again. I also need a moment to remember how to speak. "You look like a man who knows better than to bang on a stranger's hotel room and tell her to shut up." I smile at him with much more confidence than I feel. I don't want him to see me sweat. Figuratively. If he says yes, he's absolutely about to see me sweat all over this damn vineyard, the forecast for today is hot as hell.

He steps out into the hallway, crowding me again. His five o'clock shadow looks darker — sexier — this morning. I have the unexpected urge to bite him.

"And you look," he says, eyes dipping to my mouth, "like the kind of woman who'd never watch a stranger jack himself off for you. Apparently, looks are deceiving."

His words are a gentle tease — seductive, even — and also a little bit of a challenge. It takes my mind away from my insecurities, and my shoulders relax. "It seems so."

He smiles warmly at me, and our gentle flirtation feels almost comfortable. "Buongiorno, Zahra. To what do I owe this pleasure?"

I like the way he says my name. It's not quite right. The first 'a' is too long, and he's made a two-syllable name stretch to three, maybe even four. It sounds almost like a moan on his lips. It's shocking and a little dirty, and I can tell by the look in his eyes that he knows that; that he's said my name this way on purpose. This man's voice makes the hair on my arms stand up, but the feeling is fleeting.

Unfortunately, his question is like a bucket of cold

water dumped all over my mood. It extinguishes the heat between us. Well, at least on my end.

I spent a lot of time figuring out what to wear and choosing my lipstick color, but did I give even a second of thought to how I was going to ask him to be my...date?

"Fuck," I mutter to myself.

Giulio's eyebrows lift nearly to his very healthy hairline, and his eyes squint with interest.

"No, wait, no. That's not what I meant."

He laughs in my face. Like, laughs his ass off. He flattens his hand over his chest, his head falls back, and the formerly quiet hallway is filled with his deep, melodic chuckling. Asshole.

"Never mind," I say and turn away. I'm definitely going to crawl back into bed now.

"Oh, tesora," he laughs around the words.

I hear his footsteps behind me, but I still gasp when his arm circles my waist and pulls me back into his strong body.

"Zahra," he moans into my left ear.

Shiver is not a strong enough word for what my body does when he says my name in that way and so intimately.

"Don't run away," he says. "Or at least walk slowly, so I can admire the view."

His cologne is warm, something like... I don't know, what does teakwood smell like? Sandalwood? Musk? Whatever it is, I like it. I like it so much that my stomach is doing all the flips right now.

"Why did you come to see me?" he asks.

I have to take another one of those slow, deep breaths. "I... I have a reservation for a tour at the vineyard, and I..." My words trail off as the arm around my waist moves. His hand flattens across my stomach in a possessive hold. I should be turned off, but I'm not. I sigh internally, weary at my overactive libido.

"I like wine," he says. I recall that image of his lips around the wine bottle again.

"S-so do I."

He chuckles. I feel myself getting wet, like turn-my-pussy-on-like-a-fountain wet. "I know." His lips brush my ear, but there's no judgment. "Are you inviting me to tour the vineyard with you?"

I sag into his arms, and that feels...dangerous...but good. Great, even. "I—" I start speaking, but I have to stop and swallow the lump in my throat at the feeling of his warm, minty breath on my ear. "I don't want to go alone," I admit in a tiny whisper. "I can't." It's easier to say these words now that I'm not looking at him.

He's silent behind me, and I think he's going to tell me no. Maybe he's trying to figure out a nice way to let me down.

"Andiamo," he whispers. "Let's go, tesora."

And we do.

THE CAR they send for us is actually a golf cart.

It's not glamorous, and I think briefly that Ryan would have hated that; he would have thought it was beneath him, but Giulio doesn't. He slides into the back seat first, which I think is rude until he spreads his arm across the back of the seat, turns to me, and smiles in invitation. "Vieni qui," he says.

My brain doesn't need to speak Italian to understand what he means, and neither does my body. As I crawl into the tiny back seat beside him, there's sweat at the back of my neck, my clit is throbbing, and my knees are weak. We're off to a great start.

It's a tight fit. Giulio does nothing to stop his body from touching mine. In fact, he spreads his legs wider, so his thigh brushes against mine. His forearm touches my bare shoulders, and his fingertips lightly brush my right arm as it curls around me.

The drive to the vineyard takes ten minutes. Ten bumpy minutes. His body bounces against mine the entire time, the bare skin of our legs and his arm against my shoulder — sticking for a humid fraction of a second and then pulling away. We make our way through the San Marco town center. The cobbled streets are not fun, but the packed dirt road as we enter the vineyard is smooth. Almost as smooth as the soft linen of his clothes against my bare skin.

Can a car ride be erotic? Because this one is. By the time we unfold from the golf cart, my pussy is somehow even wetter than when I crawled inside. My nipples are hard enough to cut diamonds.

Ryan who?

"This vineyard has been here for nearly a century," the tour guide tells us, as we move carefully through the vines.

I thought it would be a small group tour, but it's not. It's just the tour guide, me, and Giulio's silent presence at my back.

God, I hope this tour is expensive as fuck. If not, I'm going to buy all the wine to make sure it is.

As we wind through the neat rows of grapevines, I swear I can feel his breath on my ear or shoulder. Once, I think I feel his fingers at the hem of my dress, but when I turn around, he's not touching me. Not with his hands, at least. He's watching me with those dark eyes and a subtle grin on his face, and I can feel that.

The tour guide tells us a bunch of things I never hear. Lots of stuff about the strain of grapes and how long the vineyard has been owned by the same family — whose name I don't catch — because I'm so focused on Giulio.

Maybe I'll book another tour on one of Ryan's other cards.

But you know God don't like ugly, because just as that thought enters my brain, I stumble. Somehow, my foot sinks into a patch of soft dirt, and I pitch to the side. I'm just about to crash into a row of century-old vines when two strong hands grab me around the waist and haul me upright.

I yell out and then suck in a dry breath of air when he sets me on firm ground but doesn't let me go.

"Be careful, tesora," he whispers into my ear, chuckling softly.

My face heats with shame. "I shouldn't have worn these shoes," I mumble.

My ass is pressed against his front, and he might not be fully hard, but he's not soft. He looks down the front of my body, and I wonder if he can see down my dress. I wonder if he knows that I want him to.

"I like the shoes," he says before turning to brush his mouth across my ear again. "I like your toes as well."

I barely swallow this moan.

Someone clears their throat.

The tour guide's eyes are averted, but he's red-faced and clearly embarrassed. "Just this way, we have the barrel storage for the tasting room," he says nervously. "Andiamo, si?"

"Va via," Giulio says in a hard tone that makes me shiver and causes the tour guide to scurry away.

"What did you say to him?"

"I told him to leave."

"Why?"

His arm tightens around me, and he grinds his erection into my ass. It's harder now.

"Do you want me to tell you?" he whispers. "Will that excite you?"

"Yes," I say without even a second of hesitation. There's no room to second-guess or think too deeply. Literally.

He smiles against my ear, and then his tongue caresses my earlobe.

I whimper.

"You're beautiful," he tells me. "He didn't deserve you."

His hand brushes against my thigh, and I jump. I look down my body and marvel at just how short this dress is. I hadn't thought about that. Or maybe I had, who knows. Anyway, his hand is so close — too close? — to my pussy as his fingers caress the soft, ruffled hem.

"How do you know that?"

"Because no man who would make you cry deserves you," he whispers.

"Would you?"

His lips drag across my cheek. "Would I make you cry?" he asks.

I nod. My mouth is too dry to speak.

"Probably," he admits and then corrects himself. "Certainly. I'm not a good man."

I turn to him and look him in the eyes.

He smiles at me, but he looks almost sad. Or maybe that's just honesty.

"Why do you think you're not a good man?"

"Because I am not. And that is perfectly fine. You don't need a good man right now."

"I don't?"

His hand moves under the hem of my dress, and his fingers traverse the seam of my thighs. I spread my legs for him. He pushes his hand between my legs with a filthy smile.

"No, tesora," he whispers. "You need a man to remind

you that whoever he was is beneath you. You deserve better than him. Better than me."

"How do you—" I whimper and squirm in his hold. Or at least I try to, but his arm tightens around my waist, holding me still as he caresses my pussy through my wet panties. "How do you know that I deserve better than you?"

He smiles at me again in that same sad or honest way that I can't decipher.

"Because," he starts to say, but then stops.

THERE ARE some sounds that I know in my blood. The heavy, hacking laughter my nona made after a few too many glasses of wine and a cigarette. A very sharp knife cutting through the crust of freshly baked bread. My mother's singing voice tinged with the remnants of tears. A breaking bone. The sound of a gun cocking.

"Zahra," I whisper. It takes all the energy I have not to shove her to the ground or throw her over my shoulder and run. I force myself to suppress that unexpected desire I feel to protect her because it would be dangerous. Running away with her won't solve the real problem at hand. The answer to her question is like a cloud hanging over us, but she can't see it.

How do I know that she deserves better than me? Easily, because my entire life is nothing but danger, and I can't run far enough away that it won't find me. Or her.

"Yes?" she whispers.

"You need to do as I tell you, tesora," I say, our lips almost touching.

She shivers, and I wish so much that she hadn't. I also

wish that I didn't have to take my hand away from the warm heaven between her legs. Last night, there wasn't anything I wanted more than to get my fingers between her delicious thighs, but now that they're there, I can't enjoy the feeling of her smooth skin.

"When I let you go, I want you to walk back to the tasting room. Walk. Whatever you do, do not run. And don't turn around, no matter what you hear."

I watch as her eyes clear, and the lust fades to confusion and then fear. Her eyes are big and deep brown and terrified. Beautiful. Heartbreaking.

"What's going on?"

"I can't tell you that." There isn't enough time to tell her what I think is happening, but I also don't want to confirm her darkest fears. I don't want to tell her that whatever's hiding in the vines should be afraid of me, and so should she.

I reluctantly pull my hands from her body and steady her on her feet. I refuse to look down at her beautiful toes peeking out of her tall shoes. I can't let myself get distracted by the sight. "Go. Now."

I can see all the questions she wants to ask me in her eyes. I shake my head quickly. She presses her lips together and then turns slowly. I watch her take two shaky steps and stumble. I reach for her just as she rights herself. She was right, her shoes are inappropriate for the vineyard, and I doubt she'll be able to run if she needs to. That thought terrifies me for a second, but I make a decision to make sure that she doesn't have to run.

I can do that for her, at the very least.

I reach around my body to the small of my back. I take my gun from its holster and keep it at my back just in case Zahra doesn't follow my order and turns around. I keep my eyes on her small form and watch her retreat as I release the safety on my gun.

Slowly, I move in the opposite direction.

At the edge of the row, I make sure the coast is clear, take a final look at her, and then move in the direction of the sound I'd heard.

Normally I would move slowly, cautiously, and with as little sound as possible. But not today. I whisper loudly and make as much noise as possible, hoping to draw whoever is out there to me.

And away from Zahra.

ZAHRA

I'm not a fool. I know what danger sounds like, and Giulio's voice is dripping with it. What I don't know is if he's the thing I'm running from or not. I also don't understand how one second he was about to fingerfuck me in a vineyard, and the next, he was telling me to run back to the tasting room. No, sorry, walk. *"Whatever you do, do not run."*

It sounded like a cheesy line from one of Ryan's movies, but it's more believable than Ryan ever managed. It made me shiver, and not in a good way. Whatever's happening right now is something that has Giulio on high alert, and that has me shaking with every tentative step.

I've watched enough movies to know that there can only be one of two things happening right now. Either zombies have invaded the vineyard, or a serial killer is on the loose. Those are the only options, I'm certain of it. Either way, I do as Giulio says.

At the end of the row, I shuffle quickly across the dirt

path breaking up the rows of vines. I look left and right, but there's no one there. Vaguely, I wonder where the hell the tour guide went. I can see the roof of the tasting room ahead of me. It feels surreal. Nothing seems wrong right now, except an eerie quiet I hadn't noticed before.

When I dart into the next row, I exhale. I'm breathing hard even though I'm barely walking above a stroll. Nothing seems out of place besides me and my platform espadrilles, to be honest.

Maybe Giulio's mistaken?

I turn around and think to tell him that — even though he told me not to —but he's gone.

Oh. Well, that's terrifying. The hair on the back of my neck stands up. I can feel a small stream of sweat running down my back. I turn around and run. Well, I try to run, even though Giulio told me not to, but these shoes are not made for fleeing.

There's only one more dirt path walkway and another row between me and the tasting room. It feels so close and yet so far away. So, of course, my scared ass tries to move faster. If I can dart across that path — without breaking my ankle — I'll be home free, I think to myself as a comforting mantra.

And then I run right into a big, strange, hard body. The solid muscle and height of this body feels like a brick wall. I hit it and then bounce back. I hit the ground ass first, and it hurts like a bitch. So does the fact that I'll probably never be able to get this dry earth from my formerly bright white dress.

I know this body isn't Giulio by feel. It's too tall, the chest is too broad, and whoever it is doesn't catch me. Giulio would have caught me.

I'm sitting on the ground, dazed, confused, and hurting.

It takes me a few moments to catch my breath and blink back the tears. I wish it took me longer because when I look up, I come eye to...eye with a gun.

I've never seen a gun in person before. Not a real one, at least. I should be scared, but seeing the gun — having it pointed at my head, no less — makes me feel a kind of impotent rage. I didn't even get to taste any wine!

I know they say in movies that people's lives flash before their eyes, but that doesn't happen to me. I think about Zoe, though. I think about all the things I haven't said to her, all the apologies I owe her. I even think I'd do anything to see her again. To have her suck her teeth, roll her eyes, and tell me she told me so one more time. And that thought makes me angrier. Whoever the fuck this man with a gun is, isn't going to rob me of the chance to make up with my older sister.

"Dov'è?" he barks at me.

I jump and blink.

"Dov'è?"

"I don't speak Italian," I scream.

I think Zoe would appreciate me not going out like a scared bitch, even though I *am* a scared bitch right now. I also think she'd like Giulio, not that it matters right now. Well, correction, Zoe would like me letting some fine ass Italian man feel me up in the vineyard. She would smile at me, nod, and tell me that's "a whole vibe." She's a horny idiot, and I love her. I haven't told her that enough.

The man starts yelling as he starts toward me with slow steps, and it shocks me out of my anger.

Three days ago, I was supposed to marry the man that I thought was the love of my life, but now I'm about to die next to some old ass fucking grapes. Don't tell Zoe. Also, don't tell her that I close my eyes and pray. She would be so mad I didn't kick him or something. All our lives together, and she still doesn't understand that she's much braver than me.

A loud bang rends the air, and I jump at the sound. Something heavy hits the ground, and I jump again. My ears are ringing. I smell smoke. I'm waiting for the pain. I'm waiting to die.

I hear a voice instead.

"Zahra." Someone with a very thick accent says my name, and I jump again before I realize that I recognize that voice.

I open my left eyelid only, just in case. I see Giulio standing above me. His face is full of concern and rage. Am I hallucinating him? Can a dead woman still be horny?

"Zahra," he says again, and steps over something to get to me.

My gaze dips, and I see that the thing is the body of the man I'd run into before. He's face-down in the dirt in front of me. The gun I'd seen up close and personal is lying next to him.

"Zahra," Giulio says again. I only just now realize how gentle his voice is.

"G-g-gun," I stutter.

He looks down at his right hand, and I do too. I jump when I see a gun there. He moves both hands to his back. When they reappear, there's no gun.

I turn to look at the other gun, but he doesn't seem to notice what I'm seeing. How can he not see the gun a dead man had pointed at my face?

"I need you to stay calm, tesora," he says, crouching down in front of me.

Ridiculous. Calm is not a word I understand anymore.

"What are you doing?" I whisper. I have to whisper because I seem to have screamed my voice hoarse.

He kicks the gun near me away, and I exhale a harsh breath in relief. "I'm searching him," Giulio says matter-of-factly and then pushes the corpse over onto its back. *His* back.

"What the fuck?" I whisper.

"I need to see if he has any identification on him," he says.

"A-are you a police officer?" I whisper hopefully. I don't know what the fuck I'm hopeful for, but Giulio dashes those hopes anyway, so it doesn't matter.

His wry laughter fills the air. The suspiciously calm air, now that I think about it.

"No. Non sono la polizia," he says.

I get the gist. "Then, who are you?"

He doesn't answer me. I watch as he pulls a leather wallet from the man's coat and shoves it into his pants pocket.

"Who are you?" I ask again as he moves closer to me.

We make eye contact, and he frowns. "I told you," he says quietly.

I try and swallow, but my mouth is too dry. "Not a good man," I say, thinking about how different the world seemed just a few minutes ago when he was pushing his hand between my thighs.

"No," he says and then offers his hand to me. "Come, tesora."

I should scramble away. Like full-on kick my shoes off and run like a white girl from a horror movie, but I don't. Zoe would be so angry if she were here and I once again missed a moment to get the fuck out of here. But Zoe's not here.

It's just me and Giulio and the dead body between us.

I take his hand and let him lift me to my feet. I let him lace his fingers with mine and lead me out of the grapevines. I don't know what it means that I don't run from him. And I surely don't know what it means that I should be afraid of him, but I'm not. I don't know anything anymore.

I THINK I'm in shock. I'm not entirely sure what shock is or what it feels like, but I'm very certain that something's not right.

Giulio leads me through the vineyard, and for a few seconds, I feel as if I'm in someone else's body. We move toward the front of the property and dash from the vines into a small copse of olive trees. He stops and turns toward me. He looks me over from head to toe, but not in the erotic way he did yesterday or this morning. This look is assessing, almost clinical.

He shrugs his coat from his shoulders. "Put this on," he says and then helps me push my arms into the jacket. "Wait here."

"Don't leave me," I blurt out.

His hands smooth over my shoulders. He squeezes firmly but gently. "I'm just going to get a cart. You can watch me. I will return as quickly as possible. Si?"

I nod, even though I'm still not sure about this. I watch him like a hawk as he turns away from me. I see the holster at his back and the gun, and I realize that he's had that on all day, even when he was touching me just a few moments ago. I fixate on the straps of the holster, not the gun, as he walks casually toward the small bank of golf carts near the winery entrance.

I tell time by the sound of my own pulse in my ears.

There are four golf carts lined up near the entrance. I wonder where the drivers have gone. Casually, I watch as Giulio checks each of the carts. He's looking for keys.

I wrap my arms around myself and am immediately surrounded by the soft scent of his cologne. It calms me, even though I'm terrified that someone will dart out of the trees and tackle him, or I'll hear a loud blast break the strange silence surrounding us, and the next thump I hear will be Giulio's body hitting the dirt.

But none of that happens. In a few minutes, Giulio is slipping behind the wheel of one of the carts. He turns it on and backs it out of the parking spot and heads toward the entrance.

For a brief moment, I'm terrified that he'll drive away without me until the cart pulls to a stop, and he turns to me. "Come, tesora," he says.

Even my horny lizard brain doesn't react to that, which is another sign that I might be in shock.

I don't run, because I really shouldn't be running in these shoes. Also, my feet hurt, and I'm terrified that I'll fall and break my ankle. I sigh in some faint echo of relief as I slip into the passenger seat next to Giulio.

I think he's going to take off and speed back to the hotel; I want him to. But he turns to me and looks at me again. This time, I look down at myself. My formerly pristine white dress is covered in dirt and a soft spray of blood, I now realize. That broad-shouldered man's blood.

I shudder.

"Don't look at it," he says definitively, a command. "Look at me."

I do as he says immediately. And I'm not sure if it's the shock or what, but I feel myself calm when I meet his gaze.

"I need you to help me, tesora."

"Anything." I mean, he just saved my life, what am I going to say, no?

I watch as he shrugs out of his holster and wraps the straps around his gun. "I need you to hold this — hide it — just until we get back to the hotel."

I suck in a deep breath and nod. Carefully, Giulio places his gun in my lap. It feels hot, but I'm pretty certain that that's just a figment of my imagination.

He places my hands carefully over the gun. "Don't look at this either," he tells me.

So I don't. I raise my head and stare forward as he buttons his coat closed so that no one else can see — including me — that I'm covered in dirt and blood or the gun in my lap. It sounds strange, but as soon as the coat is buttoned closed, I make myself forget.

Is that what shock is? Or is this a coping mechanism? Either way, I like having someone tell me what to do, so I don't have to think.

"Hold on," he tells me.

Okay, correction, I like when he gives me clear commands. "Hold on" is unclear. I turn to him and feel myself frown so hard my jaw hurts.

He smiles. It's not the warm smile he gave me this morning, or the seductive grin he leveled at me as he slipped his hand under the hem of my dress, or even the rueful smile, from just before my world was flipped upside down — again. This smile is playful. "Hold on to me," he corrects as if he can read my mind.

And so, I do. I take one hand from his gun and wrap it around his bicep, holding onto him as if my life depends on it because I think it does.

The ride back to the hotel takes another ten minutes. Giulio doesn't speed back to the safety of the hotel. He doesn't court any undue attention. I wish he would speed, but I don't think I have the energy to tell him that, so I concentrate on not letting the gun fall from my lap or my grip on his arm loosen. My hands are full — literally — so I let him make the big decisions for the moment.

But still, I wonder at how normal the world seems as we drive back. Doesn't anyone know what happened in the vineyard? Didn't anyone hear the gunshot?

Am I going crazy?

"You are not crazy," he says.

I turn to him in confusion. I didn't realize I'd said that last question aloud.

He keeps his eyes on the road in front of us, but I know his attention is on me. "I'm sorry you had to see that," he says.

Has the single word "that" ever been so loaded?

"And I'm sorry that I ruined your dress. But you are not going crazy," he says.

It's not a brand-new dress, and it doesn't erase the past twenty minutes of my life, but I realize that he's trying to give me something Ryan almost took: a reassurance in myself.

"What's happening?" I ask him again.

He shrugs, and my mouth falls open in shock. How can he shrug in a moment like this?

"I told you I'm not a good man."

"That's not an answer."

"No, it's not, but right now, it's all I can give you."

"It's not enough," I say, "I deserve an explanation."

The golf cart slows as Giulio pulls carefully up the narrow road toward the top of the hill. He turns to me, and he's not smiling anymore; he looks very serious. "I agree. You deserve much more than I can give you. But I will tell you what I can as soon as we're back in the hotel, agreed?"

That seems reasonable, so I nod at him. To be fair, I'm not entirely sure if I'm the best gauge of reasonable right now. For instance, is it reasonable to follow a man who just killed another man in front of you? Is it reasonable to be sad that my favorite dress is ruined? Is it reasonable to care that this is the second white dress I'm going to have to throw away in less than a week? Is it reasonable to want the killer in front of you to put his hand between your legs again?

Who knows? Certainly not me. But in the new landscape of the world, most of this sounds okay-ish, so I tighten my hold on Giulio's arm and let him drive in silence.

When he pulls into the hotel driveway, the doorman welcomes us with a stately nod. If he thinks it's strange that Giulio's driving the golf cart and not one of the hotel drivers, he doesn't say anything.

I clutch Giulio's coat tight in front of me to hide the impressionist art piece on my dress and press the gun against my stomach as the doorman helps me from the cart. Giulio takes my hand from the doorman's, almost possessively, and leads me into the hotel. The world here is even more normal than the town below. There are people milling about the front desk, a family walking through the lobby toward the pool. I can even hear piano music and the clinking of silverware against dishes from the restaurant.

We ride the small elevator up to the penthouse floor. It shocks me again, somehow, that we've been sharing this floor for days purely by accident. I wonder how different my life could have been if Ryan hadn't ruined our plans, and he and I had taken this trip together. Would I have met Giulio? Would he have even noticed me if I weren't crying myself to sleep next door? Would he have preened for me by the hotel pool? Certainly, I never would have let him watch me come, or had him come for me, which means I guess I never would have seen him kill a man either.

When the elevator doors open to our floor, I move automatically toward my room, but Giulio puts an arm around my waist and leads me to his.

"What's happening?" I ask because I really can't pull together the right words to ask the right questions. I'm not sure if I know the right questions, and I know for certain that I'm terrified of the answers.

His hand snakes inside his coat and grabs his gun from my shaking hand. "Stay with me for a bit longer, tesora."

Somehow, that sounds right, so I do.

GIULIO

She's in shock; that's very easy to see.

I should take her to the hotel medic or the local hospital. Or maybe I should just leave her alone and let her process whatever she's feeling away from me, but I don't want to. I also don't know what the hitman from the vineyard knew, so I can't leave her alone until I know she's safe. At least that's how I rationalize this to myself as I lead her toward my hotel room and potentially more danger.

"Wait here, tesora."

She looks at me again with those big, brown, scared eyes that make me want to feel things I shouldn't and probably can't. Eyes that make me want to make promises I know for sure I cannot keep.

"I just need to check the room to make sure it's safe."

She wraps her arms around herself and nods.

I push the door to my hotel room open, carefully. I wait in the hallway and listen for a few seconds. Nothing seems out of place as I scan the room visually, but I pull the gun from the holster in my hands before I move into the room. I clear each space methodically, maybe even more thoroughly than I might have if I were alone; because I'm not alone.

I check the sitting area, the bathroom, my bedroom, and lastly, my closet. I check my guns and make sure they haven't been tampered with, and then I pull my holster back onto my body and slip my firearm back in place, remembering the shock in Zahra's eyes when she saw me holding it.

I need to call Alfonso and leave a message for Salvo, but first, I need to take care of Zahra. Those are the wrong priorities. I know that, but I don't care.

I rush back to the door and check the hallway again. She's standing just where I left her, shivering in my coat. I usher her into the sitting area. "Sit."

She's still holding herself tightly as she sits on the sofa. I move to the bar and pour her a large tumbler of the closest dark liquor.

She takes the glass from me with both hands. "I only drink wine," she says and then gulps down half of the liquid.

I cannot help but smile. I don't think her distress is attractive, but I think everything she does is attractive. I'm also worried for her. I move back to the bar, pour myself a small drink, and take a moment to think. I need to make those calls and get out of here. I need to look at the wallet in my pocket and figure out who's after me. I need to get somewhere safe.

Unfortunately, I'm not in a rush.

I take my drink back to the sitting area and sit on the coffee table in front of Zahra.

She's still holding the glass in her hands, but they aren't shaking anymore. That seems like progress.

"How do you feel?"

"Like I just saw you kill a man," she answers quickly, making eye contact with me.

She's wonderful.

I don't know what it is about her, except everything. There's no fear or accusation in her eyes or words. She should be afraid of me, but she's not.

"You did see that," I tell her.

"Why? Why did you do it?"

"He would have shot you."

"That's not why you killed him," she says definitively. She rolls her eyes at me, and it takes everything I have not to laugh. Brave and smart.

"No, it's not. He was after me, but I can't tell you why. Even if I could, you wouldn't understand."

She rolls her eyes again. "Because I'm a woman?"

I laugh this time and take another sip of my drink. She follows my lead. "No, because you're American and have no idea who or what I am."

"Who are you?" Her eyes are shining with interest. I wonder if she knows that she likes a little bit of danger.

"I'm someone you should forget you ever met."

"That mysterious, dangerous shit must get you so much pussy."

I laugh so hard there are tears in my eyes. "Mi piaci molto," I tell her.

"What does that mean?"

I don't translate, because it's unfair. "It means that you should get as far away from me as you can," I tell her.

"I think you're lying."

"I think you're beautiful." I shouldn't flirt with her, and I definitely shouldn't linger here long enough to fuck her, and yet I know I will. I know that if she would allow it, I would take her to the bedroom and fuck her until another armed man shows up. I'd kill him too, and then fuck her again.

I would put everything on hold to spend a few more hours in her presence. My father used to tell my mother that I didn't understand danger. He used to say the words with pride, and he wasn't wrong. I've always known that, but I feel it deep in my bones in this moment. I know that I would stay here gladly and put myself in danger to taste her skin and sink balls deep inside her over and over and over again because I feel the danger more acutely when I'm with her.

I feel everything more acutely in her presence.

"I just saw you kill a man," she says again.

"And that's why you need to forget about me."

She's still looking at me as she takes another sip of her drink and swallows slowly. I watch her tongue dart from her mouth and glide over her lips as she tastes the alcohol from the rim.

I don't groan, but I want to. I want to tell her that if she's offering, I'll stay here and lick the entirety of my bar and hers from her body, even if it gets me killed, but I have enough restraint to wait for whatever she has to say.

"Who are you? And don't say "not a good man." I got it, believe me. I want to know who you are and what you do."

"I can't give you any details," I say even as I realize that

I want to. For the first time in my adult life, I want to tell someone exactly who I am, where I come from and what I do; but that's dangerous, mostly for Zahra. I keep waiting for the moment where my words sink in, and she runs away like she should, but it doesn't come.

"What can you give me?" she says, not giving me any room to breathe. I wonder if she's a lawyer; that would be just my luck and hilarious. Also, I don't hate that she's interrogating me right now. I don't know what that says about me.

"I'm a bad man, who works for bad men, and when necessary, I kill bad men."

She stares at me, and I recognize that her big brown eyes are curious and lit with some unknown fire as she considers my admittedly vague response.

"And that man at the vineyard was a bad man?" she asks me innocently.

"Yes."

"You're certain?"

I'm not. At least I can't be entirely certain until I verify his identity, figure out who sent him and how they knew where I was, but I am. Contrary to popular belief, it's a rare occurrence to run into another armed man who happens to be innocent. It's even rarer to meet a strange man who will aim a gun at an unknown innocent woman who anyone would objectively call 'good.' I also want to give Zahra a sense of security. "Yes."

There's another moment of silence. She swallows the rest of the liquid in her glass before nodding at me and taking a deep breath. "Okay."

I squint her in confusion. "Okay? What does that mean?"

She shrugs, and my eyebrows lift. "It means I can't do

anything about the man you killed. And I'm trusting that you're telling me the truth and he was a bad man. Also, I'm pretty certain that I'm in shock. So...okay."

Definitely shock. "Okay." I don't know what this means, and in truth, it shouldn't mean anything, but somewhere deep in my chest, it means something. "I need to leave."

She frowns at me. "And go where?"

"I can't tell you that."

"What about me?"

"You're going to stay here while I check your room and make sure that everything is okay. Before I leave, I will tell hotel security to watch out for you. And once I'm gone, you're not going to think about me at all for the rest of your time here. You'll be safer without me anyway. And when you go home, you're not going to think about that stronzo either. You're going to move on with your life and forget any of this ever happened."

It sounds good in my head. I think it even sounds good as it comes out of my mouth. I don't know Zahra, but I know that I will be thinking about the last thirty-six hours I've spent with her for much longer than I should. I'll do the exact opposite of what I'm telling her. I'll remember Zahra. How could I not?

"No," she says definitively.

"Scusi?"

"No," she says again as if that explains anything.

"What do you mean, no?"

"I mean just that. No."

"What part of my plan don't you agree with?" I ask, frustrated.

I like that she takes a moment to think about my question. She doesn't give me a flippant answer, because this isn't a flippant situation. She brings her glass up to her mouth and then remembers at the last minute that it's empty. I pluck the empty glass from her hands and give her mine. She downs the rest of my drink in a single gulp. I watch her lick the liquid from her lips again and ignore the way the lower half of my body responds to the sight.

"No to all of it," she says with an energetic shrug, "but especially to the part where you leave me here. What if I'm not safe?"

"I told you I would contact security and have them keep an eye on you."

"Will they kill a man for me?"

No. I don't tell her that, because she already knows the answer. She seems like the type of woman who doesn't ask questions unless she already knows the answer. They won't kill a man for her; they might not even get to her in time if someone should show up here looking for me. But I would. And as I watch her watch me, I realize that she knows that as well. Of course, she does. I already have.

"If I leave here, you'll be safe," I tell her.

"How do you know that?"

"Because the man I killed was here to kill me."

She rolls her eyes again. I'm becoming very attached to that movement.

"Duh," she says. "I'm a boring American who works in public relations. No one is coming after me with a gun. But how do you know that they haven't connected me to you? How do you know that when you leave here, they won't ask someone at the front desk about you and find out about me?"

I purse my lips and squint my eyes at her in disbelief, because we both know that's probably far-fetched, to say the least. Even if someone were to find out that she and I had spent time together, they could just as easily find out that I fucked the waitress yesterday and go after her. Either way, once I leave here, neither of them will know how to contact me, and only Zahra even knows my real name. She'll be safer when I'm gone.

"That's ridiculous," I say.

"Maybe, but can you guarantee my safety when you're gone?"

"No."

"I didn't think so. That's why I'm coming with you."

"No."

"Yes."

"You don't even know me," I tell her, incredulous. I grab the glass from her hand and walk back to the bar. I turn my back to her because what she's suggesting is more than ridiculous and far more dangerous than her staying put. But I also don't want to look her in the eye and let her know that I'm seriously considering it. When the glasses are half-full again, I turn back to her and freeze. I watch as she stands from the couch and unbuttons my coat. I watch it fall to the floor at her feet. Her dress is stained with small droplets of blood and streaks of dirt. Her feet are covered in dust from the vineyard. She looks small and fragile, but not broken. She's looking at me with hard, determined eyes as if she's decided what will happen and is waiting for me to catch up to her line of thinking.

In fact, I think that's exactly what's going through her mind. It's written on her face.

"After I check your room, you'll give me your dress and shoes, and I'll get rid of them. No one will be able to tie you to me once I'm gone. I'm just a strange man you met at the pool. Nothing more." Those last two words burn for some reason as they pass my lips.

"I was supposed to get married four days ago," she admits.

"But you didn't?" I ask. My fingers flex around the glasses in my hands.

"No." Her eyes have become glassy with unshed tears.

I have to force myself to relax my hold on the glasses before I break them. I put them down carefully. "Why not?" I ask her.

"The night before our wedding, the paparazzi caught my fiancé heading into his hotel room with a stripper."

"Cazzo," I breathe. I'm furious.

"And my best friend met them there for a threesome. She was also my maid of honor."

I want to grab my gun. I want to fly to wherever Zahra is from and find her ex-fiancé, her best friend, and the stripper. I want to kill them. I shouldn't feel this way.

"Give me their names and addresses," I tell her.

"You're trying to scare me away," she says accurately.

"Of course, I am. But I'm also being serious."

She takes a tentative step forward. "Are you?"

I swallow slowly and take a deep breath in and out of my nose.

She stalks toward me on her long legs that are no longer shaking, watching me as intently as I'm watching her.

"Yes. Give me their names, and I'll kill them for you," I tell her in my deepest, scariest voice.

I don't expect to see her shiver or to watch as her tears dry, and her eyes begin to dance with interest again. I also don't expect to see the hard points of her nipples poking through the thin fabric of her dress.

"For me?" she asks in a small whisper.

"For you," I admit.

"See," she whispers, "that's why I'm safest with you.

You could have lied to me at any point in the last half an hour. You could have left me in the vineyard covered in blood. You could have sent me back to my room once we got back here, but you didn't. I don't understand anything about the world or my life right now, but I know safety when I see it."

"I'm dangerous," I tell her, even though I don't want to admit even this to her.

She smiles at me now, and it's the most beautiful thing I've seen in years. "Obviously," she says. "That's why I'm safest with you."

She's close enough that I can reach out and touch her. I can grab her around the waist again. I can wrap my arms around her, pull her body against mine, and let my fingers sink into the soft flesh at her hips. I can let her know what it does to me to see her looking at me this way, but I don't.

What I do instead is a mistake, I know that. It's a mistake that will slow me down and maybe cost us both our lives. It's a mistake that Salvo would never approve of. But since I don't plan to tell him about it, what does that matter? Zahra has made her decision, and I make mine.

"I'll check your room, and then you have twenty minutes. You need to shower and change into comfortable clothes and shoes. Put your bloody clothes in a plastic bag for disposal. Pack only necessities that you can carry. You can't tell anyone where you're going or who you're with. Leave your mobile phone here."

I give her these directions in the same tone I might relate a plan to Alfonso; clinical, cold, deadly. It's my last-ditch effort to get her to change her mind. It doesn't work.

"What about my passport?" she asks. So smart, sexy, brave, reckless. Perfect.

"Bring it," I tell her as I walk to the door. My hand is

already on the pistol at my back as I move into the hallway to make sure that her room is clear. A better man would take the elevator to the lobby and leave without another word. I can replace everything in my room, even the guns. I don't need to go back, and if I don't, she can't follow me. But I'm not going to do that. I'm going to check her room and then give her the twenty minutes I promised. And then we're going to run away.

Together.

WE DON'T CHECK out of our rooms, that's an amateur move. Zahra leaves most of her belongings in the honeymoon suite I now know she was supposed to share with a man who definitely did not deserve her. I've already packed light, so I take everything that I've brought with me, knowing that whatever happens, I'm never returning to Villa San Marco. The sun is still out, although it's dipped in the sky by the time we arrive at the Milano Centrale train station.

I keep a keen eye on my surroundings. The world feels even more dangerous with Zahra by my side. It's been a long time since I've felt responsible for anyone's safety but Salvo's and my own. Alfonso can take care of himself.

Both of my bags are in my right hand, so my left hand is free to reach for my gun should I need it. I walk as slowly as seems practical toward the ticket booth with Zahra at my side. I try to keep my eye on her without actually looking at her directly.

I should have been clearer when I told her to change. We're on the run. I thought she understood that and would put on a pair of jeans and a t-shirt. She's wearing another dress; another *very* short dress. We haven't even left Milan, and she's already a distraction, and yet I can't make myself regret bringing her with me.

I stop at a bank of seats and motion for her to sit. I don't like the idea of letting her out of my sight, but we're much more inconspicuous apart. Very few people will notice a beautiful woman sitting in a train station by herself, but the ticket agent will remember a beautiful woman with a man who looks as if he might break the jaw of anyone who gets too close to her.

I drop my bags at her feet and crouch down in front of her. "Wait here."

"Are you going to ditch me? Abandon me?" she asks. Her voice is small but determined, and her eyes are fierce.

I place my hands flat on her thighs. She shivers under my touch. "I said I would take you with me, and I don't lie."

"Ever?"

"Ever."

She leans forward and pins me with her beautiful dark eyes. "I believe you."

"Good." Bad. "Stay here while I get our tickets. Don't speak to anyone, and don't move from this spot."

"And what do I get if I do what you say?"

"Are you still in shock?" I ask her.

She bites her bottom lip, and it is the most erotic thing I've seen since I was looking down the front of her dress at the vineyard. "I think so," she admits. "But I think I'm running on pure adrenaline now that everything has set in."

"Eventually, the adrenaline will wear off," I remind her.

"True, but until then, what do I get if I do what you say?"

I straighten my legs and bend at the waist to hunch over

her. I brush my mouth over her cheek and kiss a soft path up to her ear. My nostrils fill with the scent of her soap. "If you stay here and don't speak to anyone and don't move, I'll make this the best train journey of your life."

She shivers. "Okay," she says. That settles something wild in my chest, comforting me in a way it shouldn't.

I stand straight, wink at her, and turn away. I choose the shortest and fastest queue. I don't want to be away from Zahra any longer than I need to. While I wait, I finally reach out. I pull my mobile phone from my pocket and type a quick text message to Salvo, telling him in code that I'm leaving San Marco. I don't give him any more information, because I know he'll be able to find me if he needs me.

When I make it to the ticket counter, I buy four tickets to Rome.

I step out of line and walk to the closest trash can. I pull the dead man's wallet from my pocket and open it. I don't recognize the picture on the identification card, but it's the surname that matters. I shake my head and dial Alfonso's burner phone. He picks up on the second ring.

"Si," he says by way of greeting.

"Tell Mama that it didn't rain, but I found a little shop with the neccio she loves."

"Si," he says before disconnecting the line.

I toss the wallet and my phone into the trash can and cut through all the human traffic to get back to Zahra as quickly as I can. I haven't been gone for more than twenty minutes, and there's probably no need to move with such singular focus. I should be monitoring my surroundings closely, but all I can see is Zahra, sitting exactly where I left her, her long legs crossed and delicate fingers laced in her lap. The only difference between now and when I left her is the worry on her face and the frantic gnawing at her bottom lip.

I imagine the adrenaline is beginning to wear off, and the shock can't be far behind it.

I don't know if she's the kind of woman who believes in therapy, I don't even know her surname, but I do know that she can only keep herself together for so long without getting some kind of help. And I am not help. I'm trouble, I'm danger, I'm a weapon, and she wouldn't be in this predicament if she'd never met me. If I were a better man, I would walk away or put her on a train to Rome with enough money to buy a plane ticket home, but she already knows that I'm not better, so why bother thinking about that? Especially not when she lifts her head. The light filtering through the stained-glass windows hits her curly brown hair, and we make eye contact. Her wet lip is red and slightly swollen. She smiles. At me.

For me.

I pick up all of our bags in one hand and offer her the other. "Andiamo."

She grabs onto me much too quickly for a woman who should know better. I'm happy she doesn't know better.

Vaguely, I realize that now my left hand is occupied, and I'll waste crucial moments, letting her hand go to grab my weapon, but I don't care. It's been barely a full day since our mutual masturbation session in her room, and I'm already getting used to throwing caution to the wind just to touch her. A mistake.

She tightens her hold on my hand and leans into my side. There are so many tactical reasons why I should not walk with her in this way, but I don't want to walk with her any other way. I imagine what we might look like to strangers, and I wish it were true.

"Where are we going?" she asks, whispering the question directly into my ear. The scent of her fills my nostrils again.

"Somewhere where I can keep you safe."

"That's not an actual answer," she says. "But that's okay, I trust you."

"You shouldn't."

The smile on her face is too bright, too trusting, too beautiful, too perfect.

"I know," she says. "If you told me I could trust you, I wouldn't. I've made that mistake before, and I never want to do it again. But while I was waiting for you, I thought of something."

"I'm listening."

"I spent nearly seven years with a man who told me I could trust him and who said he wanted to spend the rest of his life with me. I believed him, even though he was an actor, and maybe in hindsight, that was the biggest red flag. But while you were gone, I thought of every minute I spent with you. There weren't many." Her laugh is an airy, fragile exhalation. The sound is as seductive as it is wounded. Or maybe it is seductive because she sounds wounded. I don't smile with her, but I do stare at her for too long. I like the flash of her white teeth, her bruised lips, and the delicate column of her neck. I more than like all of those things, and all of her.

"I was thinking that every time I've met you, and every minute I've spent with you, you haven't lied to me. You were a cocky bastard by the pool. You were a whore through the wall. You were a jerk yelling at my door. You were a horny jerk sitting on my couch. And you kept me safe at the vineyard. You want to fuck me and protect me," she says while looking deep into my eyes. "I can trust a man who wants to protect me so he can fuck me. Your motives are clear."

I want to refute what she's said, but I can't. It sounds ridiculous, but there is a logic to it if you squint. I squeeze her hand and lead her toward the train platforms with a nod.

"Andiamo," she whispers.

Her accent is terrible, but still, somehow, incredibly sexy.

ZAHRA

I snag a rail map from a stand on the train platform. I don't know anything about Italy. I vaguely understand that Milan is in the North, and San Marco is in the mountains...somewhere. Besides that, I don't have a clear picture of the rest of the country, and I study the map, using it to distract myself from the strangeness of what I'm doing and Giulio's strong, silent presence beside me.

The map works for a while, but not nearly long enough.

We're sitting at the end of a busy car in two seats. If given a choice, I might have chosen a quieter car, and that would have been a mistake. The sound of metal slapping against metal as the train moves, the commotion from the family on the other side of the car arguing about who didn't set the alarm last night, and the juvenile teasing from a youth sports team are the real distraction. I need sound. I need to stop my brain from wandering to all the things I don't want to think about. There are so many things I don't want to think about.

Giulio isn't having any problems focusing. We're

partially hidden by the seat in front of us, and Giulio takes advantage of our position to monitor the rest of the car. I watch him watch the train out of the corner of my eye. He's looking left and right, up and down the center aisle.

I should let him do his job — both of our lives depend on it — but I need more of a distraction than sound. We haven't been on the train long, but I can feel my body beginning to settle. I don't want to go back to Milan, but I don't think I want to feel the enormity of this day — of the last few days — just yet.

"So, what's my reward?" I lean into his side and ask.

He doesn't respond immediately, but I see his jaw tick. He's heard me. When he does turn to me, his pupils are dark and dilated. His jaw is clenched. "What would you like?"

In a different scenario, that would be a perfect question. A question I don't think Ryan has asked me in years, because he assumed he knew me so well. But I barely know myself well enough to know what I want — especially not right now — and I don't want to give an answer any thought.

That's what I like about Giulio; why I wanted to come with him. I shake my head and press my breasts against his arm. His jaw ticks again.

"That wasn't the question," I say. It hasn't escaped my notice that he has a knack for skirting around direct answers. I believe him when he says that he doesn't lie, and now I can see how he avoids it. I file that tidbit of useful information away.

"What if you do not like my reward?"

There's no one in the aisle seat in front of Giulio. I move my right hand to the seat back in front of him and unlock the tray table. It's not enough cover, but it'll do for the moment. I move my hand to his right thigh and feel him jump under my touch.

"Tesora," he says in a playful warning.

"Why do you think I won't like my reward?"

He shifts toward me, and his hand slides over my leg. His fingertips are rough as they move from my knee up my thigh. "You might not think it's a reward."

"There's only one way to find out."

"That is an excellent point. Sit on my lap." His words come out in a desperate, relieved rush.

I turn to look at the crowded car on instinct.

"No. Look at me."

I sink into those words. I let myself go knowing that I don't have to hold myself together right now; that I don't have to decide. I nod and stand, smoothing the skirt of my dress into place, even though it doesn't cover much.

"Wait," he says and stands, stepping into the aisle. "Come."

I follow him into the aisle. There's a woman napping in the seat in front of the one I'd just vacated. Giulio doesn't care. We trade seats. He presses his back against the wall and spread his legs in invitation.

"Maybe we should switch back," I suggest in a whisper.

"Sit, tesora," he tells me again. He's enjoying this.

My eyes flit to the woman in the seat in front of us. She's snoring lightly. I shimmy onto his lap carefully, trying not to sit directly on the hard mound in his pants and using my skirt to cover more of my legs than the bit of fabric will allow, but Giulio's not interested in that. He pulls me firmly onto his erection and juts his hips up into me, almost as a reflex. He sighs softly, and I realize that he likes the weight of me on top of him. I do too.

I smooth my skirt over my thighs again, lock my knees

together, and cross my ankles, but once again, Giulio intervenes.

He pulls my legs apart at the knees, and I swallow a shocked, aroused gasp. We both watch as his index finger circles each of my kneecaps and then moves up my right thigh. When he reaches the hem of my skirt, he plays with the fabric, teasing me.

"Someone might see," I pant.

"Si, that's the point, tesora. That's your reward." As he says these words, his hand slips under my skirt. He massages each of my thighs slowly, clenching and relaxing his hand, pressing into muscles I hadn't realized were tired and sore. Actually, now that I think about it, my entire body has been wound tight for hours, ever since I ran into that armed man in the vineyard. Feeling those aching muscles allows me to let my body relax and lean back into Giulio.

"Better?" he asks, his mouth brushing against my cheek as he speaks.

"Yes."

"Tell me when to stop," he says, pushing my thighs apart. His other hand settles against the small of my back for a moment, and I relax just a bit more.

His hand moves down my back to my butt. I feel him start to pull my skirt up. My eyes dart down the train car as I shift from side to side on his lap, helping him expose my body. He grunts when my weight shifts on the erection that feels much harder now. When my skirt is free, he places his hand on my bare back. His fingers dip into the back of my underwear, toying with me.

"You aren't worried someone will see, and we'll get kicked off of the train?" I ask, gulping as his hands massage my thighs and back, and my temperature rises.

"I couldn't care about anything less right now. There's a condom in my jacket pocket. Get it."

I swallow a whimper.

There's a moment of hesitation between us, as I'm thinking, and he's giving me the space to think. Is this what I wanted? Is this what I was asking for? He keeps massaging me.

I haven't been with anyone besides Ryan in nearly a decade. I'm clearly mourning the end of two relationships, not just one. I just saw a man die in front of me. That man aimed a gun at my face. I'm letting this stranger take me to places unknown. I don't have my cell phone, so I can't even call for help. I'm 100% sober. My clit is throbbing.

My hands are shaking as I turn and push his coat open, searching for the pocket at his chest. I feel the square wrapper through the linen pocket and dip two fingers inside to pull it out.

"Are you sure?" he whispers, touching me lightly, unhurriedly, no pressure.

To be honest, I wasn't until he asked me. "Yes."

I feel the loss of his hand between my legs and frown.

He takes the condom from my hands and shifts me onto his thighs. He unzips his pants and pulls out his erection. I use my body to block him as best I can. Giulio doesn't care; he doesn't even seem to notice that we're so exposed, even in our small alcove.

When the condom is in place, his hands circle my waist again, and he lifts me back onto his lap as if I weigh nothing, turning me so that my back is resting against his chest. I lock my knees together. Instead of his erection underneath me, I feel the length of him up the small of my back. I reach around to grab him at the head.

He groans before grabbing my wrist and pulling my hand away. I whimper again.

"You haven't earned that yet," he tells me.

I'm not sure if those words should be sexy, but they are. "Tell me how to earn it."

"Sei troppo tesora per essere vero," he says to me.

"Non parlo Italiano," I remind him.

"Si," he says, but doesn't translate. "Spread your legs."

I do as he says without a second of hesitation this time, propping one foot onto the empty chair next to us.

He's still holding my wrist behind my back. His free hand goes to my thigh. He starts caressing and massaging my muscles again as he moves slowly up my thigh.

I watch as his hand disappears under my skirt, and I lay myself over him, my entire body open not just to him but to this experience and, incidentally, anyone who happens past. I shiver when his other hand gently cups my sex.

His mouth moves to my ear again. Has any man ever spent this much time whispering filthy things into my ear?

"Tell me when to stop," he says, and then peels my panties aside. I hold my breath. He traces his fingers up and down my lips, grazing over my clit. His touch is too light to get me off, but enough to make me moan and shudder.

"Is this too much?" he asks. I can hear the laughter in his voice.

I move my free hand to the back of his head and gently pull his mouth closer. "No. More."

I feel his smile against my ear before he gently sucks my earlobe into his mouth, licking and biting at me as he pushes a single finger inside of me. I gasp, loudly, before I press my lips closed.

The woman in front of us shifts in her seat.

I freeze, but Giulio doesn't stop. While I'm waiting for

her to fall back to sleep, Giulio is busy working that first finger and another and then another inside of me with careful and increasing pressure. By the time the woman in front of us has gone back to snoring louder than before, Giulio has four fingers so deep inside my pussy that I can barely breathe. I'm gasping and moaning and trying to keep my voice down, but I know I'm failing, and I can't care.

"Is this how you like it?" he asks, licking the outer shell of my ear.

"Yes," I moan, and I mean it.

Each time his fingers stroke as deep inside me as our strange position will allow, his palm presses into my clit. He memorized how I like to touch myself even though he only saw it once. Ryan had never. Could never.

Every one of Giulio's touches is full of intention, even the way he's licking and sucking and biting at my ear. Giulio's known me for a handful of hours, and he's already figured out all the things that get me hot, and more importantly, he wanted to know them. It took years of careful instruction in the bedroom to teach Ryan how to make me come more than once when we had sex.

Fuck Ryan forever, to be honest.

"I can keep doing this, tesora," he tells me. "I can make you come so hard that you'll forget the train and everyone on it but me."

"God, yes," I exhale on a full-body shiver. My orgasm is so close.

"Or, you can let me inside your wet cunt, and we can let the movements of the train get us off."

I come so hard that I lock my thighs around his hand and bruise my lips biting them shut. The orgasm hits me like a rocket. Even though I felt it coming, I'm unprepared for what it does to me, the way I shudder, the sweat that covers my body, the way I drench my ass, and surely Giulio's pant leg.

But I'm also unprepared for the new door of my own sexual desire that opens for me in this moment. It isn't just how expertly Giulio touched me or his filthy words; it's the way he gives me choices with only so much room to think as if he knows I can't handle more in this moment. The way he gives me limits, so I don't have to think too hard about the things that hurt. The way he gives me a safe space to feel.

There's no Ryan in this moment. There's only Giulio's fingers buried in my pussy, my orgasm, and the hot length of him against my overheated back.

Sometimes when I was with Ryan, I felt as if I had no choices, no say in my life, because his job exposed me to any and everyone, no matter what their intentions. Being in the public eye felt stifling. Ryan's career expectations and his batshit fans shrank the world around me the longer we were together. I'd had to move out of the little apartment Zoe, Shae, and I shared after college because the paparazzi were camping out outside my building. Some of my friends stopped inviting me to brunch because they didn't want to be on the celebrity gossip sites the next day.

Being with Ryan might have given me access to his money, but it didn't make my life better. Zoe had been right. *He makes you hide yourself away. Even if he doesn't mean to. Being with him puts you in a box.* How hadn't I realized the truth in this before? And *why* had I been about to bind myself to him?

I don't have the wherewithal to work through any of these realizations, not consciously at least. My brain notes them and moves swiftly away because accepting just how unhappy and unfulfilled I'd been in my previous relationship is much less important than attending to Giulio's options.

I know the answer as soon as I can breathe again.

I relax my thighs and plant my feet on the slightly sticky train floor. I don't stand fully, just enough to grab the head of his dick and position him at my opening. I look briefly over the seat in front of me at the crowded car, but this time, it doesn't affect me. I don't care. Besides, no one notices when my sweaty face pops up over the seat or my look of pure erotic ecstasy as I sink back down out of view onto Giulio's hard, throbbing dick.

I try to lower myself onto him slowly, but he doesn't let me.

He grabs me at the waist again — at some point, I should consider telling him how much I like that — and yanks me down. I yelp and groan.

His mouth is at my ear again. I adjust to the welcome intrusion of him inside me and his familiar panting breaths, and what I'm assuming are Italian curses. I don't know what they mean, but I *know* exactly how he feels.

GIULIO

"Cazzo. Ti senti caldo. Voglio restare qui per sempre."

I've had good pussy before. Correction, I've had great pussy before. The best money can buy. Zahra is better.

She's wet and warm and still shivering from her orgasm, vibrating around my cock like the best sex toy ever made. I could get used to this. I *want* to get used to this.

"Aspetta un secondo," I whisper to her. "Give me a moment."

She doesn't answer, but she doesn't move either. Somewhere on the other side of the train, a small spat erupts and is quickly quieted, but it's as if it's happening on a different car or a different train — maybe even another world — because in the little world of these two small seats that we've occupied, it's as if nothing can touch us. She leans into me, fully relaxing in my arms for the first time, and I hold on tight. After a while, she turns her head and brushes her soft lips across my cheek.

"Whenever you're ready," she whispers to me. Her voice is as soft as her cunt and her skin.

I'm ready.

I'm not an exhibitionist, and maybe Zahra isn't either, but I think we both like this relatively tame flirtation with danger; that at any moment, someone could discover what we're doing. I push my hips upward, rocking into her slowly and then retreating. There's not much room to maneuver myself in and out of her the way I imagined last night after I left her hotel room, but that's okay. We'll make this work.

I sink down in my seat and pull her on top of me. From this angle, I can pull out a few inches more and press into her a few inches deeper, heightening the pleasure of each stroke. She buries her face in the crook of my neck and moans as quietly as she can. I feel the vibrations of her breath all over my skin, and it pushes me closer to the edge. I won't last long inside of her.

She shivers around my cock in another orgasm. "Cazzo."

"Fuck," she says, echoing my thoughts. "So good."

"Si." I wrap both arms around her. "Are you ready?"

"God, yes," she moans against my cheek.

Now that I have a hold on her, it's easier to lift her from my lap, pulling her up the length of my shaft as I retreat and lowering her onto my lap as I push inside her again. There is something so delicious and wrong about the way we have to fold into one another to make this position work without rousing the person in front of us — again — or dislodging the thin cover provided by Zahra's skirt.

But it works. We make it work.

"Oh, God," she moans again. "Fuck me, just like that."

"Solo Dio può fermarmi," I tell her, my breath ruffling her curls. I pump up into her with a singular brutal thrust to accentuate my promise.

Zahra rewards me by sinking her teeth into my neck to muffle her moan, but I hear it loud and clear — I feel it vibrating over my skin — and it sends me into a frenzy.

The seat we're in squeaks each time I pull out of her, and every time I push back inside. Zahra's muffled moans turn to cries as she shivers in my tight hold, and her cunt grips me like a vice. I'm breathing so hard I feel as if I'm running beside the train. If we cared about being quiet before, we don't any longer.

Our little corner of the train feels like a sauna. We're both covered in sweat, and I can smell the delicious scents of her cunt and soap and perfume mingling in the air. I want to suffocate in it.

This is temporary. We both know that. But when I fill the condom between us, and she grunts out yet another release, it feels endless. It feels like this moment — this thing between us — could be something that we both know it can't.

She breathes a soft, exhausted laugh and raises her eyes to mine. I brush a few wet strands of hair from her face. Her eyes are soft and unfocused. She's here, but not quite.

"Bellissima," I tell her.

She shakes her head. "I know that word."

"Bene."

This moment is softer than anything I've ever experienced before, and of course, it's ruined.

The heavy metal door between the cars scrapes open. "Biglietti," the conductor calls as he steps into the car.

Zahra reacts faster than I can. She reaches inside my jacket pocket, snatches the tickets, and shows them to the conductor. Her other hand moves to the skirt of her dress and smooths it down, trying to cover the place where our bodies are joined. I don't help her because I don't care.

When the conductor moves away, I tell her again. "You are beautiful."

She looks at me and licks her lips.

The movement reminds me that I haven't kissed her yet. I move to sit up, stretching my neck to get my mouth nearer to hers, but she mistakes my intentions and leans away. I groan as she carefully lifts herself from my lap. I already miss her wet warmth around me.

"I made a mess," she says. She sounds shocked.

I'm not. I look down and am thankful that I changed into dark trousers before we left the hotel. The wet spot she's left on me is barely visible, but her smell is everywhere, as it should be.

"You should go clean up," she says.

She's still perched on my thigh, still trying to cover me with her body.

I nod and stuff myself back into my pants carefully with the condom still on my dick. She steps into the aisle, and I follow her. Out of the corner of my eye, I see the woman in the seat in front of us close her eyes quickly and grin.

"Do you think we should move?" she asks.

I nod and grab our bags from the overhead luggage rack. As we walk through the train, I use our bags to cover the wet spot on my pants. We find another secluded pair of seats, two cars over. I make sure Zahra is settled before I promise her that I will return and then go in search of the closest toilet.

When I'm locked inside the toilet, I take off my soiled pants, discard the used condom, and clean up as best I can in the facilities. Before I leave, I look at myself in the mirror. I seem normal. I might look a bit tired and sweaty, but I look more or less like myself. That feels strange. I don't feel the same as I did this morning and certainly not a week ago. I feel better.

I lean forward and pull the neck of my shirt down, turning my head to the side to see my neck in the mirror. I can feel a throbbing at the base of my throat, and I see why. Zahra's adorable teeth left a faint bruise on my skin, where she bit me.

"Merda," I hiss. "This woman is going to kill me."

And I'll like it, I think, as I head back to our seats.

We change trains in Florence.

"Stay with me," Giulio tells me as we step from the train and walk briskly through the train station.

I don't have any plans to run away. It's not like he kidnapped me or anything. Also, I'm holding onto his hand so tight I worry I might be cutting off his circulation; I'm certainly cutting off mine.

I think we're both just nervous about the large crowds in the train station. He hasn't told me directly, but Giulio is clearly worried that we might have been followed, which is why I guess he bought the tickets to Rome even though we got off long before then, and why we have to route through the main train station to buy new tickets, this time to a station I can't even pronounce. It's also why he stays as close to me as possible at all times.

I'm not worried about the danger, or at least not the same kind of danger. I hadn't realized it, but while I was in San Marco, I'd forgotten what it was like to be in the public eye. The only public interested in seeing me day drink by the pool was Giulio, and no one besides the woman at the front desk seemed to recognize me or care about my life blowing up all over American reality television. If things were any different in Milan, I didn't notice as we passed through. But Florence feels like a much larger city from the train station alone. I feel exposed. I haven't checked into American entertainment news since the morning of the wedding. I know what I *think* they're reporting about me — well, Ryan really — but I don't know for sure, and I don't want to.

Being up to date on the celebrity news cycle is my job, but I haven't thought about it once since I met Giulio. Now that we're in Florence, I'm thinking about it. I'm wondering if a paparazzo is going to pop out of an alcove and shove a camera in my face. I'm imagining Giulio beating the man with his own camera. I'm imagining how all of that would play on a 24/7 news loop.

And I'm terrified.

So while Giulio buys our new tickets, I shove my sunglasses onto my face and keep my head angled down toward the floor. I don't look anyone in the eye. When Giulio is back by my side, I do exactly as he says; I stay with him, and I don't let him out of my sight either.

GIULIO

"Po...Puh...?"

She's adorable.

"Poggibonsi," I tell her. I say the name of the city again, slower still.

She frowns at me. She's tired. There are dark circles under her eyes, and her normally luminous skin is dull and tinged with gray. She's pulled her big curly hair into a bun on top of her head. We've been traveling all day, except for a quick standing lunch in the train station during our transfer. Besides that short break, we've been sitting for hours, and the journey has taken its toll on Zahra. Her frown only accentuates her weariness.

"Say it slower," she commands.

"I don't think it's possible to say the word any slower, tesora," I tell her.

Her frown deepens.

We're waiting outside of the train station for a hire car. This station is small but still full of tourists. We don't stick out as much as I was worried we might, and that's a good thing, but it does nothing to assuage the growing anxiety in my chest as we move closer and closer to our destination, a place I haven't visited in two years and hate more than any other location in the world.

"Po-ggi-bon-si," I tell her, my eyes darting down the length of the street behind her.

I jump as Zahra presses herself against my right side. When I turn, she's smiling up at me, and I wonder if this is what she looks like first thing in the morning. I shouldn't think that, but I do.

"Slower," she commands with a smile.

I face her fully and wrap my free arm around her waist, bending forward until our lips touch. She doesn't flinch away like she did before. I smile against her mouth.

"Poggibonsi," I say again, whispering the word against her mouth, moving her lips with mine. It's not a kiss, but it feels like lightning shooting up my spine. Her lips are smooth and soft, and I want to sink into them. It doesn't take much to imagine all the things I'd love to do to those lips. I want to linger on her lips with mine until the sun sets, but I can't.

I reluctantly move away from her mouth. She missed a small curl in her bun, and it's blowing in the soft wind. If I were a better man, and if the world were a better place, Zahra and I could stay here in this moment forever. Those are fantasies I can't afford to entertain, even though I do.

"We're not staying here," I tell her, looking away.

"Where are we going?" she asks for the third or fourth time today.

I haven't told her before because I can never be overly cautious in my line of work, but now that we're in this small town and the closest person is out of earshot, I tell her. "San Gimignano."

She smiles and bounces onto the balls of her feet. "I like those words," she says and taps her index finger against her lips. "Slower." Her mouth splits into a smile.

I can't tell her no in that moment, and I don't want to. I lean forward, and our mouths touch again. "San Gimignano."

She thanks me by swiping her tongue across my lips.

I moan. She smiles.

"Kiss me," she says.

And I do.

<hr />

ZAHRA

I fall asleep almost as soon as Giulio pulls the car away from the train station. I want to stay awake and see where we're going for myself, but all the boredom and fear from our train ride catches up to me as soon as my ass hits the car seat. I'm out as soon as the engine roars.

"Come on, Zahra."

His voice wakes me gently, but not fully. He undoes my seatbelt, and then I feel his arms shimmy behind my back and under my knees.

"I can walk," I tell him even though I make no move to do so.

"I know," he says gently as he pulls me from the car. "Hold on to me."

I wrap my arms around his shoulders, bury my face in his neck, and let him carry me inside. I don't even open my eyes to see where we are. I'm too tired, and I trust him.

I startle a bit as he lays me on a bed. The sheets smell fresh. The mattress is a little firmer than I like but comfortable.

I feel his hands on my ankles, taking off my shoes. I groan and bury my face in the pillow beneath my head.

"Sleep, tesora," he whispers.

I'm already asleep.

GIULIO

I dig a new SIM card from the bag I packed. I send Alfonso a text, letting him know that I've arrived but not where I am. I assume he knows, or if he doesn't, he's not meant to.

I call Salvo.

"Are you safe?" he asks instead of saying hello. I always appreciate the way that he doesn't mince words. He's clear, and he likes to get to the point as quickly as possible. So do I. It makes my job very easy.

"I am."

"Are you where I think you are?"

"I am."

"Is that wise? For you?" he clarifies.

I'm in the kitchen. I don't hate this room as much as the others. This room and the bedroom where I put Zahra to sleep are about the only two rooms in the house that don't make my skin crawl. No, this isn't a wise decision, I think. If I were on my own, I wouldn't have come here. In fact, if I were on my own, I might not have left San Marco. I could have stayed on holiday, armed and prepared for someone to come looking for the man I'd killed. At least there, I could have enjoyed the pool and avoided stepping through the landmines of my past.

"I'm not sure," I tell him.

"Then, come here."

I turn to the wall behind me. On the other side, Zahra is fast asleep in my childhood bed. I can't take her to Naples. I know why, but I don't want to admit it, and I don't want to tell Salvo about her. I don't want these two parts of my life to actually touch. She knows I'm not a good man, that's fine, easy, but I don't want her to understand the depths of it all. That's why I brought her here, a place most people who know me don't know exists, and no one would ever think to look for me.

I just want to ride out the storm and enjoy this fleeting moment with Zahra. Alfonso and Salvo can fix this problem. I'm on holiday, I remind myself.

"You told me to get away," I remind my boss with a false smile, hoping it will lighten the severity of my voice. "I've never had a holiday before."

Salvo takes a deep breath and exhales slowly. "If you're sure."

I am.

"Did you call just to check in?" he asks.

"No. I have news," I tell him.

His voice brightens. "Do you?"

"Yeah. My visitor up north?"

"Si."

"His identification card had a surname you might be interested in."

There's silence on the other end of the phone.

"Necci."

Salvo huffs out a breath. "Certo. Is every branch of this bitch's family full of thorns?" he asks.

It's not a real question, but if he were actually asking me, I'd tell him that the answer is yes. I know intimately that one bad apple doesn't just spoil the bunch; it poisons the soil. But he's not asking, so I keep my mouth shut.

The other end of the line is quiet again. I don't interrupt, and I don't hang up until Salvo dismisses me. I let him think even as I try not to do the same. I'm waiting for orders. I'm waiting for permission to set my course so I can distract myself from where I am right now.

"Okay," Salvo says. "You stay there until I tell you otherwise."

I nod, even though he can't see me.

"I'll check in with Alfonso to see how he's enjoying his holiday."

"Okay. What if I have another visitor?" I think the chances are low, but I wouldn't be able to do my job right if I didn't ask.

"You're a hospitable person," he says with a laugh. "Do whatever you like." He hangs up without another word.

I turn the phone off, take out the new SIM card, and wash it down the kitchen sink. I turn around in the middle of this old stone kitchen, looking at — but trying not to see — the kitchen as it used to be. It barely takes a minute for the silence to get to me.

I rush back into the bedroom with a tight chest that begins to loosen when I see Zahra. I haven't been gone long, but in my short time away, she's somehow tangled herself in the sheets and turned over onto her back. She's snoring loudly. She looks peaceful.

I watch her for a few minutes, letting my mind settle. Eventually, I grab my bag and move quietly to the bathroom across the hallway.

I shower and throw on a pair of pajama bottoms and a fresh t-shirt.

This house has three bedrooms. It's not a big house, but it sits on a large plot of rich, fertile land, bordered by the vines from a local vineyard. On paper, this place is a paradise. In reality, my skin began crawling as soon as I walked through the front door. I don't want to see any of the rest of the house. I hurry back to the bedroom.

Zahra's flipped onto her stomach, and her snores are softer now, or maybe they're just muffled by the pillow. I didn't imagine she'd be such a wild sleeper. My eyes move involuntarily to the empty side of the bed. I consider slipping under those covers. I wonder if she would roll onto me in the night. If she'd kick me, or steal all the blankets. I wonder what she'd think about waking up in my arms tomorrow morning.

I smile, imagining a rude awakening of her palm against my cheek, and shake my head. If she's going to slap me, I want to see it coming. I grab a blanket from the foot of the bed and settle into the comfortable chair by the window.

I move the curtain aside and look out into the night. There's nothing but darkness outside. Good. I wrap the blanket around my shoulders, slump into the seat, and fall asleep to the sound of Zahra's heavy breaths.

You KNOW when you sleep so hard you wake up still kind of tired and groggy? That's me this morning. I'm somehow refreshed but still tired. I think the exhaustion from the last few days is finally starting to catch up with me.

It takes me a few seconds to realize where I am. I don't recognize this room or this bed, but then I hear him snore. I turn onto my right side and see Giulio sleeping in a chair with a blanket thrown over his body. It isn't until I see him that I realize I'd expected Giulio to sleep with me, especially after that train ride. But he didn't.

Like so much of my life right now, I don't know how to feel about that. Should I be happy that he didn't cross any boundaries we hadn't explicitly discussed? Should I be frustrated that after fucking me so publicly, he couldn't even sleep in the same bed with me? Should I be confused that I let a man fuck me on a train when sometimes I was nervous to let Ryan hold my hand at press events? Should I be concerned that all of this — masturbating for a complete stranger, running away with a man I know is a killer, the great public sex — is very unlike me?

If Zoe were here, she'd probably roll her eyes and tell me that life is full of contradictions and to stop obsessing over all the details. And maybe because I'm not rested, and also she's thousands of miles away, I decide to lean into the advice from her imaginary self.

Also, Giulio is sexy as hell when he's sleeping. His arms are crossed over his chest. I swear I can see his muscles flexing under the blanket. His head is lolling to his left, and his face looks so serene that he almost looks like another man. His lips are parted the tiniest bit, and every time he snores, he wrinkles his nose adorably. He doesn't look like a killer, I think out of nowhere.

And there goes Zoe's voice in my head. *What the hell does a killer look like?*

Great question, imaginary Zoe. To clarify, this man doesn't look like a killer to me — even though I know that's exactly what he is — because he looks like a man I want to fuck again.

Imaginary Zoe pipes up again. *And that's all that matters.*

I shake my head and roll onto my back. I stretch my arms and legs wide, moaning as my stiff muscles loosen. Yeah, last night was definitely the best sleep I've had the entire time I've been in Italy. I crawl out of bed carefully, trying not to wake him. My bag is right where I can see it next to the bed, and I snatch it up, holding it to my chest. The only door in the room leads to the hallway, so I head toward it. I have to pee so badly I'm practically jumping up and down. Thankfully, as soon as I step out of the room, I see the open bathroom door across the hall. I rush inside and close the door quietly.

Since Giulio is asleep, I decide to take my time relieving

my bladder, showering, brushing my teeth, and washing my face. And then I see my hair.

"Jesus," I whisper to myself, gently touching the frizzy, dry curls as if they're someone else's. I didn't wear a scarf last night, and it shows.

I dig into my bag and find the small pouch of travel-sized hair products. Since I'm in no rush, I spend another indeterminate period of time gently wetting, moisturizing, and setting my curls, trying to look less like a tumbleweed, even though I kind of feel like one. I've moisturized my entire body and my hair, but my mouth and throat are so dry I don't even think I can speak.

But I can scream.

And I do, just as soon as I open the door and find Giulio, looking bleary-eyed and menacing in the hallway outside the bathroom door.

"Troppo forte," he grunts at me.

"What the fuck does that mean?" I croak. My hand is resting on my chest, and I can feel my heart beating a wild rhythm.

"Too loud," he says. "Are you done?"

"I wouldn't have yelled if you hadn't been standing out here like a statue," I tell him, gasping. My throat feels shredded.

He rolls his eyes and shakes his head. "No. With the toilet. Are you done in the bathroom?"

"Oh. Yeah. Sorry. Let me just grab my things."

"Leave them. Make yourself at home. But move, I have to piss."

I turn to him and squint. "You're so rude first thing in the morning, apparently."

"We can talk about that after I use the toilet," he says, ushering me out of the bathroom unceremoniously.

I stand in the hallway, confused and still tired, as he rushes into the bathroom and slams the door in my face. But then I hear his voice through the wood barrier. "You smell delicious, Tesora."

"You're disgusting," I say, shaking my head. "Those are my hair products, by the way."

He laughs, and then I hear the sound of him peeing into the toilet.

I take that as my cue to find something to do elsewhere. I move into the kitchen. It's beautiful. I had a Pinterest board planned for this trip that changed so many times I hardly remember what was on it as Ryan's management changed our plans to fit his celebrity lifestyle. At first, I'd wanted to spend our honeymoon in Rome, but Ryan's agent thought that was too much of a tourist city and convinced him that he'd never get any privacy if we went there. She might have been right, but for months, I lived with a simmering resentment that Ryan had vetoed our honeymoon plans without even discussing it with me. We didn't talk for nearly a week; not that he noticed since he was shooting a film in Tucson at the time.

After that, I became obsessed with the idea of renting a small cottage in Tuscany and spending a week completely alone, just the two of us exploring a gorgeous village with lush, green rolling mountains as our backdrop. His PR firm vetoed that option because apparently, Ryan wasn't yet the caliber of star who could disappear to some rustic village in the middle of nowhere and drop off the public radar for so long. They even tried to convince him a little honeymoon photoshoot might help his fans warm to me. Maybe if they saw me as someone to envy, they'd treat me like they treated other celebrities.

I took so many exceptions to this line of thought, not

just personally but professionally. I work in PR as well. The idea that Ryan had to vacation in luxury and style based on someone else's ideas of who he was — and on our honeymoon, no less — was the exact opposite of the kind of advice I gave my clients. I told Ryan so many times throughout our relationship that if he wanted to be an actor with longevity, he needed to be exactly who he was; advice he never took, by the way. Actually, now that I think about it, even though I had just as much experience as his current PR rep, he never valued my input. I had never stressed the point at the time because I firmly believed in separating our personal and professional lives, but in hindsight, it stung; I'd just refused to acknowledge it at the time.

Also, in hindsight, I guess I was wrong. Based on what I know now, it made much more sense for Ryan to project a version of who he was to the studios, the celebrity entertainment news channels, his fans — and me — because Ryan wasn't the wholesome Midwestern action star on the rise in a loving, long-term relationship. He was a cheating asshole. Who knew? Not me.

Anyway, that long mental tangent is because this kitchen reminds me of a picture I posted on my Pinterest board during the Tuscan Villa phase of our honeymoon planning. Red slab tile connects the open kitchen and dining areas and the counters. The cream walls make the dark wood and red and brown accents around the long room pop. The mix of old and new looks exquisite to me, just like something out of my Pinterest finds.

There's a huge dining room table between the two rooms. It's rustic, like someone split a tree open and threw some varnish on it and some chairs around it. But it's the entire wall of glass at the back of the house that I love the most. The views of the garden and the vineyard bordering the property are breathtaking no matter where I stand. This kitchen is just my style, but it isn't Ryan's, which is why the apartment we share in New York — the apartment I haven't thought about in days — looks like some modern spa retreat, instead of a rustic family home where we plan to raise kids.

It's ridiculous that a kitchen can make me think so much about my previous life. But I'm realizing that with the thousands of miles between Ryan and me, and without the distraction of my phone, work emails, and a packed schedule, I have lots of time to think about things that I probably should have thought about years ago.

"We don't have any food," Giulio says as he walks into the kitchen.

He startles me, and I cry out again.

He rolls his eyes as he walks past me into the kitchen. "Stop yelling. It's worse than the tears."

"Shut up."

He laughs and opens the refrigerator.

I watch his muscles flex under his clothes as he moves. I'm particularly partial to whatever is going on under his t-shirt, but I don't want to shortchange his ass. There's a lot going on there that I'm into now that I have time to really look without pretending that I'm not. I hadn't realized just how built he is. He has a swimmer's physique, which makes a lot of sense and maybe explains those very small swim briefs. Or maybe he's just European. Either way, I heartily approve.

Giulio moves around the kitchen with my full attention, and I realize that I've never seen him naked. A new regret blossoms in my chest. I know I agreed to give up on lists, but my brain rejects that premise. A page turns in my head.

"See Giulio naked" is the first thing scrawled at the top of this new list for a new phase in my life.

He makes a tsk-ing sound as he opens the cupboards and quickly closes them. When he turns to me, he leans against the refrigerator and crosses his arms over his chest. It's similar to the pose he'd been in while sleeping. It's much less adorable now, though. Without the blanket, I can see the way his dark hairy forearms and biceps are covered with ropey muscle. I can fully take in how sexy he looks first thing in the morning, with his hair sticking up in every direction, five o'clock shadow darkening his jaw, and his eyes dancing as if he's finally relaxed after the stress of our trip.

"There's no food," he says again. "Would you like to go into the village?"

I can't help myself, but I brighten at that single word. "There's a village?"

"Si," he says. "I told you last night. San Gimignano."

I remember those last two words. Well, I remember how they felt against my lips and how his mouth tasted on my tongue. I don't shiver, but my entire body tenses with expectation at the memory. I can tell by the way his mouth tips into a lopsided grin that somehow, he noticed my reaction.

"I didn't realize it was a village," I say weakly.

"It is. And do you know what the village is famous for?" he asks me.

I shake my head, too afraid to speak. I don't want to say something else and sound stupid again.

He pushes off the refrigerator and walks toward me. There's something about this man that's like electricity to me. Even the sound of his bare feet slapping against the tile of the kitchen floor makes my body thrum. He gets close,

close enough that I can smell the lingering minty scent of toothpaste around him. Close enough that I can almost taste it. I tilt my head back, silently offering my mouth to him.

He smiles down at me and whispers a single word. "Wine."

I'll blame this next part on my still groggy brain, on the last few very confusing days, but it takes me nearly a minute to understand that that single word isn't a command. In that minute where I think that it is, I imagine all the things he could do to make me whine. And I want him to do those things to me.

But then I realize what he's saying, and I brighten again. "Are you fucking kidding me?"

He shakes his head, "I'm not. There are vineyards all over this region, and the wine here is world-famous."

"Then what are you waiting for? Hurry up. Get dressed," I tell him excitedly, slapping his arm with my hand. It hurts, actually. He might be shorter and not as built as Ryan, but he's just as strong. Maybe even stronger.

He leans forward to brush his mouth and that spiky stubble across my cheek, before turning back toward the bedroom to get dressed.

I watch his ass as he walks away.

GIULIO

"It's beautiful," she says more times than I can count as we drive from the farmhouse toward San Gimignano. Out of the corner of my eye, I watch her crane her neck in every direction, trying to take everything in.

I know the countryside is beautiful, and yet it's hard to be here and not remember all the ugly I've seen in this place. But that's not Zahra's burden to bear, so I nod and grunt each time she sees some new thing to exclaim over. I focus on the cadence of her accent and the tones of her voice, finding soothing comfort in her, even though I shouldn't. I'm not some dark, hardened criminal who needs an innocent waif with watery eyes to save me. I've seen the movies, and that life isn't for me. But I have seen a lot of ugly in my life and done a lot of terrible things as well. Zahra isn't going to save me. She's like a beautiful respite. I know this moment won't last — I know I can't keep her — but I keep the memories I don't want to revisit at bay by focusing on her voice and let her excitement center me in today rather than tomorrow and certainly not yesterday.

I park outside the village wall. "We can walk from here," I tell her.

She looks down at her shoes, another pair of tall, strappy platforms that show off those white toes I remember from the first time I saw her at the pool.

"You could have told me that before we left. I could have changed my shoes."

I undo my seatbelt and then undo hers. I lean over the middle console and get as close to her as I can without touching. She sucks in a sharp breath, and her nervousness makes me smile. "I didn't want you to change shoes."

"And what are you going to do when my feet hurt?" she asks, disdain and lust mingling in her voice.

"Carry you."

"You're just saying that."

"You know I'm not. If you want me to, just tell me."

"Is this just about carrying me?" she asks in a heated whisper.

"You know it's not," I tell her with a smile.

She licks her lips, and there is nothing more seductive than watching her pink tongue glide over her bright red lipstick. It doesn't move, but I imagine all that I could do to smudge that color across her mouth.

"Let's go," she says abruptly and opens her door.

I blink after her as she slams the car door and walks towards the village, flouncing away from me. As I watch, she stops and turns toward the car with a smile on her bright face. She lifts her right hand, points her index finger at me, and crooks it slowly, beckoning me forward. I don't hesitate to push the car door open and rush to her side.

San Gimignano is a small place. I assumed it had gotten smaller since my mother and I left, but I think that was just a coping mechanism. As we walk around the streets — carefully, so Zahra doesn't trip and fall on the stone roads — I realize that the village is just as it was when I was a child. I wouldn't call San Gimignano lively outside of the tourism, but there's life here, and Zahra wants to see it all.

I give her a tour of what I can remember of the town, which isn't much. We stop for coffee and pastries at the first bakery we see. We visit both of the cathedrals. Zahra prefers the artwork in the Sant'Agostino. I don't care about the art, but I love watching her face light up at each piece. She carefully runs her hand across stone walls all over the town, marveling at the different textures and how long the buildings have been standing. I don't know why I find that so fascinating, but I do. Watching Zahra, I realize that everything I know about this town is personal and horrible, but not historic, so I run my hands along the walls right along with her, wanting to see this place through her eyes.

We become tourists.

We double back to the entrance and find a kiosk with maps and buy one to share, and then we set off.

"There are towers all over the place," she says, staring intently at the map. She's not watching where she's going, so I do it for her. I have a hand poised ready to catch her should she fall and a hard eye aimed at anyone who strays into her path.

"We can see them all," I tell her, leaning into the part of my brain that wants nothing more than to please her.

She smiles as she moves her sunglasses from atop her head to her face. "You can't take that back now," she tells me. "Andiamo."

I can't help the smile that forms on my face. "Your accent is horrible."

She wrinkles her nose. "I'm trying," she whines.

We set off in the direction of the closest tower. Her hand reaches out to brush my arm, and I don't think. It feels as if it's been years since she last touched me instead of just a few hours. I brush my fingers across the back of her hand. When she looks at me, her bottom lip is clutched between her teeth; the red on her lips, white teeth, and brown skin all seem to shine in the sunlight.

Her hand moves down my arm, our palms glide together, and then our fingers intertwine.

"You're going to have to work on your pronunciation," I tell her.

"You should give me another lesson," she whispers.

That sounds near enough like a command to me.

I spin her around and press her gently against the closest wall.

Her mouth falls open, and she tips her head back. "Tell me," she whispers. That is absolutely a command.

I take my time dipping my head. I want to build the expectation of our mouths touching for both of us. I want her to remember this moment because I will.

"Andiamo," I whisper against her lips, slow enough that she can feel the way my lips stretch and then contract around the word.

"Andiamo," she whispers back.

Better. "Again."

This time when she speaks, I move my tongue over her mouth and that deep red lipstick, tasting it as she speaks carefully.

"Again," I tell her.

She presses her mouth more firmly against mine. She says the word again and again as the kiss deepens until there are no more words, just her wet tongue gliding against mine, her legs spreading to invite me between them, her soft breasts pressing against my chest, her arms around my neck, her soft ass in my hands and the rough stone wall behind her.

"Verrai per me?" I whisper to her as I pull her into my body.

"Translate that," she says even as she shivers in my hands.

I smile against her lips and kiss her again, before pulling away. "I will tell you tonight," I tease. "Let's go see the towers, yes?"

"Wait," she whines.

I kiss her chin and run my thumb under her bottom lip. Her lipstick is still perfect. I'll have to work harder to dislodge it.

"No," I tell her, pulling away from her warm, soft body. I hold out my hand for her. "Come."

She looks from my face to my hand to the front of my pants and licks those red lips again.

I feel her shiver as she slips her hand into mine.

"You're going to regret that," she whispers in a fierce, excited voice.

"Dio, I hope so," I tell her. And I do.

"My feet hurt," I whine.

"But you look gorgeous," Giulio says. "We're almost done."

"Hurry," I whisper into his ear and giggle when he groans.

"Sfacciata," he hisses at me.

"Translate."

"Tonight," he says as he has so many times today. After that kiss this morning against the wall, we've settled into a playful routine. Each time he says something in Italian that I don't understand — probably something dirty — I tell him to translate, and he promises me that he will tonight, with a grin on his lips. Based on the looks he's been giving me, and the persistent semi-hard erection he's been sporting all day, I imagine that we have a long night ahead of us. I'm ready to get back to the house to get down to business. I tried to rush him out of the village when we were done sightseeing, but he wouldn't let me. Thankfully, Giulio remembered that we still don't have any food at the house where we're hiding out, and we stop inside a small grocer just off the Piazza della Cisterna for a few things to tide us over for tonight, at least.

I like to cook, but I leave the real shopping to Giulio because I can't read any of the writing on the packages. Besides, I just want to see everything, all the different kinds of fresh pasta and oil and vinegar. I smile at the grocer who seems to be hovering around us, but not, I think, in that racist American way, but in a 'let me make sure these tourists spend all their money' kind of way.

"Don't forget the wine," I tell Giulio.

"Of course not," he says, leading me to the surprisingly extensive — considering how small the store actually is — wine and spirits section.

"You said this town is famous for wine," I remind him.

"Si. You have to try the vernaccia."

I grab the sides of his head in both hands and turn his face toward me. I've always thought Italian was a beautiful language, but it's even more beautiful coming out of Giulio's mouth. I like the way his lips caress the words, the varying intonations of his gruff voice, and the way I can sometimes discern his meaning by the warmth in his eyes.

"Say that word again," I tell him.

His eyebrows dip together over the bridge of his nose, and his dark eyelashes flutter. "You have to try the vernaccia di San Gimignano."

"Do you like it?" I ask him.

The grin on his mouth disappears, and his eyebrows bunch together. I wonder if I shouldn't have asked that.

"I've never had it," he finally admits, but then his face brightens. "We'll try it together, yes?"

"Si," I breathe. He shakes his head before moving forward.

"If you are good, I will lick the wine from your skin, si?"

I swallow my own groan and wrap my arms around his neck, pressing my body into his. His free arm wraps around my waist, and he pulls me in close and tight.

"What if I'm bad?" I ask in a heated whisper.

He smiles for a brief second, but he doesn't get to answer my question.

The grocer who's been following us around starts yelling. We both turn, and Giulio's arm tightens around my waist as he moves me behind him in a protective gesture.

I expect to see a man — or many men — rushing into the store with guns drawn. Pessimistically, I think that our day has been too good, so of course, it's all crashing down now before I can learn all the translations to Giulio's dirty suggestions. But when we turn, there's just the grocer and his angry red face.

I don't expect Giulio to start yelling back.

I can't even begin to understand the rapid-fire Italian, but rage is universal. "What's going on?" I ask.

It takes a few seconds for Giulio to stop yelling and answer me. "Nothing."

"Clearly, that's a lie."

He ignores me and keeps yelling at the man before releasing his hold on my waist and snatching two bottles of white wine from the display in front of us.

"Come, tesora," he says, leading me toward the front of the store. Strangely, the grocer leads the way, yelling at Giulio over his shoulder. Giulio keeps yelling back. I stand to the side, bewildered, my eyes darting from one man to the other as the grocer inputs the prices of our groceries on one of those old-school electric cash registers and then bags them carefully. Giulio throws the money for the food onto the counter, still yelling. I've never been more relieved than when Giulio gestures for me to head toward the door and follows me.

I feel like I'm in an Italian soap opera. Actually, maybe I am.

Giulio's hand settles at the small of my back as he follows me out of the store. He doesn't stop yelling until we're outside. The piazza is full of people. It's so quiet and serene compared to that scene in the store that I feel like I've gone through a magical door into another dimension.

I can feel the anger rolling off of him as he steers me out of the village. He's pissed, but he still walks at a comfortable pace for my sore feet. I wonder if he realizes that he's doing that. I wonder why these small things matter to me.

At the car, he unlocks the doors, gently places our shopping bags in the back seat, and ushers me to the passenger side. He's still furious, but a stranger might only recognize that when he wrenches the car door open with much more force than necessary.

"Get in," he barks.

"Don't yell at me," I bark back.

He blinks and then finally looks me in the eye. When he does, I can see just how angry he is, but I can also see the moment when he sees me — really sees me — for the first time since the grocer started yelling at us.

He takes a deep breath and pushes it out through his nose. "Mi dispiace," he whispers. "I'm sorry."

I have to take a deep breath too. "Thank you. Now please tell me what that was all about. Why was that man yelling at us?"

"Not us," he corrects. "Me."

"What's the difference?"

"He didn't have a problem with you. It was me."

"Why? What did you do?"

"Nothing."

I squint in confusion. "I don't understand."

He takes another deep breath. "The man wasn't yelling at me because I did something. He was yelling at me because of who I am."

"And..." I swallow the lump in my throat, "who are you?"

He huffs out a harsh, bitter breath. "I'm my father's son. Neither of us were good men, and he thought I needed to be reminded of that. As if I've ever been able to forget."

GIULIO

The drive back to the farmhouse feels longer than this morning. Maybe it's the silence.

For a brief moment today, I stopped second-guessing my decision to bring Zahra here. I let myself enjoy her presence, her hand in mine, her teasing grin, and the soft way she looked at me as if she truly saw me, maybe better than I saw myself.

That man took that all away in just a few minutes.

I haven't been to the farmhouse in a few years, but I haven't visited San Gimignano in over a decade, and I'd assumed no one would recognize me. Why would they? I'd been just a boy when my mother packed what little we could carry and ran away with me in the middle of the night. Technically, we probably could have waited to clear out the house since my father sometimes left for days at a time, but she hadn't wanted to risk it, and knowing what I know now about monsters like him, I understand why.

For months, we lived looking over our shoulders, barely

sleeping at night, thinking he would come find us, but he never did. I was a man when I went looking for him. I didn't know what I expected to find, or what I thought I would feel when I came face-to-face with the man who made my childhood a living hell. The angry man who cursed me as soon as he saw my face didn't shock me but feeling as if I was looking in a mirror did. I'd never realized just how much I looked like my father. I've wondered since what it did to my mother to see me turn into him more and more each day.

Seeing my father again changed my life for the better. Some people believe that you can't right the wrongs of the past with vengeance. My mother was one of those people. She left my father and practically became a nun, devoting herself to the church and me until the day she died. As much as I wanted to be like her, I've always known that I'm most like my father, and I made sure that he knew that too. The last time I came to San Gimignano, I found my father, and I put a bullet right between his eyes, which just happened to be the same shade of brown as mine. My mother had been dead for six months by then. This was my final present to her, even though I wonder sometimes if it was a gift she would have wanted.

I hadn't expected to inherit anything from the man who hadn't wanted to raise me, but this house, my face, and apparently, my temperament are a trifecta of confusing endowments.

I'm not caught in some psychic turmoil over what I did. In fact, killing my father was the first decision I ever made fully on my own without worrying about how it would affect my mother. If she'd been alive, I might have been eaten away by the guilt, and she would have spent every waking hour in church praying for my soul. But if there is a heaven, I hope she knows that I did the right thing for me. I met Salvo a year later. It was easy to attach myself to him and set my own path, with my father as a distant memory.

I don't know exactly why I've kept the house, but getting rid of it never felt right, even though I hate coming here. I have an apartment in Naples that's just big enough for me and the occasional guest, and I have my work. Strolling through my traumatic past has never interested me. Were it not for Zahra, I might never have come back, and that grocer is why.

I don't know how to live in a world where people will see me and think of my father. And as I park the car in front of my family home, I don't want to live in a world where Zahra might look at me and see him either, but it's only a matter of time before that happens.

I'm not a good man, but I am my father's son, and I've somehow never regretted that fact more than right now. I shut off the car, and we sit in silence for a few minutes. I can't speak. I'm terrified that I'll say the wrong thing, not that I have any idea what's right to say in a moment like this.

"We don't have to stay here," she finally says, softly breaking the heavy quiet between us.

"This is the best place to be right now. I can keep you safe here."

"We could go to...wherever you live," she says hesitantly. We both realize just how little I've told her about myself.

"Naples," I tell her, adding this to the list of things I've shared that I shouldn't.

"I've always wanted to see Naples," she says excitedly.

"You don't have to lie," I tell her.

When she turns to me, her face is as bright as her voice.

"I'm not lying. My cousin took a trip to Rome and said her day trip to Naples was her favorite part."

"Your cousin should travel more," I say flatly.

"I'll make sure to tell her that," she says. "We can go to Naples."

I shake my head. "Whoever was looking for me in San Marco will definitely be looking for me there." I know it's the right thing to say, and staying put is the right thing to do, but I can't help but conjure an image of Zahra naked in my bed, her curly hair fanning out on my best sheets, and my entire apartment smelling like her perfume and cunt. "We can't," I say, more to convince myself than to reiterate the point.

"You said you were your father's son," she says gently.

I flinch at the words. "I am."

"Are you sure?"

"Unfortunately."

"How do you know?"

I shake my head. "Come. I'll make you dinner." I want to change the subject. I want her to keep looking at me like she had this morning in the piazza, with her eyes shuttered in lust, her mouth parted because of mine, and her legs locked around me to keep me as close as possible.

Her small hand covers my forearm and squeezes. "You said you wouldn't lie to me."

"I don't lie."

"But you do know how to evade the truth."

I turn to her and flinch again, but this time at the earnestness in her eyes. I don't know what I was expecting, maybe judgment, but that's not what I see there. All I see is warmth and empathy. I hate it because I don't deserve it.

"Don't look at me like that."

"Like what?"

"Like I deserve good things."

"Define good things," she says.

The comment shocks me, and I huff a pained laugh, which makes her smile. "I'm not a good man," I remind her.

"Yes, I haven't forgotten that. Believe me. But even bad men deserve to be understood. At least that's what every Hollywood movie for the past thirty years has told me." She smiles tentatively as she speaks, and I can't help but laugh again. "Tell me what you meant. Tell me how you're like your father. I know I don't have the right to ask. And of all the things you haven't told me, this seems like the strangest to want to know. It's just that I spent nearly a decade with a man who described himself as his father's son in every interview he ever gave, even though his father is a good, hardworking, faithful man. So what I'm asking, Giulio, is for you to tell me exactly how you're like your father, because sometimes the stories we tell ourselves aren't true."

She sounds naïve but also worldly. I can't fathom how she can manage the two together; how she doesn't have an ounce of bitterness in her voice after what she's been through. And above all, I can't imagine why she's wasting her time trying to understand a monster like me. But in the end, it's the way she says my name that makes me tell her. It's the way her voice dips to a whisper, almost as if my name could ever be precious, that makes me tell her an abbreviated version of my childhood.

We're sitting in the car in silence again. It's heavier than before, because everything I've told Zahra is heavy, even though I do my best to skip over the worst parts. She keeps her hand wrapped around my forearm as I speak, squeezing here and there, when my voice gets rough. Her other hand sometimes brushes along my jaw comfortingly.

It's hard to crave her and want to push her away at the same time, but I manage those conflicting emotions quite well.

She clears her throat gently before speaking. "I don't mean this in a bad way, but I still don't get it."

"Get what?"

"How you're like your father."

"I've just told you."

"So, you have a history of domestic violence?"

I flinch. "Of course not."

"Have you isolated a former girlfriend in the countryside, without a car, or money for them to live their lives?"

"I don't date. I have no children. I'll never have children. And I never would have brought you *here* if I thought I had a choice."

"And why don't you want children?" she asks.

"I think two generations of monsters is enough." There's nothing more to say as far as I'm concerned.

"Did you terrorize the locals so much that decades later they still remember and hate you so much they also hate your son?"

"No," I grind out. "But I'm working on it in Naples."

"Right, well, get back to me in a generation about that."

It's my turn not to get it.

She squeezes my arm again. "I'm not a psychologist or anything so, you know, don't run with what I'm saying, but it strikes me as significant that you don't want to be like your father, and you're doing all you can to make sure that you don't repeat his crimes."

"I'm committing my own crimes," I tell her. "I killed my father."

"Yeah, and congratulations. Again, not a psychologist. I'm just saying, you're not a good man, but it's possible to be a different kind of bad man than your father was. Also, no judgment, but it sounds like he kind of deserved it."

I stare at her in complete confusion. The car is quiet again for a few seconds. This time, the silence is broken by the sound of Zahra's stomach rumbling.

"Oh, wow. I'm really hungry." She looks into the back seat at our bags of groceries. "I'm going to take those inside and get started on dinner. But you can stay out here for as long as you want. I have no problem eating alone."

I open my mouth, but no words come out, and Zahra takes that as an invitation to leave.

She squeezes my arm and brushes her hand along my jaw again. I watch as she pushes the car door open and pulls open the back door to grab the grocery bags. We make eye contact, and she smiles as if I haven't just told her all that I've seen and only a fraction of what I've done, before slamming the door and carrying the bags toward the house.

Her shoes are too tall, and there are too many bags. She stumbles, and I rush out of the car before I can think. I grab the bags from her arms, unlock, and push open the door to the house. I walk in first and take mental note of the gun at my back — the gun I'd honestly forgotten I had on me all day — and make sure that nothing looks out of place as I walk through the house toward the kitchen, with Zahra on my heels.

I help her unpack our bags, and we move around the kitchen together as if we've done this before. As if I've known her longer than two days. It feels so normal, it aches.

This is where I'm supposed to be, I think. Not in this house, but with her.

"So do you want pasta? Or pasta?" she jokes, holding up the packets we picked up at the grocers'.

"That's it?" I ask her.

She laughs, "That's all we got, yes. Maybe next time we'll do better."

"No," I say, shaking my head, still confused. "You're not going to go running into the night to get away from me? You're not going to interrogate me about all the other bad things I've done? You're not going to hit me over the head with something heavy repeatedly and do the world a favor?"

She rolls her eyes. "You know, for someone whose job probably depends on them being very levelheaded, you're very dramatic. Also, we've established that I can't run in any of my shoes. So, pasta?"

"Pasta," I tell her.

"Excellent choice," she laughs to herself.

I'm still confused. None of this makes any sense. And yet in this moment, I only feel even more certain that Zahra would do best to get as far away from me as possible. The problem, I can see now, is that I think we've passed the point of no return.

I don't want to let her go.

"Do you want more?" he asks.

I shake my head, even though I kind of do.

I wanted to come to Italy for the food, but I've been here for days, and I've only had a single real meal since I arrived. I've been surviving on wine and fruit and the occasional piece of chocolate. But a good homemade Italian meal like the ones that I'd imagined and pinned to every version of that Pinterest board? This is as close as I've gotten, and I cooked the pasta.

Giulio made the pesto, though, and he's Italian, so I guess that counts. And it's great, by the way. I could eat all of the leftovers, but I don't want Giulio to think I'm greedy.

"I'm stuffed," I tell him.

He nods and then scoops another serving of pasta onto my plate. "It won't taste the same tomorrow."

"If you say so," I say around the bite of pasta I've already shoved into my mouth.

He shakes his head and scoops the rest of the pasta onto his plate. He refills our wine glasses and sits back in his seat across the humungous dining room table from me.

He watches me eat for a few seconds, which is enough time to scarf down half of what he's given me.

I eye his plate and the untouched seconds. "Are you going to eat that?" I ask with full cheeks. I have manners. My mother drilled good table etiquette into Zoe, Shae, and I, but my fork is involuntarily moving across the table toward his plate. He blocks it with his own.

"Yes."

I frown and move my fork back to my plate. I scoop up another forkful of pasta and shove it into my mouth.

Giulio laughs, but he doesn't eat. Rude.

"Who taught you how to make pesto?"

"My mother, obviously."

"Did she teach you how to make anything else?" I ask, popping an olive from the antipasti into my mouth.

"You know you can buy an Italian cuisine cookbook at any bookstore, right? Or you can order one online. They are not rare," he says gracefully, eating a forkful of pasta. Finally.

"It's not the same," I tell him, hoping he ignores the whine in my voice.

"It's close enough."

I roll my eyes. "We have to eat dinner tomorrow night," I remind him.

"You can cook me something American."

"I boiled the water for this pasta," I tell him. "You've seen the extent of my cooking capabilities."

He chokes on the food in his mouth and washes it down with another sip of wine. He sits back in his chair and wipes at his wet eyes, still laughing at me.

I would be annoyed, but I'm busy eating.

"I know you're just saying that so you can steal more of my mother's recipes."

I smile sheepishly at him and take a sip of wine before I answer. "I never said I didn't lie. It's actually kind of a job requirement for me."

"What exactly is your job?" he asks, squinting at me.

"I work in PR. Public relations," I clarify.

"Yes, I know what PR stands for. You might say that I work in PR as well."

I raise my eyebrows at him. "Oh yeah?"

"Si. It's my job to...handle anything that might negatively impact my organization."

I blink at him, waiting for more or a better explanation. It doesn't come. "I really like that moment of hesitation, the specific word choice, and the way you almost looked legitimate as you said it. You might not lie, but you certainly have a loose relationship with the truth. If you were my client, though, I'd tell you to lose the shrug. It's a tell."

He shrugs again. It's a sexy as fuck tell. "I'll remember that."

"If I were to ask you what you did for real, would you tell me?"

"Yes. But please don't ask me."

That shouldn't work on me, especially after the train wreck that was my recent relationship. A man asking me to avoid the deadly elephant in the room should be a red flag, but it doesn't feel that way. Why would his answer be more important than seeing him standing over a dead body with a smoking gun? Figuratively speaking. I don't know if the gun was actually smoking; I was too busy looking at all the blood seeping into the soil.

"Okay," I tell him. "I won't ask."

"Thank you."

"You're welcome. So," I say, forking the last of the pasta into my mouth. I feel both excitement and sadness, knowing that there's no more. Well, no more on my plate. "What is there to do around here at night?"

His glass stills against his bottom lip, and I can just see his smile through the wine. He lowers his glass to the table and stares at me before answering. "Not much, actually. That's why this was a good place to hide out."

I nod. "Makes sense. So that means we'll have to entertain ourselves?"

I see his throat bob as he swallows.

"I believe we were discussing the possibility of Italian language lessons this afternoon?"

So here's a new thing I've just now learned about myself: I'm always horny. Someone — someone like Zoe, for instance — might ask how I've made it to my late twenties and am just now learning that I have a libido the size of Italy. Here's the uncomfortable answer: I never wanted Ryan this much. That doesn't mean I didn't love him, and it doesn't mean we didn't have a real relationship, but it does mean that after just a couple of days with Giulio, I'm realizing that maybe Ryan wasn't the only one who was unfulfilled in our relationship. Maybe having sex two or three times a week was more than our married friends, but not nearly enough for me. Maybe Ryan and I were never going to work, no matter who he cheated on me with.

Now I'm not saying that Giulio is the love of my life or anything, but I am saying that I go from feeling full and happy to hungry and needy in a single breath. When he picks his wine glass up again, and his dark eyebrows bunch together over the rim as he takes a deep sip, I realize that if this day ends without me feeling this man's mouth and hands on me, I will consider the mostly lovely day we've spent together a waste.

I push my chair back from the table and stand. He takes

another sip of his wine as he watches me. I don't know if he looks at every woman he's with this way, but I do know that no man has ever looked at me with such singular intent.

"I'm going to take a shower," I tell him.

He nods slowly as I move away from the table. I walk toward the small bathroom across from our bedroom and stop at the door into the hallway. I peek at him over my left shoulder.

"You can join me if you want," I tell him in my most sultry voice.

He's already halfway across the room before I finish the sentence.

GIULIO

I'm not a young boy who's not sure what gets his dick hard. I know, and as a shortcut, everything Zahra does makes me hard. I also know that I don't have to rush. I know that we have all night and tomorrow and however long until it's time for Zahra to go back to America. I know that, and yet I'm fumbling as I strip my clothes off in front of her. I kick my shoes from my feet and rip my shirt over my head, desperate to get naked and to get her naked. I take a careful second to unstrap my holster and set it on the bathroom counter. But then I push my slacks and underwear down my legs at the same time.

Zahra isn't in a rush. She moves her hands to her back to unzip her dress lazily. The sound rips through this small room and me in an instant. I watch her move the straps of her dress over her shoulders with hunger. When she pushes her dress over her breasts, my entire body freezes. My hands still at the button of my pants. Blood rushes through my body when I see Zahra's lacy purple bra, bare, flat stomach, and black lace underwear come into view. Her dress pools at her dainty feet, and I take her in from head to toe before I kick my pants from my ankles.

She's still refusing to rush. She's enjoying torturing me.

I'll never tell her, but I enjoy it too.

She unclasps her bra and holds it to her chest.

I blow out a harsh breath and laugh. "Stuzzica," I hiss.

"Does that mean tease?" she asks in a sultry voice that makes my balls ache.

"Si."

"Good." She drops the bra to the floor.

My mouth is actually watering.

Her breasts bounce as she squares her shoulders, preparing herself for me to see her. And I do. I think I could spend the rest of my life just looking at her.

She cups her breasts in both hands. Her fingers skim over the dark brown tips.

I lick my lips. She giggles.

She's torturing me.

I love it.

"Your underwear," I say. My voice has fallen to a whisper.

Her hands smooth down her hips over the front of her underwear. "Yes?" she asks.

"You know what I want," I tell her.

"Do I?"

My gaze moves back to her face. She's a work of art. I want to tell her that, but I have to swallow the words. It's unfair, even if it is the entire truth. What I say isn't a lie, it's just not *as* true as my first impulse.

"I want you to take your underwear off."

"Good to know. Do you want to hear what I want?"

"Yes," I breathe as soon as she's done speaking. *Desperately,* I stop myself from saying.

"I want you to tell me what to do." She shivers as she says the words. "Tonight, I want you to decide every way we fuck."

My dick is so hard it hurts, and I groan.

"I don't want to come unless you tell me to. I don't want to come until you say it's okay."

I can hear my breath in this small, quiet bathroom where I used to hide as soon as my father walked through the door. A part of my brain wants this, wants to let Zahra rewrite my memories of this place. I know it's dangerous to lean into that because it won't work, but I want to try. In a year, I want to remember what she looked like in this moment and remember only that; nothing that passed before.

I slide my hands up her arms, and she shudders violently at my touch. "You don't strike me as the kind of person who likes to take orders."

"A week ago, I would have said you were absolutely correct, but now I'm not so sure." She blinks up at me and frowns. "I'm not sure about anything right now, and I've decided not to force it. Right now, this is what I want, and I want you to help me explore it." The smile she levels at me is small and uncertain and still beautiful.

My hands move up her neck. I caress her jaw and chin. Touching her makes me shiver. My dick is bobbing, tapping against her hip excitedly. I'm leaking from the tip, and just knowing that I'm smearing come on her makes me feel weak and strong at the same time.

"Did you ever do this with that stronzo?" I ask. I can't hide the jealousy in my voice.

"No. There's a lot we never did."

"What else?"

"Too much for the little time we have," she says. "I fly out of Milan in two days."

"Troppo presto," I whisper to her.

"Yeah," she breathes.

"So we will make the most of it."

She nods and licks her lips again. "You take control tonight," she says.

I nod, leaning toward her.

"And I'll take control tomorrow."

I freeze, and we make eye contact. She touches my waist, tentatively at first and then boldly. She flattens her palm against my stomach. I hold my breath. I hold myself completely still. For her.

"I didn't even know that I would like someone telling me what to do, but you haven't stopped since the day we met," she says, lifting onto the balls of her feet to rub her cheek against mine. "But for every command you give me," she whispers against my lips, "you take two from me. Whatever I want?"

I feel weak and strong again. "Yes," I whisper against her mouth.

"Tonight, you're in charge. Tomorrow, it's my turn."

"And then you go back to Milan and get as far away from me as possible," I finish.

We stare at one another. I can see that she's unhappy at my words — or, maybe how I've said them — but I think we both need the reminder that all of this is temporary.

She grabs hold of my cock boldly, stroking me once.

I hiss out a breath that sounds like a groan. "Cazzo."

"Deal," she says, swiping her tongue along my jaw.

He's not gentle with me, but he is.

I don't know how Giulio manages to embody this dichotomy so consistently, but it gives me a thrill.

He spins me around to face the shower, and then he rips my lace underwear down my legs so hard I'm surprised he doesn't shred them. I'm glad he doesn't, though; I don't believe in wasting good lingerie.

"Don't move," he tells me, palming my thighs and hips and ass as he stands up again as if he can't bear to stop touching me.

He's adorable. I'm not going anywhere but down to my knees. God, I want him to make me get on my knees.

I shiver when he lets me go to turn the shower on. As we wait for the water to heat up, I take the opportunity to drink in every hairy inch of him; the way his jet black hair contrasts with his skin, his dark nipples peeking out from under his chest hair; the neatly trimmed pubic hair hiding his balls, and the proud, erect weight of his dick between his legs. That's my favorite part, actually. It's sticking out straight and hard and staring right at me.

On reflex, I reach out to grab it. Giulio's reflexes are too good. He grabs my wrist and tsks at me with a slow shake of his head and a wicked smile on his face.

"Tomorrow, you can touch me whenever and however you want, but tonight, you have to ask for permission."

I don't know how to describe how those words make me feel except as if there's electricity in my veins. I cross my hands in front of my body, trying to hide the small patch of hair between my legs from him. His eyes follow the movement, and he smiles and shakes his head. The bathroom is warmer now, and he opens the glass partition for me.

"Step inside."

I nod once and step forward carefully, but before I step into the shower, I touch the ends of my shoulder-length curly hair. It feels like it's been days since I washed my hair, days since my hairdresser put every cream and holding product imaginable on my strands for the wedding that never was. I can feel all of the remnants of the products, days of sweat, and pollution on my scalp suddenly. I feel dirty in a way I hadn't immediately after realizing that my life was a bunch of sentient lies in a trench coat.

I turn to Giulio and look him in the eyes. I don't know what he sees when he looks at me. I barely know exactly how I feel, but I know what I want from him. "Will you wash my hair?" I ask.

He's in charge tonight, and I could make this request tomorrow when it wouldn't be a request, but I want to ask him tonight.

I don't know if it's the memory of the anguish in his face as he compared himself to his father sticking in my head. I don't know if it's the personality flaw that Zoe has been telling me about my entire life; that I feel this ridiculous need to save everyone around me, but not myself. It could also be that I'm done. I'm not sure exactly when I made the unconscious decision to stop mourning my relationship with Ryan, but it's over. I can't undo what Ryan and Trisha did, and, to be honest, I don't want to.

So what I'm asking Giulio in this moment is to help me wash away all those years I spent with the wrong man, a man who didn't respect me enough to be honest, a friendship I'll never get back, and all the regret I've been bearing for months about how I chose other people over my sister.

I'm asking him to make me feel clean again, a ridiculous request of a hitman.

"Sarebbe il mio piacere," he whispers to me. "Si."

I get the gist.

When we step into the shower, I move immediately under the spray. The stream of water engulfs me. I can feel him behind me, his body making the shower that much warmer with the heat of his desire at my back, followed quickly by his fingers.

"I'll clean your body first," he tells me. I nod sheepishly.

He moves to the shelf at the back of the shower, and I turn to him. I watch as he opens the small bottle of body wash I left there after my shower this morning. *You smell delicious,* he'd said this morning, and I think of that as he opens each bottle there and sniffs them deeply, a look of pure ecstasy washing over his face.

He grabs the small towel I've thrown over the towel rack and squirts some of the liquid inside. I stand in the middle of the shower with my hands crossed in front of my chest, watching as he prepares to bathe me. When the towel is lathered, he approaches me with a singular focus, as if scrubbing my body is the most serious job he'll ever do.

"Turn around."

I do.

He gently moves my hair aside and runs the towel over my shoulders and upper back. He follows each swipe of the towel with his hand, and the contrast between the fabric and his slightly calloused fingers against my softest skin makes me swallow a moan. He moves down my back slowly. At this rate, we'll be in here all night. I don't hate the idea.

When he reaches my hips, I hear him move. When I turn around, he's not there. I look down at the top of his head because he's squatted behind me. His face is so close to my skin that he could lean forward and kiss my body without much effort. He's watching the towel swipe through the suds over my skin with such dedication that I feel like a work of art.

"Is this a...voglia?" he asks. I don't know that word, but his fingers run over the small constellation of moles on my right hip — a constellation of moles my sister, cousin, and I share.

"Birthmark," I translate. "Yes."

He nods and runs his fingers over the small moles again.

His hands and the towel move down each leg in turn. I lift my feet so he can run the towel over the soles and between each toe. When he's done, he stands up, his hands moving across my skin again before settling along the curve of my waist.

"Turn around," he commands.

And I do.

"I should have asked you sooner," he says with a pained look on his face. "Is there anywhere you don't want me to touch?"

If he weren't in control, I would jump this man now and ride him into next week. Who cares about my return flight? "Anywhere. You can touch me anywhere," I tell him.

I know that I don't know this man at all — tragic childhood stories notwithstanding — but I can see that he's swallowing a response in the way his Adam's apple bobs, his breathing constricts, and his fingers flex against me.

"Si," he breathes in a rough whisper.

He touches me just as reverently as before, but this time he works his way from my ankles up. The towel and his bare hand move up one leg and down the other. At my left ankle, he looks up my body and lifts his eyebrows.

"Open your legs, tesora."

I spread my legs a bit.

"Wider."

Just a bit more.

I don't mean to bait him, but I'm not running from it either. I don't know what I expect him to do, but I am not disappointed.

He stands quickly and presses me against the tile wall with his hands and his body. I can feel his hard erection against my stomach and my pussy clenches.

I feel empty. I want him inside me. I've wanted him inside me all day. "Fuck me," I tell him.

"Spread your legs," he repeats.

"Are you going to fuck me?"

"Only if you behave." He says the word as a warning, but then his hips jut toward me.

"Are you lying to me?" I tease.

His jaw ticks. "I'll fuck you," he says, and it sounds like a promise, "when I'm good and ready. Now spread your legs."

This time, I do as he says.

He swirls small circles over my left thigh as his hand travels up and between my legs. I suck in a harsh breath. His fingers mix with the running water and ghost over my pussy. He caresses the hair over my mound, running his fingers through the curly hair before he moves to palm my entire sex in his big hand.

I react without thinking and grab his wrist to hold his hand there. I press my pussy down into his palm and shudder. He's finally touching me.

"Zahra," he warns.

I groan and ignore him.

"You wanted this," he reminds me.

"I also wanted you to fuck me."

"Hands on my chest."

I whimper even as I comply. But once I'm touching him, I don't mind it. I run my hands through the mass of dark hair there, scratching lightly at his skin.

"Good girl," he says, and I cut my eyes at him in annoyance.

He laughs and presses his middle finger against my opening.

I squirm. I'm not wet enough.

His hand retreats, and his fingers massage my clit instead.

My head falls back on another groan. I close my eyes and let myself enjoy how good it feels to have him touch me everywhere.

His other hand cups my breast and rolls my nipple between his fingers, sometimes pinching, sometimes caressing before moving to the other and doing it all over again. Good isn't a strong enough way to describe how he's making me feel.

"Do you know what I wanted to do to you the first time I saw you by the pool?"

"God, I hope it's fuck me."

He laughs and kisses me quickly, a gentle brush of the lips. "Obviously. But I also wanted to worship you. The first thing I thought when I saw you was that I would crawl behind you on my knees." His finger moves back to my opening, and this time he slips inside easily. "I still feel like that," he says, pulling his finger out to the tip and pressing inside again.

I open my eyes and groan again at the heat in his eyes.

"Do you want another finger?" he asks.

I nod.

"Beg me for it."

I don't even think. "Please, Giulio. Please fuck me with two fingers. All your fingers. Please. Oh, God."

He slips another finger inside at the same time as he pinches my nipple harder than before.

I hold my breath until he releases that nipple and moves to the other. I'm shaking. Already. "Do you know what I thought the first time I saw you?" I ask in panting breaths.

He laughs. "Do I want to know?"

I nod.

"Tell me." He wedges another finger inside me.

"I thought you were a cocky asshole."

"You weren't wrong."

"I thought you were a cocky asshole who could fuck me until I couldn't remember my own name."

His hand is moving faster between my legs now. He shakes his head. "That's impossible."

I scoff. "I was damn close on the train," I admit.

He shakes his head again. "No, tesora. It would be impossible for you to forget your name because it's the only thing I can remember when I'm inside you. Now, wrap your arms around my neck."

The spin from that unexpected admission to another command is so beautifully disorienting. It's exactly what I need, even if I never would have thought to ask for it. I don't know if I can handle the force of him, even though I've asked him to give it to me; to give himself to me.

I wrap my arms around his neck and hold tight.

He pumps his fingers into me a few more times before grabbing me at the waist with both hands.

I gasp and whine at the same time. That's a new sound I've never made before and might never make again. He lifts me into his arms. I wrap my legs around his waist without hesitation. I feel his dick against my ass and shudder.

This seems to remind him that he's bare. "Fuck, I'll go get a condom."

"Fuck me raw," I tell him hurriedly. "Please."

I think it's the word 'raw' that sends him over the edge. He doesn't tell me that it's not my turn to give him orders, or that he'll fuck me on his schedule and just how he wants. Instead, he presses my body back against the wall, and he pushes his dick into me painfully slow.

I feel every ridged inch of him stretching me and filling me. "Fuck."

"Tesora," he breathes against my cheek.

"Please," I beg, now that I know he likes it. He wants it.

I'm stuck between the wall and his body pounding into me, and I love it. I love knowing that I can't squirm; that every inch of pleasure I get, he'll have to give me. I love the solid presence of him. But most of all, I love that he's watching me as closely as I'm watching him. He's studying me, I realize now, watching to see what makes me moan and cry out. What makes me shudder in his arms. What makes me dig my nails into his back.

And eventually, what makes me come.

"Tsk, tsk, tsk." He tuts against my chin. "You were supposed to ask me before you came," he says.

I groan, still shivering from the force of that orgasm. "How do you say, 'I'm sorry,' in Italian?" I ask in a drowsy voice.

"Get on your knees," he says with a laugh.

I squeeze my thighs around him and my pussy around his dick. We both groan. "That sounds like English."

He nips at my chin and then sets me down on my feet.

I sink gratefully — but not gracefully — to the tile floor. I know what he wants, and thankfully, it's what I want too.

I reach for him, and he tsks again. "Aren't you forgetting something?"

My hands and mouth are hovering around his dick. I look up at him with an open mouth; open, and ready to receive him. "Please," I whisper, my breath caressing the tip of his dick.

He curses under his breath. "Say it in Italian," he tells me.

"Per favore."

He licks his lips and nods. "Maybe your accent will sound better with my dick in your mouth."

Only one way to find out, I think, but can't say because I've already wrapped a hand around the base of his dick and engulfed the head with my lips.

"Ah, fuck your mouth," he groans.

"You can do that," I lean back and tell him before I suck him between my lips again.

He bends over me and digs his hands into my hair, holding me still for a second as he does exactly what I offered. His hips press back and forth, and his dick moves into my mouth in swift thrusts for a few seconds before he releases me. It's almost as if he just needed to take the edge off before he fell apart. Just the thought of that makes me shudder in another mini-orgasm.

I might be on my knees for him, but I can feel him losing control to me. This is a very cliché thought — though to be fair, my life for the past few days has been very straight-to-DVD-movie levels of cliché — but knowing that I can make him weak with desire makes me feel stronger than I have in...forever. It won't last, but right now, it feels damn good.

When he lets me go, I move my head back, gasping for

air before suckling at the tip of his dick. I love the taste of him on my tongue.

He slaps his hands against the wall and looks down at me and growls. "Keep going."

I make eye contact with him as I suck him as deep inside my mouth as I can get him, stroking the rest of his length with both hands. My hands touch my lips as I work him into my mouth over and over again. I watch until I have to close my eyes so I can enjoy the feeling of him inside my mouth and palms as his come leaks into my willing and waiting mouth.

I feel his hands in my wet hair again, but this time, he's massaging my scalp and my strands with careful touches. When I feel the slip of his fingers through my curls and smell the herbal scent of my conditioner, my eyes fly open. I keep sucking him as I look up his body in confusion.

He looks down at me and groans as I suck his dick and he co-washes my hair.

I didn't know I could come with no one touching my pussy, but I can. I really fucking can.

I really need to keep better track of all the things I'm learning about myself with Giulio; all the things I never even thought were possible with Ryan.

Not that this is a time to think about Ryan, but Ryan has never washed the sheets on our bed, let alone my hair. Maybe if he had, I would have given him more blowjobs. Actually, I think as I move my fingers across Giulio's balls and between his legs, I would have given him the best blowjobs of his life if he'd ever carefully detangled my hair the way Giulio has just done, and with the tip of his dick brushing against my throat, no less.

Amazing.

As soon as he finishes carefully maneuvering his fingers through my curls, I push two fingers between his ass cheeks.

"Fuck. Fuck. Fuck," he hisses just as I press a finger against his sphincter and swallow his dick whole.

He lets go of my hair to press his slick hands against the wall. I think he's close.

I pull back, gasping. I have to use my hands on him to finish. One hand strokes his dick in a tight hold while the other presses against his asshole. His grunts and groans and wheezing breaths are music to my ears.

He cries out in Italian. "I'm coming," he translates. He sure the fuck is.

I watch with rapt attention as his come erupts from his dick in thick, creamy spurts. It covers my hand and drips onto the shower floor, washing quickly away. I stroke him until he's completely empty and shivering at my touch.

"Fermare. Fermare. È troppo," he says, pushing my hands away.

He helps me stand, and I step under the shower spray to rinse the conditioner from my hair. I let him wash my body again, but he doesn't let me do the same.

"We'll run out of water before you get above my waist," he says. He has a point.

When we step out of the shower, I let him wrap me in a thick, fluffy towel.

"I need to comb my hair," I tell him.

"I can do that," he offers.

"Don't get cocky," I tell him with a laugh. "It won't take long."

He pinches my ass. "Bene. Sbrigati. I'll clean the kitchen while I wait," he says.

He wraps a towel around his waist and walks from the bathroom.

"Um," I call after him. "Aren't you forgetting something?"

He turns to me with a raised eyebrow and a smile on his face. He walks back into the room, but instead of wrapping me in his arms, he reaches around me to snatch his gun and holster from the bathroom counter. He moves to leave again, and I pull him back.

He's smiling when he turns to me again.

He wraps his arm around my waist and lifts me up his body. I wrap my legs around him. We both shiver when my bare pussy presses against his stomach. I crush my mouth against his, and this kiss is the best one yet. His tongue sweeps into my mouth; his teeth snag my lip. He bites down gently, and his lips massage mine.

It's a great kiss. It was a great shower. Against all odds, this has been a really wonderful day that I deserved more than I knew.

I FEEL like a teenage boy with his first erection.

As soon as I leave the bathroom, I rush across the hall and throw on a pair of briefs. I put my holster and gun on out of force of habit before heading to the dining room to clean up after our meal.

If it were up to me, I would have left it all there until the morning, in favor of burying my face between Zahra's legs or falling asleep with her body in my arms and my dick buried inside her. But I want to give Zahra — and myself — some space.

And thank God, I do. If I'd been in the bathroom combing through Zahra's hair or crawling between her legs, I wouldn't have seen the flash of headlights extinguishing just before a car turns onto the packed dirt lane leading onto my property.

I freeze with my hand hovering over the empty wine bottle, and I watch the vehicle I can only see now because I know that there should be something in its place. The car inches slowly toward the house. It can't be going anywhere else, and there's only one reason a vehicle would turn its headlights off so late at night.

I hesitate, wasting a few precious seconds. If I'd been alone, I'd already have moved into action; it's second nature by this point. But I'm not alone. I can hear Zahra humming to herself in the bathroom. I never thought of a contingency plan for her because I hadn't *really* thought anyone would show up here of all places, but they have, and I can't do anything until I figure out what to do with Zahra. My priorities are perverted again, but I don't care.

Thankfully, figuring a way out of dangerous situations is my specialty.

Once my brain kickstarts, I let instinct take over, and a plan — however imperfect and hasty — comes together. I rush from the dining room into the bedroom. I dig my burner phone from the bottom of my bag. There are clothes spilling out onto the ground. It takes me ten seconds to dig a new SIM card out of the carrier I have full of them, insert it, and turn the phone on.

It feels like ten seconds too long.

I shoot a quick text to Salvo's cell phone and dial Alfonso's number. He doesn't pick up. I speak rapidly into the phone in quick, unguarded language, because, again, I'm not alone. Zahra doesn't have time for codes.

"Se non ci sono, trovala e riportala a Milano," I tell him, rushing back to the bathroom.

She jumps when I push the door open, and it hits the wall next to the shower.

"Holy shit, you scared me," she breathes, clutching the knot of the towel against her chest.

"Good," I tell her.

"What?"

"Here." I shove my phone into her hand.

"What's this?"

"There are some people coming now. Right now," I say, struggling to speak slowly. I need her to understand me quickly. We don't have time to waste.

"What?"

"Take this phone and follow me." I don't give her a choice. I grab her hand and drag her back to the bedroom. I open the wardrobe and push all of the linens aside. "Get in."

"What's happening?"

"We don't have time for questions," I hiss at her. I can see the confusion and fear in her eyes. Good. She should feel both of those things, and if I want her to live, I can't coddle her or promise that everything will be okay. I don't know that it will, and I refuse to lie to her. "Get in the wardrobe. I'm going to hide you behind the pillows. *Do not* come out unless I come and get you, or until tomorrow morning."

Her eyes are wet with tears. "Giulio?"

"There's one number saved in the phone. If I'm not here when you come out, you call that number. It's to a restaurant in Naples called La Casa Colonica. You ask for a man named Salvatore and tell him that you're my wife and need help. Do you understand me?"

"Where will you be, if you're not here?"

The question breaks my heart. I didn't think my heart could still do that. "Don't make me lie to you. Just promise me that you'll call the number."

"But—"

"It's still my night. You have to do as I say."

Her face hardens. "That wasn't about this."

My shoulders sag. I swear I hear a door slam shut outside, but that's probably just my nerves. "I know, but we don't have time for questions or for me to figure out how to explain what's happening to you without lying. All that matters is that *it is* happening. Get into the wardrobe. Don't make a sound. Call the number if I'm gone. Please."

I think she decides to do as I ask because of that last word.

She nods stiffly and then crawls quickly into the wardrobe. I heave a sigh of relief. It's premature, but I feel as if the only task that really matters is complete. Still, the entire exchange takes two minutes too long.

It takes another minute to cover as much of Zahra as I can see with the bed linens, extra blankets, and towels. I close the door to the wardrobe. I pull the suitcase with all of my weapons from behind the seat where I slept last night. I open it and grab a gun for each hand — gun at my back notwithstanding — and extra rounds.

I shut the lights in the bedroom and bathroom off and move back into the kitchen to shut those lights off as well. I turn on the light under the stove exhaust fan at the same time as the front door creaks open. It's an old house, and I say a silent prayer of thanks that it makes more noise than it should, while also hoping that this doesn't bite me in the ass.

I crouch behind the kitchen island, waiting, listening. If I'd had more time, I would have met them at the door. That would have been more fun. It also might have kept them farther away from Zahra.

I hope I never have to tell Salvo about the decision I made to protect her over myself.

Since I couldn't meet my new friends at the door, I do the next best thing.

The door behind me leads out into the back garden. Most of this room is glass, and I plan to use that to my bene-fit. I stay low to the ground and walk to the door. I turn the lock on the patio door slowly; it's newer than the front door and turns without a sound. I pull the handle down slowly and hold it, and then I train my eyes on the panel of glass that should show me the hallway leading to the front of the house. Right now, all I see is the pitch-black night outside, but I wait. I'm used to waiting as long as it takes to get the job done. As usual, I don't know what I'm waiting for until it arrives. The light from the exhaust fan hits something metallic — probably the butt of a gun — and that's all I need.

Someone young and brash might take that moment to pop up from the floor and start shooting, hoping to use the element of surprise. I'm neither young nor brash and the element of surprise is overrated. I also hate getting shot. It fucking hurts. So instead of doing something that almost guarantees a bullet wound, I push the patio door open hard and loud. This time, it squeaks.

A barrage of gunshots burst into the silence. I jump back from the door as quickly as I can, but not quick enough. I can feel the heat as something large slices through my forearm, and then the warmth of blood flowing down my hand.

It hurts like hell, but it's not a gunshot wound, and I want to keep it that way.

In the reflection, I see two dark figures making their way into the kitchen, heading toward the door. Instead of popping up from the ground and firing, I wait until I see feet shuffle around the island. I'm aiming high and shoot the first person I see in the temple. The body crumples to the floor. Whoever was behind them darts back toward the hallway, which is the opposite direction of where I want them to go — closer to Zahra — so I draw their attention toward me as I sprint out into the yard.

I wish I were wearing clothes, shoes at least, something I can pretend would be a barrier between me and the shower of glass and bullets that follow my path into the night. But in my line of work, wishing for something you don't have is a waste of energy, and there's no time for that when you're running for your life. I have to work with what I *do* have, and right now, I have a gun in each hand, a backup in my holster, and a head start. I've had less.

I run around the perimeter of the house, ducking low to the ground. The grass is soft and wet on my feet, a lovely thing on a hot summer day, a terrible thing on a dark night, where every footfall matters. My feet almost slip with every step.

I duck under what would be the bathroom window trying to devise my next move. I don't have any keys on me, but I can hotwire the car in a few minutes, and potentially lure whoever is inside away. But they could leave someone behind, and that person could find Zahra. I could rush back into the house, but the idea of that spray of bullets aimed inside instead of outside makes me queasy. I feel sick at the lack of possibilities. How had I convinced myself that coming here was a good idea?

This is the problem with intimate connections, and why I don't have any. They're a liability. I don't leave.

Instead, I dart away from the house toward an old oak tree where I used to play by myself as a child. Like so many other things on this property, I have mostly bad memories. My father used to send me out here for branches to "discipline" me and my mother with, and sometimes I used to hide in it for a moment of safety.

I push the memories away. I can't afford to get distracted. I make it to the tree, and from this vantage point, I can see most of the back garden and the entirety of the front with an eye toward the road. I can also dash into the vineyard to the north of the property, which could provide some cover. Those are possibilities.

There are two cars out front besides my own. I must have missed the other in the darkness. Now that my ears aren't ringing with shattering glass, I can hear the sound of an idling car, maybe two. There's someone else out there. Of course.

I turn back to the house just in time to see dark figures making their way across the back garden. They're spreading out to cover the width of the yard, trying to find me like the worst game of nascondino I've ever played in my life. I wonder if that's military training I'm seeing or just deadly preparation. The good news is that as they spread out, it's easier to see exactly what's going on. There are three men in the garden, one dead in my kitchen, and maybe one by the cars in front of my house. Five men to kill me isn't a bad decision, but it's a bit of an insult. If Zahra weren't here, this might already be over.

Salvo always told me that the best way to get through any situation was to hold onto your most destructive emotion and expend that energy on getting the job one. It's advice I've always liked, so I usually follow it. Tonight is no different.

I crouch low against the tree trunk. I wait patiently until I can see the outline of the closest man clearly, but I still have to guess at where I think his head might be. I lower my gun minutely to make sure that I hit something vital at the very least. When I shoot, I have to duck around the tree as his compatriots begin to shoot indiscriminately in my direction, but even the blasts of their guns don't mask the sound of a body hitting the ground.

Two men in the back garden, one dead in the back

garden, one dead in the kitchen, and maybe one in front of the house.

I can hear them rushing toward me, shooting as they come. This is where it gets tricky. They slow down as they approach, and then one of them calls out.

"We could have made this easy," he yells, "but now I'm going to spend the night with you, my guns, and your kitchen knives."

As threats go, I've heard worse — I've definitely given worse — but it's not bad.

"And when we find the girl you been traveling with—"

I don't know what he planned to say after that, and I never will. I run around the tree, take aim, and shoot the dark figure closest to me. I don't even know if he's the man who was speaking, and I don't care. What I do know is that there's now one dead in the kitchen and two dead in the back garden, and I think whoever is left will think twice about mentioning Zahra to me again, even if they don't know her name.

A bullet grazes my arm. I'm lucky, but that was far too close for comfort.

The other man is close enough now for a clean shot between the eyes, but that goes both ways. Alright, I know I said the element of surprise was overrated, but it's all I have to take the second man down.

I take aim at the only man left and begin to shoot as I rush toward him. When I'm out of bullets, I drop that gun and switch the gun in my right hand to my left, barely missing a beat. I grab the gun from my back holster with my right hand. Sometimes Alfonso accuses me of having too many guns, but better too many than too few because I'm not really a hand-to-hand combat kind of guy. I love guns. Knives are okay if the situation calls for it. Sometimes explosives are nice, but I hate loud sounds. Hands are messy, but sometimes they're the only option, like right now.

I ram my shoulder into the midsection of the man in front of me. He uses the butt of his gun to hit me right in the kidney. Now, that's excruciating — maybe even more than a gunshot wound — but I can't dwell on the pain. I compartmentalize it. I tackle the man to the ground, and I fall on top of him, losing the gun in my right hand. Unfortunately, he holds onto his gun and uses it to smash me in the left eye. It's harder to compartmentalize that pain because I see stars, and they seem brighter against the dark backdrop of the night.

I start punching him in the face with my right hand and try and aim the gun in my left at his head. But I can't leave my left side open long enough when he still has a gun in his right, so I make a calculated decision to toss my gun to the side so I can hold his right wrist to the ground.

This is everything I hate about hand-to-hand combat. One bullet in the head and this could have been over so, many minutes and bruises ago. But with only one hand — and my non-dominant one at that — the outcome of this fight is well out of my control, and I hate when situations aren't in my control.

A gunshot rings out.

We both freeze for a second, waiting to feel the sting of a bullet entering our bodies, but only I make the mistake of looking toward the front of the house.

I shouldn't be thinking about anything besides putting a bullet between his eyes, but in reality, I'm only terrified that Zahra didn't listen to me.

What if the gunshots scared her?

What if she snuck out of the cupboard?

What if she heard all the commotion in the backyard and ran to the front door?

What if there were two men out front instead of one? Or three? Or four?

What if that gunshot was for her? What if I've been trying to punch this guy and stop myself from being shot, while Zahra is bleeding out on the front porch?

Once again, I take Salvo's advice, because it's still good. I take my strongest and ugliest emotion, and I let it fuel me, even as I refuse to name it. I stop worrying about getting shot. I slam this asshole's right hand to the ground, and his grip loosens on his gun. I smash my fist into his left temple. I feel bone smash against bone. I smash his right hand against the ground again and again and again. He tries to grab my face to dig his fingers into my eyes, and I cry out.

"You fucking pussy," I scream. I let the rage and pain I'm feeling fuel me. I stop punching him and circle my hand around his throat. He's scratching at my face, but I don't let up on his windpipe.

It takes a few seconds for him to register the lack of oxygen, but when he does, he starts scratching at my face for real and finally drops the gun. I let go of his wrist and his neck. He sucks in deep pulls of air, trying to refill his lungs. I grab him by both sides of his head and twist. He goes limp under my body.

I don't take a moment to catch my breath.

All I can see in my mind is Zahra's lifeless body at my front door. I snatch one of the guns from the ground — I don't even know if it's my gun — and race barefoot on the wet grass toward the front of the house.

I don't move tactically. I don't try and look for cover. I just run until I'm skidding to a stop around the front of the house, where I find Alfonso leaning against one of the cars, with a .357 in one hand pointed at the ground and his cell phone pressed to his ear.

"You sound tall. Are you tall?" he asks the person on the phone. He sees me and frowns. "Why are you in your pants? And what happened to your face?"

"Ai, sfigato. Why are you just standing here? Why didn't you come help me?"

"Help you with what?"

"Some asshole just tried to claw my eyes out, and you're here on the phone with some woman?" I look around as I spit these words at him, looking for any signs of Zahra. "I heard a gunshot."

Alfonso nods his head toward the driver's side of the other car. I see a body on the ground, the face beaten to mush. "He shot at my rental car. I made a deposit. Stronzo."

"What are you doing here?" I ask, checking each car for more people with guns and any sign of Zahra's dead body.

"Salvo told me to come check up on you. He thought something was wrong."

"Nothing's wrong."

"You haven't seen your face."

"I handled it."

"Yeah, but why come here?" he asks.

My fingers twitch around the gun in my hand.

We both turn when the front door wrenches open. Alfonso raises his gun on instinct, and she freezes.

"Put your gun down, deficiente," I yell at him. "I told you to wait until I came to get you."

"I heard you on the phone. And don't yell at me, you fucking prick," she yells at me and then rushes into my arms. She wraps her arms and legs around me, just like she did in the shower.

I know what the phrase "the hammer drops" means in

that moment because having her in my arms after everything that just happens feels right. And I know it shouldn't.

"I thought she'd be taller," I hear Alfonso say.

"Sta' zitto," I breathe into Zahra's neck, squeezing her tighter than ever.

I DON'T KNOW how I fall asleep after everything that happened, but I do.

Okay, that's a lie, and I really need to stop lying to myself after all this, if nothing else.

Giulio carries me into the house and tells me not to look into the kitchen. I've already seen the body, but I do as he says because I don't want to see it again. He lays me on the bed and tells me that everything will be okay. It's not a lie, technically, so I don't push him on it. Besides, the only thing I care about is the request I make.

"Sleep in the bed with me tonight," I tell him.

"I have to clean up," he says. It's not a bad euphemism for what I can only guess he's about to do.

I know," I say, "but after."

He nods and brushes a curl from my face. I crawl under the covers. He sits with me for a few minutes. I'm not sure if he stays to calm me down or to calm himself, but I appreciate it, nonetheless. I wake up in the middle of the night because I'm thirsty. I think about going into the kitchen, but I remember that body on the floor and the pool of blood. I decide to wait until the morning. Besides, Giulio is in bed beside me, his arm thrown over my waist holding on tight enough that I know it won't be easy to move anyway.

I drift contentedly back to sleep.

When I wake up the next morning, the room is painfully bright. I'm groggy and a little sore from all of the action yesterday — and not just the hit squad that apparently showed up to kill Giulio — but I feel rested. How fucked up is that?

I'm in bed alone, and that sucks. I turn onto my back and look up at the ceiling.

My mother believes that the best kind of clarity comes first thing in the morning. Well, this morning, I'm wondering what the hell my life has become, and not just because, you know, the aforementioned hit squad, but like everything. The Not Quite Wedding Day, the sister I need to make amends to, and the memory of my time in the cupboard, when the only coherent thought I had was, *What if something happens to Giulio?*

It didn't make sense last night, and it sure doesn't make sense today. Unfortunately, staring at the ceiling doesn't give me any answers.

I hear muffled voices coming from the kitchen.

When I finally get out of bed, I realize that I'm still naked, wrapped in a towel. I move across the room to my bag. I sit on the floor and rummage inside for a t-shirt that I throw over my head. Thankfully, I remember that Giulio's big, kind of terrifying friend showed up last night at the last minute and pull a pair of shorts on as well. I'm not sure if he's still around.

Giulio seems like the kind of man who'd have a friend show up, beat a man to death apparently, and then disappear before breakfast. But just in case, it's better to be clothed than sorry.

When I walk into the kitchen, my eyes move immediately to the spot on the floor where I'd seen the man last night. There's no one there and no trace of blood. In fact, besides the jagged shards of broken glass around the door and windows, everything looks just as it had the night before, when we'd eaten Giulio's mother's pesto and drank the best wine I've ever had in my life.

Giulio and his scary friend are sitting at the table, sipping what look like espressos. They look normal, even kind of sexy, which probably says more about me than them. This whole fucking morning is surreal.

I'm so caught up staring at them and wondering what's happened to me in less than a week that I don't immediately realize that they've turned to me.

The scary one sees me first. "Buongiorno, bella," he calls.

My smile is tight. I nod and mumble, "Buongiorno" in return.

He grimaces. "Let's stick to English."

I frown.

Giulio laughs. "She's still learning," he says. I wonder if he's thinking about all the Italian words he whispered against my lips. Or maybe remembering all of the times he's been so overcome with parts of him inside of parts of me that he forgets his English. If he's not, I am.

"Good morning, tesora," he says to me.

"Tesora?" the scary ones teases and then mumbles some more words in Italian.

I don't know what he says, but I see the way Giulio's

jaw clenches for a second. "Do you want breakfast? Coffee?" he asks me.

"Coffee. Please."

He stands from the table, espresso cup in hand, and walks toward me. He makes his way to the coffee machine, and I follow. I stand next to him at the counter, wanting to touch him, but not wanting his friend to notice.

"Do you want an espresso?" he asks.

I nod and place my hands flat on the counter so that I have something to hold onto. I watch as he grinds fresh beans and puts them into an expensive machine I don't even want to touch. I watch his hands move with rapt attention as he makes me a small cup of coffee so dark it looks black. He places the cup in front of me when it's ready. I reach for it. Our fingers brush innocently.

That small bit of contact sends a shiver up my spine.

He picks up his own cup and watches as I carefully bring my own cup to my lips. I take a small experimental sip and wince.

"Jesus Christ, that's strong," I cough.

"Americans," the scary one mumbles under his breath.

"Sta' zitto," Giulio hisses.

"What does that mean again?" I ask.

"Shut up."

We make eye contact for the first time since I walked into the kitchen. I don't have to wonder. I know we're both thinking about all of those words passing between the small sliver of space left by our mouths almost touching now.

"I'll leave you two alone," the scary one says.

I turn, embarrassed, and watch as he takes his espresso outside. The glass door has been blown out, and yet he opens it as if it's fully intact and then begins to walk leisurely around the backyard.

"Well, he's terrifying," I say. It's a joke. I mean, his friend is terrifying, but I'm not actually worried that he'll hurt me, especially with Giulio around.

"We have to leave," he says, changing the subject.

"I figured. Where are we going this time?"

Giulio takes another sip of his espresso. He doesn't look at me when he starts speaking, which makes my stomach drop. "I'm taking you to the train station. I'll get you a ticket back to Milan, and I've already bought you a plane ticket back to America."

"You don't even know where I'm from," I say. It's true, but it feels ridiculous.

"You don't have the most common name, and apparently, your fiancé is famous."

"*Ex*-fiancé," I say through clenched teeth.

"I Googled your name and the words 'wedding' and 'cheating'. There was only one result."

My stomach feels like a boulder in my gut.

"Actually, there are many results, but the same event."

I don't know why it matters that Giulio knows what happened to me, I've already told him. But it's one thing for him to hear whatever I was willing to share from me, and a completely different thing for him to read about my life as tabloid fodder. I've always hated that.

"You shouldn't have done that." I feel betrayed, and I'm not even sure that I have the right to.

"I know."

"Why did you?"

"Because you have a life—"

I scoff.

He starts again, placing serious emphasis on those first five words. "Because you have a life that doesn't have anything to do with mine. It's normal and safe, and even though that stronzo betrayed you, whatever life you have in the States is better than getting shot because you're too close to me."

"I disagree," I say. "I mean, I don't actually know you—"

"Exactly."

"But—"

He shakes his head and turns away from me. I watch his back as he moves to the kitchen sink to dump the rest of his espresso. He washes his cup in silence. When he turns to me, he still won't look me in the eye. "This isn't a discussion, Zahra. I shouldn't have brought you here. You're much safer as far away from me as possible. Even you have to admit that after...after last night."

What a shit day to commit myself to telling the truth.

"Okay, I'll give you the safer part, but the thing you need to know about my life in New York is that I was so unhappy." I've never admitted that to anyone before, not even myself. I'd loved Ryan — even though I apparently didn't know him at all — but I'm not the kind of woman who ever wanted to date an actor. I'm not the kind of woman who should have dated an actor.

I like to be behind the scenes. I don't necessarily need a man who works a regular nine-to-five and comes home every night for dinner, but I do need a man who thinks my opinion is more important than a fan site run by a sixteen-year-old girl in Brazil. I need a man who challenges me. I need a man who looks at me as if I'm the only person in the world, not just the room. I think all of these things, but I don't tell them to Giulio. I can't, because he won't look me in the eye.

And I guess on the long list of things I need in whatever relationship I end up in next — besides the obvious fidelity — what I need most is a man who'll look me in the eye when he has something bad to tell me. I need a man who won't push me away.

"Okay," I tell him.

He looks me in the eye then.

I imagine that it's hurt I'm seeing when we make eye contact, but to be fair, it could just as easily be frustration or exhaustion or, hell, constipation. I don't know this man from Adam, and I've already wasted enough time on someone I think I know but don't. I can't make the same mistake twice.

———

GIULIO

I wanted her to agree to this. I wanted her to agree to this. I wanted her to agree to this.

But I didn't know that it would hurt.

She turns and rushes out of the kitchen. She slams the bathroom door. I want to follow her. I want to finish what we started in the shower yesterday, but I don't. I walk into the garden to find Alfonso instead.

"So, do you have a girlfriend now?" he asks me. "I don't think you ever had a girlfriend."

"Shut up."

"Oh, you don't have a girlfriend. I'm sorry," he says, sounding anything but. "You have to admit that she's out of your league."

"Shut up," I tell him again.

"We both know that's not going to happen. What's the agenda?"

"I'm taking her to the train station."

He laughs. "I meant about all the bodies," he clarifies.

I feel the heat of the late morning sun on the back of my

neck mix with embarrassment. "I'm going to take her to the train station," I say as if that had been the plan all along. "You take the car with the bodies to the vineyard on the other side of the yard. I know the owner. Tell him I need to use the plot at the back of his field. He'll give you shovels and leave you alone. After I drop her off, I'll come find you, we'll get rid of the vans and head home."

"Nice recovery," he says, laughter lacing each word.

"Ti odio."

His laughter follows me into the house.

While Zahra is getting ready, I call a local tradesman I know to be discreet. I arrange for him to fix the broken glass in my kitchen, and then I check the train times. If Zahra is ready in the next twenty minutes, she can be on a train within the hour, and back in Milan by late afternoon. If she takes longer, there's another direct high-speed train in three hours. She should be ready in twenty minutes, but I want the three hours.

"I'm ready," she says just as I let thoughts of what I could do with that time blossom in my mind.

When I turn to her, she's standing just inside the kitchen with her bag clutched in both of her hands. She's looking at her shoes instead of at me.

"Do you have everything? Are you sure?" I want her to say no.

"Yes."

I swallow the first thing I want to say. "Va bene. Andiamo," I say instead.

I want her to ask me to slow down, to say the words again so she can hear them. I need her to ask me to whisper them against her lips. She doesn't. Instead, I watch as she turns and walks stiffly toward the front door. "Let me get your bag," I call after her.

She ignores me.

The drive to the train station isn't long, but it feels as if it takes forever because Zahra sits next to me in silence. And I let her.

At the train station, Zahra stands next to me without speaking as I buy her ticket. I waste money on a business-class seat because I want her to be comfortable. And even though I know I should give her the ticket and leave, I don't.

She reaches for the slips of paper, but I snatch my hands away.

"Come." I lead her out onto the train platform. The train is due to arrive in five minutes, and I want to wait with her. When she boards the train to Milan, I know I'll never see her again. And even though the part of me with a conscience knows that's the way it should be, the part of me that wants her can't fathom that this is how it all ends.

"You don't have to wait," she grinds out.

"I know."

"Then why are you?"

"You know why."

She turns quickly toward me. Her eyes are narrowed in severe slits, and her beautiful skin is flushed red in anger. I realize that I've never seen her angry before, and now I wish I hadn't, because I love it. Even though it doesn't make any sense and I barely know her, I realize that I love her.

"No, I don't know why. Tell me."

I could maneuver my way around this request; correction, command. I could find a way to tell her something rude and terrible. I could say something to break her heart, so she boards this train and never thinks about me again. I could tell her something vague and frustrating that lets the embers of whatever was building between us smolder, something that will make her think of me when she's on a date with another man and realize that he's not enough. Maybe if I do that, there's a chance she'll come back to Italy one day, and find me, and we can start over. But if that were to ever happen, it would all be for nothing. She could stay away for a few months or years, and when she returned, I'd still be exactly who I am. Or dead.

So, I decide to tell her the truth. "If I asked you to stay with me, would you?"

"Yes."

I didn't know that I could feel elated and devastated at the same time.

"That's the problem. This isn't some romantic movie; this is real life. And in real life, a woman like you should go back to New York, move out of the house you share with that stronzo, and start over. In real life, a woman like you, elegant and beautiful and smart and brave, should find a man who deserves you. You should marry a man who wears a suit to work, have a few kids with your birthmark, and grow old but still beautiful in a house that doesn't have to be guarded by armed men. You should die peacefully in bed, surrounded by children and grandchildren. In real life, you should never think about me again."

As I speak, the train rumbles into the station. The wind whips her beautiful curly dark brown hair around her head. Her cheeks are red and full of life, and so is her mouth. But her eyes start to water.

And my heart constricts painfully.

She wants me to take back everything I said. I can see that in her pleading eyes. And, truthfully, I want to do just that. I want to promise her that I can be the kind of man who wears a suit to work. I want to tell her that I can give her as many children as she wants and a safe, normal life. But if there's one thing my parents' relationship taught me, it's that wanting something doesn't make it so. My mother died devoting her life to God and me, always hoping that one day my father would change his life and come searching for her. He never did.

Zahra deserves more than what my father could give my mother. She deserves so much more than me.

We stand, staring at one another. I wish we had more time, but I can't tell her that.

"That's it?" she asks me. "Those are the last words you're going to say to me?"

"Yes."

I can see all the damage that word does to her; all the hurt and frustration she feels is written on her face. I can see it, but I can't fix it. She shakes her head and turns toward the train. I can't fix it, but I can give her a proper goodbye.

I grab her by the elbow and pull her toward me. I wrap my arm around her waist and dig my fingers into her soft, curly hair. She tips her head back and offers her mouth to me without hesitation, even now. I dip my head and kiss her the way I wanted to kiss her the first day I saw her by the pool and every day since. I part her lips with mine and slip my tongue into her mouth. Her tongue meets mine immediately. Our mouths move together perfectly, pressing and slicking and biting. She moans into my mouth, and I moan in return.

We don't have time for this kiss to last as long as I would like it, because as long as I would like is forever. So I press my lips against hers and let our tongues tangle, hoping that she understands all the things I can't say.

We kiss until the conductor yells that her train is set to depart.

I don't linger when we pull away from one another. I

can't. If I do, I might never let her leave. I rush her to the closest car and usher her inside.

And instead of going to her seat, she stands at the door until it slides closed, looking at me with wet, sad eyes. I stay with her until the train begins to move away.

I'm not a man who has regrets, plural, just the one.

ALFONSO and I are a well-oiled machine.

We've buried the bodies, disposed of the vehicles, and caught a flight back to Naples by nightfall. I shouldn't, but I track the passage of time by the distance between Zahra and me. By the time we land in Naples, I've Googled the exact number of miles between San Marco and Naples and New York. Now I know. I wish I didn't.

I want to go back to my apartment, shower, and then crawl into bed for the next five days, maybe two weeks, but my schedule isn't my own. We go straight from the airport to Salvo's restaurant. Usually, we use the back door, but since technically we haven't done anything wrong — we've just been on holiday — we walk through the front door like regular people. Besides, the police know that Alfonso and I are Salvo's associates. What they think our association means, I don't know. All I know is that they can't prove it in court.

"Benvenuto a casa," Salvo says warmly as we walk into the restaurant.

He turns to the waitress — she's new, I can't remember

her name — and sends her off into the kitchen. I'm not hungry, but sometimes Salvo is like my nona, obsessed with feeding everyone in the room. He ushers us to a small booth at the back of the restaurant. Salvo has the restaurant swept for bugs daily, sometimes multiple times a day, and every time we meet in the main dining room, he moves us around. We never sit in the same place to talk business two times in a row. And we never talk business outright.

"How were your holidays?" he asks casually.

"Hot. Boring," Alfonso says. "Loud."

Salvo shrugs. "I've always hated the sea." He turns to me. "And yours?"

Alfonso snickers, and Salvo's eyes shift from me to Alfonso and back. His eyebrows lift with interest.

"Tiring. I'm exhausted."

Alfonso bursts into laughter.

Salvo leans back in his chair and crosses his legs. "There's a story here."

"Si. Una storia d'amore," Alfonso says, giggling like a child.

I roll my eyes.

"I love love stories," Salvo says. I want to roll my eyes again, but he says those words so earnestly that I believe him.

"I don't want to talk about it." I've never said anything like that to Salvo before. He's my boss, and technically, I can't keep secrets from him. I've never needed to keep a secret from him before now, but I don't want to share even the memory of Zahra.

"Did it get in the way?" he asks me.

It takes me a few seconds to crawl out of the sadness and grief I'm trying to ignore before I can realize what he's asking. "No."

The thing I think but refuse to admit to myself is that I think it would be impossible for Zahra to get in the way. I think it's possible that she and I could have made something work. If I were a romantic, or at least just slightly less damaged, I imagine that I might have been able to turn this realization into a last-minute flight to Milan and make promises to her that I shouldn't. But I'm not, and thankfully, Salvo doesn't push me.

"What did we find out about my wife's family?" he asks.

I'm happy to be on more solid ground. I take the lead in telling him what we've learned. "I ran into some Neccis while I was away. It was surprising because I was certain that that branch of Flavia's family didn't go any farther north than Rome."

"They haven't as long as I've known them," Salvo says. "They must have been motivated to find a new place to holiday."

"Maybe," I shrug.

"You have some thoughts?" he asks, making eye contact.

He looks as tired as I feel, but looks are deceiving. Salvo might look like a warm older restauranteur, but he's really the man half the city would shrink into the shadows to avoid.

"I was in the middle of nowhere," I say, choosing each word carefully as I try to piece together bits and pieces of information that I'd collected but hadn't spent much time considering because I was so preoccupied with Zahra. "I chose the hotel because I didn't want to run into anyone I knew. So running into a Necci was a bit surprising."

Salvo nods slowly, encouraging me to continue.

"It probably doesn't mean anything," I say casually, even though I know no one at this table believes that, "but I just wonder if maybe we had the same travel agent."

Salvo keeps nodding for a few more seconds, and then he smiles. "Interesting," he says.

Alfonso and I wait in tense silence as he starts nodding again. We both know this look on Salvo's face. He's digesting the information, slowly, carefully. On his own time, he straightens his back and smiles at both of us. "Well, welcome home. Go. Rest. I'll see you tomorrow."

Alfonso and I nod and stand from the table. Salvo doesn't move. We walk to the front door of the restaurant, and I steal a look over my shoulder. Salvo's still sitting in his chair, his hands resting on his knee, and his head bowed in thought.

If I were a better man, I might feel bad for what's coming and who Salvo will set me on, but as I've spent the last few days reminding Zahra, I'm not a good man. My fingers twitch around the strap of my bag in anticipation.

If I can't have Zahra, then I need to channel all that grief into something productive. Salvo will give me a target. I don't feel bad for them at all.

I'M REALLY FUCKING sick of crying very publicly on a mode of transportation over men who've broken my heart. Zoe would never do this. I haven't spoken to her in over a week, and all I want to do is call her. I want her to give me all of the I told you so's ever and then listen to me cry and whine and complain. And then I want her to tell me what to do. Also, I really just miss my big sister.

By the time I make it back to San Marco, I'm so tired, and I've cried so much that my eyes are nearly swollen shut. Walking back into my hotel room is surreal, even though I've only been gone two days. For a second, I feel sharp jolts of anxiety crackling under my skin, and I consider calling down to room service for another bottle of wine. I don't, only because something about that makes me think of Giulio, and I can't do that anymore. I don't even shower, which is very unlike me. I strip off all of my clothes and crawl into bed and fall asleep crying. Unfortunately, I now know that there's no one on the other side of my bedroom wall to hear me and be angry.

When I wake up the next morning, I feel hungover. I can't believe that I slept in a clean bed with a dirty body; my mother would be scandalized.

I crawl out of bed, step into the shower, and immediately push my entire head under the spray. My hands feel nothing like Giulio's, and I'm somehow resentful of that, but since my detangling session was so strangely interrupted, this wash is necessary. I shampoo, condition, and detangle my hair, and then wash my body just as thoroughly. When I step out of the shower, I won't lie and say that I feel better per se, but I don't feel as lost, and that feels like the best I can ask for right now.

Unfortunately, I can still hear Giulio's voice in my head telling me that I deserve better. I deserve better than Ryan, certainly. But Giulio and I... I don't let myself finish that thought. I decide that he knows himself better than me. Maybe he's right. Maybe I do deserve better than him as well.

According to my original trip itinerary, I should be leaving Milan tomorrow. The plane ticket Giulio bought is scheduled to leave this afternoon. On the train ride back, I considered not getting on that flight just to waste his money. It sounded petty and oddly gratifying, but in the cold light of day and considering everything that I saw while I was with him, I decide to put my pettiness aside. I can nurse the bitterness I feel at his rejection on a transatlantic flight. I've done it before, why not one more time for the hell of it?

It takes me less than half an hour to pack. I never really unpacked, to be honest. I'm ready to go in no time. I sit on the bed and reach for the hotel phone, but then remember that my cell phone is in the bedside table. I pull the drawer open and collect it. On a whim, I power it on for the first time since I arrived. While I wait for it to connect to some cellular service, I pick up the receiver for the hotel phone and call down to the front desk.

"Buongiorno," a female voice I recognize says on the other end of the line.

"Hello, this is Zahra…" My voice trails off as I consider whether or not I can bear to say my would-be married name, even just for simplicity's sake. I can't. "This is Zahra Port in the honeymoon suite. I'd like a car to the airport."

There's a moment of silence, and some wrestling on the other end of the line. When the desk clerk speaks, her voice is a small whisper, but louder, as if her mouth is very close to the receiver. "Miss Port, I was just about to call you. There's someone on the way up to see you."

"Who?" I know who I want it to be. But it's not. I know it's not.

"Your husband."

"I'm not married," I clarify, just as the door to my hotel room opens. "The fuck?"

"I know. But that's how he described himself," she says. "It's Ryan Fuller. He's on his way up, and he told us not to tell you."

I shake my head in utter disbelief. It literally cannot be, I think to myself. I hang up the phone without saying goodbye and walk through the bedroom into the sitting area. And there he is.

I can't believe it's been almost a week since I've seen Ryan, and I really can't believe that I don't feel much of anything now that I have. Not even rage.

Ryan's standing just inside the hotel room with a

bouquet of flowers in his hands. He has that smile on his face, the one that he uses in the movies. He had an agent who'd told him once that his smile was his moneymaker. He spent three weeks perfecting that smile in the bathroom mirror before his first movie audition. Over the years, his movie role smile completely supplanted the lopsided grin he used to aim at me when we first started dating. I wonder if he even knows that I know that this smile is acting. Actually, maybe it's not even acting anymore.

"What are you doing here?" I ask him.

"Well, this was supposed to be our honeymoon," he says, much too nonchalantly for my taste.

"You didn't show up to our wedding. Why are you showing up to our honeymoon?"

He winces at my words, so I guess he's not a complete lost cause. "Zahra, what can I do to make it up to you? How can I make this right?"

I don't mean to laugh, but I cackle so loudly that my throat feels raw. I need to drink some water, eat some food, and get the fuck out of here.

Ryan's face falls, wiping that million-dollar grin away. Thank God for small miracles. "Zahra, I was an idiot."

"Yeah, I realized that. Tell me something I don't know."

"I never loved her."

"Is that supposed to make me feel better? You fucked my best friend behind my back, and you didn't even love her. Besides, you already told me that in front of her. I said, tell me something I *don't* know."

"I want to be with you," he says, as if it's a heartfelt admission, as if it's supposed to make my heart swoon, and my eyes fill with tears. I wonder what his fans would think if they knew how absolutely useless he is without a good script, lighting, and time to do as many takes as he needs.

"Why?" I ask him. I don't actually care, but I realize that I was in such a rush to run away on our wedding day that I didn't ask the questions that really needed answers.

"Why do I want to be with you?" He relaxes, as if he spent the entire flight across the Atlantic, thinking of the perfect answer to this question. Maybe he did.

I suck my teeth and shake my head. "No, I get why you would want to be with me. Hell, I could even understand why you would want to be with Trisha. I want to know why you wasted damn near a decade of my life and asked me to marry you and then fucked my best friend. I want to know why you weren't man enough to just break up with me or be faithful. I want to know why you thought flying here would make any difference in my life."

"Zahra—"

"I'm not done. I also want to know which one of your agents had to convince you to come here. I want to know which journalist you've chosen to conduct our reconciliation interview. I want to know which movie role has you running all the way to Italy, thinking you can win me back to try and minimize the bad PR. Oh, or is it the contract for our wedding special? Is there a film crew in the lobby? I want to know why you think I'm so stupid that I don't see exactly what you're doing. And I guess I want to know how you've spent nearly a decade with one of the best public relations managers in New York, and you think I'm dumb enough not to see the work. Now I'm done. Answer."

Cathartic isn't a strong enough word to describe how I feel seeing Ryan red-faced and dumbfounded at what I've said. I feel as if a weight I had no idea how to unload has completely vanished in the span of a few minutes. I feel — necessary therapy notwithstanding — as if this moment is closure.

"You stole my credit card," he says.

Technically, that was Shae, but I would never snitch. "And what if I did?"

"I can press charges."

"You sure can. Are you going to?"

"Not if you give me another chance."

"Ugh." I wait for a second to see if he realizes how absolutely disgusting what he's just said is. That moment of realization never comes, and that's sad on a human level, but wonderful on a this-relationship-is-really-fucking-over level.

I realize that I'm still clutching my cell phone in my left hand, only when it vibrates. I look down and see so many message notifications that my phone can't even display the number. My phone vibrates with a new text message. From Zoe. I unlock my phone and pull up my text messages. I open the text chain between my sister and me and see days of missed messages.

Where are you?
Are you OK?
Do you want me to fuck Ryan up? 'Cause I will.
Call me.
Call us.
Dad's worried.
Okay, I'm really worried now. Are you alive? You need to check in. WTF Zahra. This isn't like you.

The messages go on like that for days. She even has the nerve to threaten me a bit. But the new message is so different in tone that it shocks me.

I saw on the celebrity rags that Ryan is in Italy. Are you

*okay? I know you always hated that I didn't like him, and I
still don't, but if you get back with him, I promise to try and
make it work. Please, just text me back.*

There are tears in my eyes. I'm about to cry again, but
not because of Ryan or even Giulio. Knowing that Zoe,
who's hated Ryan fiercely, would be willing to put all of that
aside just to be in my life makes the guilt bubble over from
terrible to unbearable. I can't believe that I was about to
marry someone who would come between us. And I can't
believe that that man has the fucking audacity to be
standing in front of me trying to blackmail me into getting
back together with him after cheating on me for so long.

I don't cry, but I do laugh again. Who knew the sham-
bles of my life were so fucking funny?

"Here's what we're going to do," I say. When I look up
at Ryan, he has a smug shit-eating grin on his face that I
recognize for its honesty, if nothing else. "You're not going
to file a police report about your stolen credit cards."

I see him relax again.

"But I'm not getting back together with you."

"That's not the deal I gave you."

"Yeah, you're not a great dealmaker, that's why you
have an agent and a team of lawyers. You should have come
here with one of them. Hell, you should have come here
with anyone, someone smarter than you. But you didn't, and
that was your big mistake. Remember that I always told you
that you should never negotiate on your own. I meant it.

So, here's my counteroffer. You're not going to go to the
police to report your stolen credit cards. You're going to
chalk up this honeymoon I went on without you, and all of
the expenses incurred, as a kind of one-time alimony

payment. It will cost you much less than marrying me only to have me divorce you and take half of everything. Maybe even more than half.

In return, I'm not going to sell my story about how Ryan Fuller, up-and-coming action movie heartthrob, fucked around on me with my best friend and a stripper who's more famous than him. I'm not going to get on *Good Morning America* and cry my eyes out perfectly and prettily on live television, so all of your fans realize just how much of a douchebag you are.

I'm also not going to get a literary agent to shop a memoir about my life with you or actively seek a movie deal for it. I'm not going to negotiate that my contract include a clause that the film be released within weeks of your latest big budget action movie.

I'm not going to then create an entire brand as the scorned woman rising triumphantly from the clutches of a terrible man and mediocre actor. And most importantly, I'm not going to tell TMZ about all of the plastic surgery you've had done. I think eating a few thousand dollars for my solo honeymoon is the deal of the century. Wouldn't you agree?"

I feel so light I'm floating.

Ryan is sweating and falls into the closest chair.

I don't tell him that I sat in that chair and watched another man masturbate for me. That would be cruel.

I don't know what Ryan's thinking, and to be honest, I don't care.

I turn back to the bedroom and snatch the hotel phone receiver from the base with a little too much force. The same clerk answers. "This is Zahra Port calling again about that car."

"Yes, madam, I'll call a car right away. Would you like someone to help you down with your bags?"

"Yes. Please."

Ryan sits slumped in the middle of the sitting room as I prepare to leave.

There's not much left to do besides grab his credit cards from the hotel safe and throw them on the coffee table in front of him.

I wait for the porter at the window, looking down on the grounds below.

I think about Giulio and his tiny swimwear and feel a tiny tug in my chest, but I ignore that. Or, at least I try to.

I fail.

I mean to catch my flight back to New York. I do. But when I look at the screen of departing flights, my eyes keep straying up to Naples. So many flights to Naples.

I should go home, call my sister, move out of Ryan's apartment, and start over. I should find a man who *doesn't* have a gun strapped to his body all the time. But I was also supposed to marry Ryan and grow old with Trisha, but that didn't work out, and those plans were years in the making. Giulio only bought this plane ticket this morning. Plans change.

I rush to the closest ticket counter. I keep one eye on the departures board while I wait. When I make it to the counter, I tell the agent the flight I want to board, and she frowns at me.

"That flight leaves in two hours, ma'am," she says as if I haven't been watching the clock on my phone inch toward the time to boarding.

"I know. I still need a ticket."

"It will be more expensive than normal," she says with

raised eyebrows. She's looking at me the way Shae looks at me when I talk about buying a designer handbag or something else equally as frivolous. She's looking at me with a mixture of judgment and pity as if I need someone to tell me that there are other flights to Naples.

Hell, I could even take a train for less than this last-minute flight is going to cost me. Yes, I get that, but saving money right now is not the point.

I brush off her judgment because she doesn't understand, and I don't have time to tell her. I'm not even sure I could explain what I'm thinking or what I'm about to do. I only half-understand it myself. But I don't need to understand it, because I feel it.

I'm the thinking sister, Zoe's the feeling sister. We've fought all our lives because I can't make a move without thinking about it for too long, and Zoe's motto is to never overthink or else you run the risk of missing the crest of the wave. Or something like that. I don't know. Neither of us has ever surfed, but whatever, she thinks it sounds good. Anyway, in this moment, what I'm saying is that I see the wisdom in her weird water-based motto. I don't know what I'm doing, but I can feel the rightness of it in my bone marrow. No overthinking necessary.

"I understand," I tell the ticket agent. "I'm willing to pay whatever it costs."

She frowns but starts typing on the computer in front of her, and that's all I need. She asks for my passport, and I rush to pull it from my purse along with my wallet.

When the ticket agent tells me the price of my ticket, I want to faint. I hand over the credit card with my highest limit and pray. In an hour, I've checked my bags, and I'm on a plane to Naples, a city I've never been to, hoping to find

Giulio even though I have no idea where the hell he could be.

Okay, maybe I should have thought this through a little more.

I GET A LATE START this morning.

After years of having to share my home with a woman I hated, I'd been accustomed to spending as little time in my apartment as possible. Now that Flavia is gone, I find myself lingering in the mornings, enjoying my home for the first time in years. These days, I enjoy waking up later, taking longer showers, and then sitting at my kitchen table to enjoy an espresso in peace and quiet. Some mornings, I even stay in bed longer than I've ever been able. I lie flat on my back, close my eyes, and conjure every image of Shae I can.

There's no shame in the fact that sometimes I don't start my day until well after daybreak because I stay in bed touching myself thinking about a woman I never should have met and will probably never see again. This morning is one of those days. As soon as I open my eyes, the idea of leaving my bed is the worst thing I could imagine. I stay in bed until mid-morning, ignoring all of my responsibilities, stroking myself to the still vibrant memories of Shae's smile, taste, smell, and the warm grip of her cunt around my cock.

If left to my own devices, I would have stayed in bed all

day, but I can only delay the start of my day for so long. The restaurant can open without me — the restaurant can run without me — but my organization won't. I need to be where I can be seen, by people who need me, and people just waiting to take me down.

Eventually, I do get out of bed. I shower — stroking myself to one more orgasm I wish I could share with her — and then I head to work. I walk through the front door and nod at Massimo, the bartender, and the waitress, a new girl whose name I can't remember.

I make my way to my office — the fake one — and check my messages. I check the safe, even though there's nothing of real importance inside. And then I throw my pristine apron over my head and tie it at the back. I walk back out into the main dining room and sit heavily in the chair at the small table where I sit every day. The small table where I was sitting the first time I saw her. The new waitress brings me an espresso and the morning paper. I unfold the paper and begin to read, sipping slowly at my drink. For the next hour, the restaurant traffic ebbs and flows. Tourists arrive; tourists leave.

A man and a woman masquerading as a couple walk through the doors and ask to sit across from me in the restaurant. I hear them say it's so they can enjoy the scenes of the piazza, but I know that's a lie. They're polizia, obviously, but I don't even bother to lift my head. I know who they are, and so does Massimo. I don't have to look behind me to know that he's watching them even more closely than I am. They linger over lunch, and I forget them. When they leave, I suspect they'll return to their station and file another report that says that I haven't done anything but sit at my table, read my newspaper, and sip my espresso.

Once the lunch rush is gone, the new waitress brings

out my lunch before she leaves. While we're closed, most of the staff leaves, except Massimo, who busies himself, cleaning his guns behind the bar.

After I eat, I walk to the back of the restaurant, stopping briefly to take off my apron, before I go to my real office. Giulio and Alfonso are already there.

"What's the word, boss?" Alfonso asks.

"Have a seat." They do.

I sit in my regular chair and look at my two lieutenants. Alfonso looks the same as ever, eager, and deadly. But Giulio looks different.

"Are you sure you're alright?" I ask him.

If it had been up to me, I never would have let him go to his father's home in the countryside. I understand why he did, I've used the location for business more than once, but the house doesn't mean anything to me. Even though Giulio has only ever told me about his childhood in the vaguest terms, I looked into his background before I offered him a position, so I know what he lived through. If he had asked me, which he normally does before he makes any big decisions, I would have told him to go somewhere else. Anywhere else. But he didn't ask me, and that is enough of a sign that he's not alright. I don't know what happened while he was gone, but the Giulio who returns isn't the Giulio I sent away.

Unfortunately, whatever is going on with him has to wait.

"We have a mole," I tell them.

If any of my wife's *other* crooked family members had tracked Giulio on his holiday, I could have believed their resourcefulness, but the Neccis are so reviled that even Flavia pretends as if they don't exist. They don't like her either. When I was planning to take Flavia's father position,

I found that the Necci branch had been screwed over by her father for decades. I correctly assumed that when I took him down, they wouldn't object, and I was right.

So, their reappearance is shocking, to say the least. But the thing about operating in the lowly underbelly of society that most people don't realize is that the lowly underbelly has an underbelly of its own. And the Neccis are the nocturnal leaders of that under-underworld.

"Who do you think it is?" Giulio asks. He sounds as eager as Alfonso, which is very unlike him. It's not that Giulio doesn't like his job, but to him, it is a job. Alfonso is eager to do what needs to be done in as brutal a manner as possible for the thrill of it. Giulio likes to complete his jobs cleanly and efficiently. They're polar opposites, and that's always been very useful to me. But I don't focus on his strange behavior. If I've learned nothing in all my time at the top of the food chain, it's that nothing stays hidden forever.

"I don't know who it is, but I have some ideas," I say.

"Just point us in the right direction, boss," Alfonso says.

"Not yet."

"Why not?" Giulio asks.

I squint at him through the naked illumination of the hanging light bulb. It's not the best lighting in the restaurant, and as I age, my eyes can't adjust as quickly, but Giulio doesn't need to know that.

"Sorry, boss," he says quickly. "It's just that anything could have happened to you while we were away, and that doesn't sit right with me."

"Me either," Alfonso agrees.

"I'm touched by your concern," I tell them. "I have some ideas, but the best way to make a mistake is to rush in foolishly. My predecessor did it regularly, and that's how I took him down. I'm going to go down eventually, but I refuse to repeat history. I called you here just to put you on notice. You need to watch what you say and who you speak to. If there's something I need to know, you come here and tell me in person, and I'll do the same. This could be nothing, or it could be the end as all things end. Who knows? Be prepared."

They look at one another in confusion or concern or both, before turning back to me. "Yes, boss," they say in unison.

"Dismissed." They stand to leave and head to the back door. "Giulio, stay for a minute."

He and Alfonso exchange a look. Alfonso has a smug smile on his face as he pushes out of the back door into the alleyway.

Giulio turns to me and straightens his back.

"Are you going to tell me what happened while you were away?" I ask.

"Boss—"

"Is that a no?"

He shakes his head, and I see his internal struggle written on his face. "It's not about the job."

"I know it's not, or else you'd be dead already."

"Do you ever wish you hadn't gotten married?" he asks unexpectedly.

"Every day."

"Was it just Flavia? Or was it marriage in general?"

"What do you mean?"

"I mean... I don't know how to say it. Did you wish you had never been married because you married the wrong person? Or is marriage just horrible?"

I exhale a harsh breath and stand slowly. "Oh. I see what you mean. A few months ago, I would have told you that marriage is the worst idea anyone has ever had. My own parents went from one relationship to another, and they were all the same, abusive spectacles. I decided when I was just a boy that I never wanted to get married. But then I needed Flavia to consolidate power, and we both know that I like power more than anything."

"I don't know, boss, you have a soft spot for zeppole," he says with a soft chuckle.

He's not completely incorrect.

"Hold on," he says, squinting at me in confusion. "What changed a few months ago?"

What didn't change a few months ago?

This room has been sprayed with every disinfectant known to man, but still, sometimes, I can smell her. I can picture her bent over the table. I can see her cunt, wet and gasping, waiting for me. I can taste her on my tongue, and I can feel the sublime release of coming inside her with nothing between us. Everything changed a few months ago. "Let's just say that I learned that every relationship is about the people who are in it. My parents' relationships and my marriage were terrible because the people in it were terrible. Other kinds of relationships are possible."

"I'm not a good man," he says, with a conviction that surprises me.

"So many aren't," I concede. "But there's a difference between someone who does bad things and someone who is bad. I don't know exactly where we stand on that spectrum, but I've known a lot of really bad men in my life, and you aren't particularly high on the list." I decide not to ask him about his time away. "Dismissed."

Giulio nods absently and strolls from the backroom.

I spend the rest of the afternoon thinking deeply about the threat I can see coming, but not clearly. Just before the restaurant opens again, I allow myself a few moments of respite, wondering where she is and what she's doing.

The night falls, and I'm back at my small table, with another espresso, and the evening paper. I've spent my entire day doing nothing of any use besides being visible and keeping all of the attention on myself while my lieutenants get to slink around the city doing all of the activities that I used to love.

As soon as the waitress unlocks the front door, a woman rushes inside. I look up, and for a brief, beautiful moment, I think it's her. From far away, it looks so much like Shae that my stomach flips, and my cock hardens in my pants. Under the restaurant's lights, her skin is the same shade of light brown, her eyes look near enough the same, and her curly hair makes my fingers itch as I remember digging my hand into Shae's and yanking her head back. God, and I remember the melodic sound of her moan. But it lasts only a moment because this woman is not Shae. She's a little taller and slimmer at the waist. And when her eyes scan across the restaurant, they don't stop at me.

"Table for one, ma'am?" the waitress asks.

"Actually, no, or maybe yes."

She's American, which makes it all the worse. I take my glasses from my face and watch the exchange, mostly because anything that deviates from my regular schedule is fascinating, especially if I don't get shot in the process. Also, without my glasses, I can pretend that she's Shae for a few more seconds. I can let myself imagine how I would feel if she walked through those doors again.

"I'm looking for a man," she tells the waitress.

"Aren't we all?"

The woman smiles, but it doesn't reach her eyes. "Okay, this is going to sound really crazy, I understand that, but I don't have another option. So look, I'm here on vacation, and I met a man, and then he just disappeared."

I put my glasses back on my face and look at her clearly.

The waitress is looking confusedly from the woman to the bartender and then to me. She's new. I'll have to tell her to not look at me in moments like this. Not everyone knows I own this restaurant, and I would like to keep it that way.

"Ma'am, this is a restaurant."

"No, I know, I understand that. But he gave me the name of this restaurant and told me that if anything happened and we got separated that I should call a man named Salvatore at La Casa Colonica in Naples."

The waitress looks at me again, and I realize that I'm going to have to fire her.

The woman follows the waitress's line of sight, and her eyes land on me. "Are you Salvatore?"

"It depends. Who are you looking for?"

"Giulio."

"And who are you to him?" I ask her.

"His wife?" Her voice lifts at the last word, turning what should be a declaration into a question. It's incredibly endearing.

"I don't believe he's married. If he were, I'm certain he would have told me about it."

"I'm also pregnant with his child," she says desperately.

It's a great lie. Well, no, it's a terrible lie, and she's a terrible liar, but in terms of making up a ridiculous story, it's great; interesting. If I wanted something to break the monotony of my day, this girl is it. Her arrival isn't as good as Shae turning my entire world upside down in an afternoon, and nothing would be better than her coming back to me, but this will do. For the moment, at least.

I can't help but laugh softly and sit back in my chair. "And where did the two of you meet?" I ask her.

"In Milan," she says.

"Milan is a big city. Where exactly did you meet? *When* did you meet?"

She straightens her back and peers down at me, pressing her lips closed.

Oh, I like her. And I bet Giulio did as well.

"That's between my husband and I," she says. I so badly want to laugh. "Do you know where he is or not?"

"Giulio is a very common name in Italy," I inform her.

"Of course, it is, but I think you know exactly who I'm talking about."

"Have you had supper?" I ask.

She reels back and shakes her head. "I'm not hungry. I'm just looking for my husband."

"I understand, but it will be easier to search for him on a full stomach. And if you're telling the truth, maybe he'll show up here while you wait."

"That sounds ridiculous," she whispers, but I can see her calculating her options and then deciding to accept my offer.

"Okay," she says.

"Wonderful. Join me."

She wheels her two large suitcases across the restaurant and pushes them against the wall. I stand and pull out her chair, ushering her into the unused seat at my table. I send the waitress in search of menus and nod surreptitiously at Massimo, knowing he'll understand my silent command.

I return to my seat and clear the evening paper out of the way. Up close, unfortunately, she looks enough like Shae that if she weren't here to find Giulio, I might try and convince myself to take her home. Try.

"What's your name, bella?"

"Zahra."

"And where do you come from?"

"New York."

"Is this your first time in Italy?"

"Yes."

"So, on your first trip to Italy, you meet a man, marry him, get pregnant, he leaves you, and you chase after him? This has been an eventful holiday."

"When you say it like that, it sounds better than I thought."

My eyebrows lift, and I can't help but chuckle, "Better?"

"Yeah, much better. You don't even know this was supposed to be my honeymoon with another man."

I can't help myself. I laugh so hard and loud that for a few minutes, I forget about Flavia and her deceitful family, about the mole, and about my own boredom. I don't forget about Shae, but the ache I feel in my chest from missing her lessens the tiniest bit.

GIULIO

I just want to crawl into bed and try to sleep tonight instead of thinking about Zahra.

I'm on call twenty-four hours a day because Salvo's summons is never a suggestion. I haul myself out of bed, throw on a pair of joggers and a t-shirt, and return to the restaurant.

When I walk through the front door, my eyes move immediately to Salvo's table.

I stop walking and breathing.

I think she's an apparition. She better be a fucking apparition.

"What are you doing here?" I yell across the restaurant.

She turns at the sound of my voice, and her beautiful mouth breaks into a smile.

I feel like I'm floating just having her look so excited to see me, but then I crash back to Earth. "You shouldn't be here."

She rolls her eyes and sighs. "Well, hello to you, too." She plucks a wine glass from the table, and I watch as she takes a sip.

I turn to Salvo. He grabs a water glass and takes a sip while looking at me over the rim. He gestures for me to come forward. I'm making a scene.

I try and calm myself as I walk toward them, but I can't; I barely know what the word 'calm' means when I'm around Zahra.

When I'm close, Salvo places his water back onto the table. He looks up at me with amusement in his eyes. Salvo never looks amused.

"Do you know her?" he asks.

"Biblically," Zahra mutters.

Salvo smiles. I fight my own smile. I refuse to give her the satisfaction.

"Yes," I grind out.

"We opened our doors for dinner, and she rushed in here looking for her husband."

Zahra chokes on her wine.

I glare at Salvo because I can't look at her. I refuse.

"Her...husband?"

"I was surprised. I didn't realize congratulations are in order."

"This is so embarrassing," she mutters.

"Maybe you should have thought about that before you showed up here," I say, still refusing to look at her.

"Well, maybe if you'd given me your address or cell phone number—"

"Why would I do that? You were supposed to be on a plane back to America. That ticket wasn't cheap."

Zahra stands abruptly from her chair and glares up at me. "I didn't ask for that ticket."

"We talked about this."

"No, we didn't. You told me I had to go home, kissed me, and that was it."

"Yes," I say, trying not to scream, "that was it."

"But that wasn't it. I'm not done talking."

I shake my head. "Go home."

"No," she spits back.

My response is cut off by the sounds of Salvo's chair scraping against the floor. We both turn to see him crossing his legs and settling back in his seat. He motions to Massimo for a drink.

"Salvo," I say. No, I plead. "Tell her to go home, please."

Zahra huffs out a small annoyed breath.

Massimo places a tumbler on the table in front of Salvo, and his eyes shift between the two of us. We watch as he lifts the glass to his mouth. Before he takes a sip, he looks me in the eyes and smiles, "No."

"Salvo. Per favore. È innocente. Lei merita di meglio di me."

"Hey," Zahra says, snapping her fingers in front of my face. "English."

I roll my eyes at her. "You don't even speak the language. Go home, tesora."

"No," she says again, like an obstinate child. She's fucking beautiful. "Besides, I was taking lessons."

I squint at her until I realize what she's referring to, and my eyes go immediately to her lips. I miss the window for my response, and she knows it.

"Tell him to stop telling me to go home," Zahra tells Salvo.

"Oh, no," he says. "Please, pretend I'm not here. Continue."

"Wow," Zahra says, tilting her head to the left. We're close enough that her curls brush my arm. "I like you," she tells Salvo.

The man smiles in a way I've never seen him smile before. "That warms my heart," he says. "Now, please, continue."

"No," I say. "There's nothing else to talk about. Let's go. I'm taking you to the airport."

"No," Zahra shoots back. "You can't. I'm pregnant."

My entire body freezes. "What the fuck are you talking about?"

"Ah, yes. She did tell me that. I believe her," Salvo offers.

"We met four days ago." I lean forward and whisper to her. "And we used a condom."

She walks two steps forward and pushes her body against mine. It takes every bit of strength I have not to grab her. "On the train. Not in the shower," she corrects, whispering the words back to me.

God, I wish she hadn't whispered. Or said the word 'shower.' Or touched me. Or come here. "Cazzo," I breathe.

"That means 'fuck'," Salvo offers helpfully.

Zahra smiles. "Oh, good to know," she breathes against my lips.

"Zahra. Please."

She licks her lips, and her tongue just brushes my mouth.

I groan.

"Please, what?"

"Yes," Salvo interjects. "What exactly are you asking her?"

"You need to leave," I tell her. "I'm not good for you."

She smiles and places her hands on my chest.

I suck in a sharp breath. "My ex showed up in Milan," she says.

"I'll kill him."

"You would, wouldn't you?"

"You know I would."

"I do. That's why I decided to stay."

"I told you—"

"You said," she interjects, "that I deserve a man who deserves me."

"You do."

"You're right. I do."

"Then you have to go home."

She rolls her eyes and steps back. She shakes her head and turns to Salvo. "Thanks for dinner," she tells him.

Salvo stands and reaches for her hand. She offers it to him, and I watch as he kisses her knuckles. I squint my eyes until he lets her go. When he sees the look on my face, he chuckles, grabs his drink, and walks to the bar.

"Hey," Zahra says, pushing at my shoulder. "Grab my bags. Let's go."

"To the airport?"

She rolls her eyes again. "Absolutely not. Your apartment. I'm tired."

"Zahra—"

"That wasn't a request," she says, dropping her voice

and leaning into me. We make eye contact, and I feel that same jolt of electricity I felt in her hotel room all those miles away. "You got to be in charge in San Gimignano." She absolutely mangles the word gorgeously. "It's my turn now."

I swallow a lump in my throat.

"Tell me when to stop," she whispers.

I don't.

I can't.

"Great. Let's go," she says and then pushes past me.

I watch her walk through the restaurant full of dread and excitement. She waves at the bar, and I turn to see Salvo and Massimo waving back.

I make eye contact with Salvo. I'm on the precipice of making the best or worst decision of my life, and I want to run into it, but I look at my boss, hoping that he'll give me an out.

He doesn't. He nods his head toward the door, and I sigh slowly, before snatching Zahra's suitcases and rolling them toward the door.

"What the fuck is in these things?" I yell at her.

"Clothes. Shut up," she yells back.

I hear Salvo and Massimo laughing at me, but I don't care. The only person that matters in this moment is Zahra.

Correction: She's the only person that matters at all.

I'm vibrating on the drive to his apartment. I can barely sit still. I want him to touch me.

When we arrive at his building, there are two armed men standing out front. They unlock and open the gate for Giulio's car, and he drives inside. The building is small and modern and surrounded by a low retainer wall.

"Are you having second thoughts?" he asks after he parks. "We can still go to the airport."

"I was just thinking," I say, licking my lips, "that I hope the walls of your apartment are thick." He sucks in a breath, and I turn to him. "Because we're going to be loud."

He mumbles something in Italian, and then his fingers are digging into my hair, massaging my scalp. He pulls my face to his, and I moan into his mouth.

"I missed you," he whispers, biting and licking at my lips.

"Then you should have come for me," I tell him.

"I wanted to be a good man."

I push him away with a frown. "Sta' zitto."

He frowns.

I roll my eyes. "Shut up. You understood what I said."

"Did I?" he laughs.

"You would have really let me go all the way back to America?"

His thumbs brush my cheeks. "Yes."

I roll my eyes. "It's a good thing you're not in charge then."

"Si, tesora. That's a very good thing."

"Show me your house," I tell him.

"Whatever you want."

His apartment is definitely a bachelor pad.

It's clean, but there's not much in it; just the necessities. "You're going to need more furniture," I tell him as he pushes my suitcases out of the way.

"I have enough furniture," he says, patting the back of his couch.

"That's cute."

"You're going to be trouble."

"That's rich, coming from you."

He laughs. God, I love the way he laughs.

"Get naked," I tell him, power and excitement pulsing through my veins.

He lifts an eyebrow at me. I lift an eyebrow back. He pulls his shirt over his head.

I hold my hands behind my back because I want to touch him so badly, but I need to wait. Also, I want to watch him undress again.

"Sit on the bed," I say when he's naked. He rushes to sit on the edge of the bed, facing me, legs splayed and his semi-hard dick bouncing in the air. "You're much better at taking orders than I am," I breathe.

"Remember that when it's my turn."

I grab the hem of my dress and pull it up my legs slowly.

"Faster," he grunts.

"Say it in Italian, and I'll consider it."

"Piu veloce," he says.

I pull my dress over my head and throw it on the floor.

He grunts in approval.

I move my hands behind my back and unhook my bra, but I don't take it off.

"Voglio vederti adesso," he whispers.

"I'm glad you're catching on." I drop my bra on the floor and walk toward him. I lift my right leg and place it on the mattress between his legs. He moves without any direction necessary. I watch him unclasp my shoe and pull it from my foot while I stabilize myself with both hands on his shoulders and give him my other foot. He leans forward and takes the other shoe off. He turns his head and brushes his lips along the inside of my elbow. He drops my shoe to the floor and grabs me at the waist, sucking my nipple into his mouth.

"I didn't tell you to do that," I say, even as I run my fingers through his hair.

He ignores me and laves each of my nipples with his tongue, slowly and thoroughly.

"Take off my underwear." The cool air hits my wet nipple, and I shiver.

He almost rips my underwear, pulling them down my legs. His hands caress and massage my thighs before sliding around to my backside. I whimper when he grabs ahold of each cheek.

"Never mind," I gasp. "You're just as bad at taking orders as I am."

He chuckles against my rib cage. The soft puffs of his warm breath against my skin are everything. I let him kiss and massage me for a few more minutes before tightening my grip in his hair and pulling his head back.

He laughs up at me. "Giusto. Proprio così."

"Lay back."

"Si, tesora."

"What does that mean?" I ask as he climbs onto the bed. His dick is hard now and pointing at the ceiling.

"Yes," he says and laughs.

"Smartass. 'Tesora,'" I say, trying to mimic his accent as I crawl onto the bed over him. I straddle his stomach and feel his body jolt when my pussy touches his overheated skin. I'm wet. I've been wet since he was yelling at me at the restaurant.

"Treasure," he breathes.

I place my hands on his chest. I can feel his heart pounding against my palm.

"Sei il mio tesora," he says, and I can figure out what that means from context clues and the matched pounding of our hearts.

"Say it slower," I tell him. "Against my pussy."

"Como sei così perfetto?" he says, grabbing me by the hips and hauling me over his face.

My knees settle on either side of his head. His big, rough hands circle my waist, and he pulls me to his mouth greedily.

My groan is so loud it's a scream.

If someone had asked me to explain why I was apparently willing to upend my entire already mess of a life for this hairy, cocky jackass, I honestly might have had a hard time explaining myself. I know. That sounds like a train wreck waiting to happen. Don't tell Zoe. But I have an answer now.

Giulio eats my pussy with the same kind of energy he gave to pushing me away for my own safety. He's thorough and methodical in everything he does. He parts my folds with his tongue, tasting me in deep, long swipes. When his lips close over my clit I fall back, and my hands land on his abs. He flinches underneath me and sucks my clit harder.

"Oh fuck," I scream. "Your neighbors are going to hate me."

"I don't care," he breathes against my pussy. He covers my clit with his fingers and starts to fuck into my opening with his tongue.

"Yeah. Me neither. Oh, God."

I'm coming. So soon. That wasn't the plan. The plan, if anyone's wondering, was to make him come so hard he'd think three or four times before he tried to put me on another train without consulting me.

That's okay; I'll get around to that next time.

He keeps eating me until my back bows, and I hunch forward over his head. I grind my pussy along his tongue and come so hard that if he does try to put me on another train, I'm just going to double back again like I did this time. I've decided. I ride his mouth from one orgasm into another, and then one more before my pussy is so sensitive that I have to crawl off of his head — pushing his hands away because he's trying to keep me in place. I flop onto my back on the bed next to him with a heaving chest.

We're both panting.

"You taste wonderful, tesora."

"Thank you. That's the nicest thing you've ever said to me."

He scoffs. "I had very nice things to say about your tits in your bikini."

"Did you? I can't remember. I was too busy watching your dick get hard in those tiny swimming trunks."

"So you did like the view?" he asks me.

I try to get up from the bed with a laugh, but he grabs me around the waist. We turn onto our sides, my back to his front, and he holds me.

"Tighter, please," I whisper, settling my head onto his bicep.

"Si, tesora."

I relax into the strength of his hold. He brushes the hair from my face and twines a single curl around his finger, caressing it lovingly.

"I won't tell you to leave again," he whispers against my cheek.

"Good. But I decided while you were eating me out that I'm not going anywhere anyway."

He smiles and kisses my cheek, but I can feel his frown against my skin. "But my life is dangerous, Zahra."

"I've noticed. Thanks for the warning. Only a few days late."

"Have you thought this through?"

"Not really," I admit. "My heart is very on board, though."

"Zahra—"

I shift so that we can make eye contact. "Look, you don't know this about me yet, because we don't know each other at all, but I've never done anything on a whim ever in my entire life."

"Then you shouldn't start now."

"Yes, I should," I tell him. "I've spent months thinking about very big decisions and never felt as sure about anything as I did when I bought the plane ticket to come after you. I'm not going anywhere. Now, if you would please put your dick in my pussy and stop talking about breaking up with me? We haven't even been on our first date yet!"

I groan as he slips inside with ease.

"You aren't pregnant, right?" he asks me, as his hips meet my ass and retreat. We both shudder.

"God, no," I breathe. "I've been on birth control since I was sixteen. Let's hold off on kids until after we've had a few very uncomfortable conversations about baby names or have been together longer than a day."

"Deal," he breathes into my mouth and pushes inside me again.

We stare at one another as he slowly pumps into me with patient strokes as if we're not in a rush. As if there's a real future between us. I'm happy he's finally come around.

"Cazzo," he breathes.

"Yeah. Fuck. I remember. We're definitely doing that."

"It also means 'dick'. The fuck you're thinking about is 'scopare'," he grinds out as his hand moves between my legs to circle my clit.

"This is the best way to learn a language," I moan. "How do you say 'faster' again?"

He doesn't tell me, but he does speed up his thrusts. I reach around his body and squeeze his ass, encouraging him to fuck me with everything he has. And he does.

We stay like that well into the night, grinding against one another, slow and then fast and then slow again. He whispers so many Italian words and phrases into my ear and against my hot, sweaty skin that I feel certain I'll be fluent in Italian in no time.

At the very least, I'll become well-acquainted with the Italian tongue.

My favorite phrase, though, is the one Giulio breathes into my mouth each time he comes inside me.

"Penso di amarti."

"Shut up. We barely know each other," I tell him just before we pass out in his bed. "I think I love you, too."

EPILOGUE

ZOE

I'M PACING around the living room, and I hate pacing in this apartment. There's a squeaky floorboard around the coffee table, and it annoys the shit out of me. I've tried pacing around the bedroom, down the hallway, and through the small galley kitchen. There are squeaky floorboards in all those places too. This place is a minefield of sharp sounds that make it hard to think while doing the one thing that allows me to think.

I could go to my apartment.

There aren't any squeaky floorboards there.

There aren't any dicks there either, though, so I'm kinda trapped at the moment.

Trapped and pacing around my boyfriends' apartment while I type a very long email to my younger sister that she probably won't reply to. The squeaky floorboards are worth it if it means that they'll help me work out my frustrations once I press send. It's better than burning through a pack of batteries with my sex toys, I think.

Now, back to this email:

Zahra Christine Port-

This is the third email I've sent you in as many days. If you have not responded to this email within 24 hours, I will be forced to take drastic measures to ascertain whether or not you're dead in a ditch, were kidnapped by that shithead you almost married or joined some weird European cult. If you're wondering, I would prefer the cult, but since I promised you that I would try and accept that douche nozzle, I will.

Sorry, I should probably call him by his name, but I'll wait until you've confirmed a reconciliation before I give him that courtesy.

Look, I know you, and this isn't like you at all. Call me. Call mom and dad. Call Shae or the aunties. CALL SOMEBODY!

You better be safe. I didn't go to journalism school to have to spend the golden years of my career running around Europe looking for your remains. I refuse! I'll do it, but I'll be so mad at you. And it'll kill our parents.

I love you.

Stop being a dick and check in.

I read over the email a few times, but honestly, I think it's perfect, so I press send.

"Hey babe, dinner'll be ready in ten," Kevin calls from the kitchen.

"Okay, thanks," I call back with false cheer and start typing another email. This one is quicker and much less formal and emotional.

KeKe -

Hack into my sister's credit card accounts, please. She's disappeared in Italy. Let me know when you find anything.

My best friend's response is much faster than my little sister's.

Done. Will send a report in the AM. Hope she's getting that good vitamin D.

Faster, but much crasser. No one is perfect.

"Z," Tyrone calls from the kitchen, "you want wine?"

"God, yes," I breathe, walking toward the dining room.

I imagine that each step brings me a bit of calm, because, for the first time ever, I have a plan; a promise, really. I promise myself and my annoying, overthinking sister — wherever she is — that if I haven't heard from her in twenty-four hours, I'm going to find her, even if I have to hop on a plane to Italy. I'm willing to make the sacrifice of a few days in a beautiful country with lots of wine and the best food to find her.

If I have to throttle her with a bunch of grapes when I *do* find her... Well, she's been MIA for a week, she deserves it.

ACKNOWLEDGMENTS

As usual, I want to thank you, whoever you are, for making it this far. I started writing this story when the world seemed decidedly less terrible and finished it when I realized that I was wrong. It wasn't the most fun I've had writing a book, but I loved these characters and the world I created for them. A world where there's wine and travel and a brooding stranger who can kiss the hell out of you in a train station because he loves you even though you just met. I'm not living in that world, so please wear a mask and stay safe.

Thanks to Tasha L. Harrison and the #20kin5Days Facebook group for your write-ins. Without you this book would still be stuck with Zahra in a bloody dress in that vineyard wondering what the hell is going on. Thanks Lucy Eden for writing with me even though your internet hates you or me or both of us. Thanks Kai for gently encouraging me to finish this and all the other stories but also for being the keeper of my too many ideas. Keep that airtable to yourself though. And thank you to everyone who read Beautiful & Dirty and lovingly harassed me for more Salvo and Shae.

You didn't get much of them but... ya got something. :/ The next book in the series is Zoe because she's always right and she makes good on her promises, so Zahra (and Giulio) better watch out. And if your name is Alfonso, you maybe would like to know that Zoe is tall, fat and doesn't take shit from anyone.

And after that is Salvatore and Shae's book! PROMISE!

If you liked this story, please consider recommending it to a friend or reviewing it on any site where you feel comfortable.

Follow me on these handy social media sites where I'm not wasting time. Seriously:

Twitter| Instagram | Bookbub | Newsletter| Amazon

The Family

Beautiful and Dirty

The Hitman

Standalone stories

Encore

Layover

Office Hours